CONJURING FATE

DYSTOPIAN FANTASY

SANCTUARY

ANN GIMPEL

CONTENTS

CONJURING FATE

SANCTUARY, BOOK ONE

Dystopian Fantasy
By
Ann Gimpel

**Tumble off reality's edge into a broken world
fueled by lore and despair**

Copyright Page

Gone. Everything. In one fell swoop.

Maybe it didn't happen quite that fast, but it sure seemed like it.

I remember everything like it was yesterday. Or, more accurately, I couldn't forget even if I tried. And I have, tried that is. With every fiber of my being. But the damned tape reel has an automatic replay button, and it blasts through my brain over and over again.

I was just nineteen then. One very long year ago. I'd finished my first year at university and was on vacation between semesters. We were in Mexico at a sorcery retreat when our phones beeped and screamed warning of impending doom. Details didn't emerge for a long while, but our relative isolation in the Sierra Madre Occidental mountains saved us from immediate annihilation.

We should have remained there, but hindsight is always twenty-twenty.

In an ill-conceived attempt to escape, we finally gave up navigating clogged roads, left our bus, and teleported back to the States. I'm not sure if that was the beginning because it felt like the end of everything I've ever known.

Survival has reduced me to someone I barely recognize. Some days, I wonder why I bother, but then I pick up the banner and face another day. Better not to think too hard or pick reality apart. If I did, I'd loose my power and burn down the world.

BOOKS IN THE SANCTUARY SERIES:

Conjuring Fate, Book One
Conjuring Chaos, Book Two
Conjuring Promises, Book Three

This series has been percolating for months. I finished writing *Promised,* last of the Bound by Shadows books in early June 2023. It was slower than expected because I'd begun penning chapters for *Alive, Surviving Modern Oncology,* my passion project aimed at helping other cancer patients navigate challenging waters. It took far longer than I'd anticipated. Here it is mid-August already, but *Alive* is loose in the world, and I'm ready to return to my first love: fiction.

Many of my other series feature a dystopian near future. Bitter Harvest and Earth Reclaimed are the two that jump to the forefront. *Icy Passage* is a standalone novel with a similar dystopian cast.

I'm excited to jump back into my comfort zone. Bits and pieces of this book have been rattling around in my head since I wrote the blurb a couple of months back.

<cracking knuckles> Let's get to it, shall we?

CHAPTER ONE, ALIA

"Your turn, Alia."

Drat.

In my few weeks at the sorcery retreat, I'd come to dread those words. Why had I assumed anything would be different here? Probably stupidity or a crash course in wishful thinking. I shuffled to the center of the room. Shadows cast by a multitude of burning candles played over the walls of a mountain hut in Central Mexico. Everyone sat on cushions in a rough circle, their attention so intense it raised the fine hairs on the back of my neck.

A woman started a soft chant; everyone else joined in.

Incense—patchouli with overtones of cinnamon and mint—thickened the air. I sucked in a breath, then another, before raising my hands. Tonight's task was visualizing spirits of the dead who'd been laid to rest beneath this hut. Rhys, the man who'd organized the retreat, believed they held wisdom relevant to our age—if we could only get them to talk with us.

So far, no one had conjured more than a partial image.

Closing my eyes, I reached deep within me, channeled my astral body, and sent it scurrying downward in the direction of a crumbling graveyard. Shock nearly tossed me out of my trance, but I held steady. Usually, the dead are quiet, cast down. Not this batch. Spirits, way more than I'd expected, milled about, crashing through my essence and out the other side.

Pretty beefy ghosts. I floated a few feet away and did my best to project a welcoming ambience. No one paid me the slightest heed. I can't talk in this form, but when I've visited the spirit realm before, they were more than aware of my presence.

What was going on? My Spanish isn't very good, but even if it had been, this bunch spoke in some dialect, probably a Native tongue.

I was running out of time. The longer my astral self is free, the tougher to reincorporate it. Learned that the hard way. After watching for another minute, I selected two women, lassoed them into a spell, and headed for where I'd left my body.

At first, I thought I'd get away with it. My astral self clicked back into place about the time the spirits turned on me, hissing, spitting, clawing with long-dead nails.

The screams I heard were my own.

Guttural commands in a language I'd never heard blasted my ears, followed by, "Let go of them, Alia Eve McVie. Do it now."

My full name caught me dead in the solar plexus. Too late I realized I still held the ends of my spell tight against me. When I tried to release it, I couldn't. Frantic to undo what madness I'd invoked, I stopped thinking. Fire—my primary element—raced to my aid and chopped through what remained of my casting.

Still shrieking imprecations, the spirits burst into motes of black and gray. At least they were gone.

Panting as if I'd run a marathon, shaking from an overload of adrenaline, I told the fire I'd summoned to stand down. It wasn't any more cooperative than the spirits had been. Flames joined with two nearby candles, rendering them into puddles of fragrant goo that spilled across the wooden floor.

"Control your magic. Now." Rhys's tone was icy.

I'd have told him to go fuck himself if I weren't so obsessed with gaining the upper hand over my ability. That was the problem. My old problem. My only problem. Once freed, my power had a mind of its own.

It might have taken an hour. Or maybe only a handful of minutes. Finally, the flames sank into my body, dead center into my heart chakra where they lived when they weren't wreaking havoc.

Rhys's voice boomed. The words bounced off me, making no sense.

I bolted into the velvety darkness of a Mexican evening with all my senses on fire. My heart was still pounding; a sour taste coated my tongue. Magic thrummed along every nerve ending. Stars stood out in bas relief. The moon was almost too bright to look at. A million insects buzzed and chirped and hummed. Night hawks swooped overhead, drawn by the power swirling around me.

I hunkered into a crouch and threaded my arms around my knees willing the episode—or whatever it was—to pass. This had happened to me before, but not often. Usually, I kept the fire scalding me from the inside out under wraps.

For obvious reasons. Fear it would eat me up alive, spit me out, and turn me into something other than human gnawed at me.

"Who am I kidding?" I mumbled. "I've never been anywhere close to human."

Maybe I'd be better off giving into the inferno boiling within. Every time it got loose, I moved one step closer to a point of no return. I touched my face and forearms expecting to find wounds from the spirits, but my skin was intact.

How? Their nails had been real enough.

"Alia. You okay?" sounded from behind me.

Damn it. Last thing I wanted was to interact. With anyone. Before I could shout I was fine and for whomever to head on back inside, a hand grabbed my upper arm.

"Don't touch me," I gritted. By now, I knew who'd come after me by his smell. Like I said, my senses are hyperacute when I'm in this headspace.

Connor let go as if he'd been scalded. For all I knew, my residual magic had done just that. "You don't have to be such a bitch."

I shot to my feet and pivoted until I faced him. Dark hair hung to shoulder level, framing stark cheekbones and a square jaw. Blue eyes with silver flecks around the irises bored into me.

"You don't know shit about me," I protested and gulped air to quiet my racing nerves.

Furrows formed between his black brows; he angled his head to one side, annoyance shading to speculation. "True, I don't, but you were the only one who connected with the sprits. It was looking really good, until they turned on you."

"Your point?" Crap, I was being rude, but I wanted out of this conversation.

"It might have been okay, but you got upset when they attacked you, and—"

"Stop right there. It wasn't your spell. I suppose you'd have stood your ground and let them shred you to bits?"

"They can't hurt you," he pointed out.

Great. Now I felt like a fool. If I'd been braver, had a cooler head, maybe I could have pulled this off. It's not as if I've had jack in the way of training for my magic. Only what I've pulled off the dark web.

I took a step back. "If you came outside to chastise me, I'm hard enough on myself."

"I came out here to see if I could help. I tried inside, but you bolted from the circle. Knocked down two of us before you ran out the door."

Oops. I had zero memory of that part. "Sorry," I mumbled, avoiding his gaze.

He held out a hand. "Truce."

I shook my head. "Can't."

"I don't get it. Can't what?"

Can't touch you. Can't be part of anything with other people. Ever.

Words scored my throat. I hated talking about myself.

My magic had always been secret. Until it jumped the gate and demanded acknowledgement. I'd ridden herd on it since it first showed up when my moon blood came. Mercifully, I was older than the norm: fifteen before I crossed the threshold into womanhood.

The almost four years between then and now had been long—and marred by many near misses where I'd run for hours to burn off residual power. No one knew, not my family, not my friends.

Not my classmates throughout my freshman year at University of Oregon. They viewed me as a loner, or a stuck-up bitch. Hard to say which since I rarely talked with any of them. Go to class. Study. Rinse. Repeat.

I'd quietly signed up on the dark web for this summer sorcery workshop in hopes of meeting others like me, except my power outstripped theirs by a factor of like a million. Some of the people who'd come to the retreat in Mexico's Sierra Madre mountains, couldn't so much as light a candle —except with a match.

"Alia?" Connor's voice had gentled, much like it might have if he approached a skittish filly. Goosebumps covered his arms. No wonder. All he wore was a pair of blue running shorts and flip-flops.

My breathing had eased, the pressure in my chest reduced to a manageable level. I dropped my hands to my sides. I didn't realize they'd been raised to summon power to protect myself.

"I'm okay. You really should go back inside before you freeze."

"You're not wearing much more than I am," he pointed out.

Yeah, but magic carries a bitch of a load of heat.

"What happened in there?" he pressed and swatted at something that had landed on his arm.

Maybe if I skirted an explanation, he'd leave me alone. "The spell got away from me." I shrugged and tried for a sheepish expression. It wasn't tough to pull off. "Working on control, but it's a process."

Breath rattled from him. He rolled his shoulders back, accentuating his better than six foot height.

"Everything all right out there?" a man shouted.

"Fine," Connor called back. "We'll be inside soon."

"Speak for yourself," I muttered. No way was I conjuring anything further tonight.

"I bought you some time," Connor explained. "Are you sure you don't want to tell me what's going on."

"Quite sure." I flapped a hand his way. "Go. I'm done for tonight. Tell Rhys I'm not feeling well and am going to turn in."

His speculative look deepened. Power tinged with the hawk he turned into hovered, reaching close. I sidestepped, avoiding it.

"You can't run away from what you are forever," he said just before he turned and loped toward the long, low stone hut where we did most of our work.

I watched him until he disappeared inside, mostly to make certain he didn't double back to spy on me. Out of the twenty of us who'd convened for the tenth annual gathering of Magick and Mayhem, only half a dozen carried true magic. Connor was a shifter. So were two of the other women. Nola was some iteration of witch. Rhys, the organizer, was a shaman. I'd been trying to figure him out for the entire three weeks since I arrived.

No dice.

He kept to himself in much the same way as me. Except he was far better at concealing his true nature.

I strode away from the workshop building. A night hawk landed on each shoulder. Deep purring told me a mountain lion was somewhere close. Animals are drawn to me, even when I'm not spewing magic like an out-of-control volcano. They've kept me sane all these years.

The retreat was slated to last two more weeks.

Could I remain? More to the point, would I try to shape power again? Tonight had gone so horribly wrong, I'd been afraid I was about to burn down the building. Except its walls weren't combustible. The thatched roof was another matter entirely.

It would have gone up like a torch.

Rhys had been egging me on. Pushing for me to try harder. Until he shouted at me to rein it in. I shut my eyes and reconstructed his words. "You'll never learn anything so long as you're afraid."

Almost the same thing Connor said.

A howl burst from my throat, followed by another. The mountain lion drew near, rubbing soft fur against my bare leg. My eyes burned with unshed tears. Why couldn't I have been born normal?

"Stop. Just stop," I snarled, pissed at myself for one more descent into self-pity. I'd come to this spot to learn, but I was just as isolated as I'd been on campus.

And at home and everywhere else since power flooded me along with menstrual blood. Unsure of my next move, I stopped walking.

Two choices. Leave. Grab my stuff and start down the mountain. Someone would give me a ride to the village in the valley. Even if they didn't, it was only about six miles. Not a dealbreaker.

From there, I'd book transportation home.

If I did that, I'd be in the same boat as when I arrived. No closer to opening the secrets of what I am. Certainly no closer to managing my brand of magic. The lioness purred again, telling me she understood completely. A hawk tucked its head into my cheek, sharp curved beak clacking in rhythm to my erratic heartbeat.

Door number two was turning around, walking back inside, and ripping my shell wide open. It held risks, the worst of which would be people mocking me, telling me I was full of it, that no one had that kind of magic.

No, the worst would be my reaction to being laughed at. So far, I'd avoided hurting anyone. Hopefully, the two people I'd barreled into were okay.

I raked my fingers through thick blonde hair and held onto my skull to keep it from bursting. Why was this so hard?

Because you want something that isn't possible, an inner voice answered.

Such a simple truth, but it cut like a knife. I wanted to fit in somewhere—anywhere. Past time to pull my head out of my ass and get into my big girl panties.

My magic wasn't going anywhere. If anything, it had grown stronger since it first manifested. If I was ever going to be whole, I had to own who I was.

It was as clear an answer as I was likely to get.

A creek burbled about fifty feet away. I walked to it and crouched, splashing water on my overheated face. Cupping my hands, I drank deep. The clear water was probably crawling with microbes, but I never got sick.

If I couldn't reveal myself here, I couldn't do it anywhere.

Determined to change what I had power over, I straightened, stood tall, and headed back the way I'd come.

"Do you want us to leave?" floated through my mind from the mountain lion.

"Only if you want to," I told her and the hawks.

Between the creek and the hut, she faded into the night, but the hawks remained on my shoulders cawing softly.

I hesitated before grasping the door latch and tugging it open. Candlelight spilled into the darkness along with the sticky scents of incense.

Rhys, all six foot two of him, aimed his ice-blue gaze my way. Pale hair cascaded down his shoulders to waist level. Sometimes he tamed it into braids or a queue, but not tonight. His cream-colored linen shirt showcased broad shoulders. Tattered jeans hung low on narrow hips. He was barefoot. A medallion, reminiscent of something out of the *Witcher*, hung from a golden chain.

Problem number thirty-two was he was so flipping striking, I had a hard time breathing when he was close. Not that he, a forty-something worldly man, would have the slightest interest in a barely grown kid like me, magic or not.

Girding myself for damn near anything, I walked inside.

CHAPTER TWO, RHYS

After Alia stormed out of the hut, I reiterated basic principles and led the group through summoning exercises, mostly to keep them from focusing on what just happened. Our visitors from the spirit ream hadn't been benign. A malevolent residue hung in the air, although I was likely the only one who sensed it. Out of all the ghosts rattling about in this remote location, why had she chosen that pair? Perhaps, she couldn't tell the difference.

Young, untrained, and terrified of her ability, Alia was rapidly painting herself into a corner. Tonight was a fish-or-cut-bait moment. I hadn't planned it that way, but magic has a way of making its own rules. Power ran stronger in her than in anyone I'd seen since the Middle Ages when I was spawned.

I've run these retreats for the past decade in hopes of unearthing someone, anyone, who possessed actual command of a wide array of power. In that time, I'd met many shifters, several witches, Druids, and those pretending ability they lacked. I'd vowed the current retreat would be the last. They cost me in both money and magical resources. To hold them so many times and come up dry meant I needed to craft a different approach.

Or give up altogether.

I'd initiated the retreat idea because I was lonely. And because something was bearing down on Earth. Exactly what hadn't yet revealed itself to me, but once it coalesced, magic would become essential to survival. I couldn't take on this task alone, and so I'd purchased a bit of land with a rundown hut and used it for my purposes. When I wasn't here, the place was concealed by enchantment. If mortals wandered near, they'd be uncomfortable enough, they'd scuttle away...

"Did you hear me?" Connor asked.

"Yes and no. Could you rephrase that?" Damn it. My mind was wrapped up in Alia and wandering all over the place.

"My hawk says it still doesn't feel right in here."

Interesting, but not surprising. The animal half of shifter duos was often far more sensitive to environmental cues. I motioned to him and the other two shifters in this group. "For now, become your animals. Take five minutes to dig deeper, and then report back."

"What about the rest of us?" a very weak witch inquired.

"Form a power circle and chant. Your magic"—I stumbled over the word since they had so little—"should help."

Once the shifters were immersed in their task, my thoughts rolled forward from where I'd left them.

On the cusp of me giving up, Alia had materialized. Just shy of her nineteenth birthday, she was so full of power it shimmered around her and sloughed off whenever she changed position, leaving iridescent trails. I'd have given a lot to know her lineage. Long, thick blonde hair shrouded a tall, slender, almost waif-like figure. Hazel eyes shaded from green to blue to violet depending on the angle of the light. Aristocratic cheekbones, thick eyelashes, a high forehead, and pointed chin suggested Fae blood. Her surname, McVie, had Scottish roots, so my assumption of Faery blood might not be so far off the mark.

If she returned, there was hope for her. If not, her power would consume her, drive her mad. Not today or tomorrow, but eventually.

No one gets to deny that kind of magic. I tried for many a long year. The results weren't pretty. Connor had gone after her and returned. I could have listened in, but I hadn't. Many masters run roughshod over acolytes; it's never been my style.

A wee overreach on my part. My few forays into gathering a cadre of shamans had failed miserably. I've been alone since crossing the Atlantic in 1889.

Enchantment hummed, thickening the air as the trio of shifters reclaimed their human forms. The group included Connor and his hawk, and two female wolf-shifters. Because I'd kept tabs on Alia's energy—especially after Connor's message she wasn't feeling well and was turning in for the night—I felt her moving closer.

This could go one of two ways. She'd decided to throw her fate to the winds and claim her ability. Or she was stopping by to tell me she was leaving.

I couldn't force her to embrace her skill, or to entrain it. That sort of thing must be accepted willingly. Power is a rocky path; magic a bitch of a taskmistress at times. It wasn't so isolating when I was born. Back then, humans revered those of us who were kissed by the goddess.

That had come to a crashing halt toward the end of the 1800s when I was relatively newly arrived in the Americas. My life has trended steadily downhill ever since. Starting over with a new name in a new place every couple of decades didn't help. With the advent of electronics, obtaining identification had turned into another kettle of fish.

What a difference a hundred years makes. I used to roll into town, say I was whichever name I'd picked, and acceptance was forthcoming. Not any longer. Even after I pull out a driver's license and credit cards, people still eye me with suspicion.

Alia was near enough, sandals crunched on gravel.

The door flew open. She marched through, head held high but avoiding eye contact. A night hawk graced each shoulder. I sucked in a breath and held it. The temptation to cull through her thoughts was strong, but I couldn't accomplish it without her knowing. She'd give voice to what was on her mind soon enough.

"Sorry I ran out of here," she said in a clear voice. "Connor tells me I knocked a couple of you down. Apologies. Didn't mean to."

I released the breath I'd been holding. She'd decided to see this through. I didn't need to read her mind. Her body language reflected her intent.

The others surged toward her, murmuring encouragement. Naturally, they'd be drawn to her power same as the hawks were. In a different group, some might be envious, but no one here was.

Smart of them. With great power comes immense responsibility. At a primitive level, Alia knew as much, and it scared her to death. In another time, she'd have had a place to go. A temple or shrine or haven run by others like her, those who could shape her ability.

The twenty-first century lacked such amenities, particularly in the United States. Had she been in Mongolia or a few enclaves in the Highlands or Northern Ireland or the Andes, she'd have had a fighting chance of hooking up with others like herself.

I walked toward the group and clapped my hands to get their attention. Conversations quieted.

"Let's wrap this up for tonight," I said. "Shifters, report what you experienced."

Connor cleared his throat. "It was the oddest thing. As soon as my hawk and the two wolves were in ascendence, the rottenness withdrew."

"Yes," one of the women chimed in. "My sister and I noticed the same."

"It must be the animal energy," the other woman noted. "Evil can't coexist in the same spot with it."

"What did you learn?" I pressed.

"To shift if we sense evil?" Connor asked, followed by, "I've always tried to protect my hawk from bad things."

"Maybe you should let him protect you," I suggested.

One of the women, Moriah, grinned. It lightened her sharp features and made her look younger than her fiftyish years. Red hair streaked with gray had been pulled into a ponytail. Brown eyes were pinched around the edges.

"Easier for us." She pointed at her sister and fellow wolf-shifter. "Wolves kick some serious butt."

The hawks on Alia's shoulders clacked their beaks as if to say, "Us too."

"Tomorrow, we're going to walk through ruins about a mile from here," I told them. "Hopefully, we'll find more cooperative spirits. Get a decent night's sleep. Practice trance work and slipping between here and the dream world."

Amid murmurs of assent, the group headed toward the door. I approached Alia and held up a hand. "A word?"

She cringed but didn't turn away. Was she afraid of me along with her power?

I waited until the others were far enough away to be out of earshot. "I won't hurt you."

She took a step back. "What do you want? I'm tired."

"I'm not the enemy."

She shook her head as if I'd slapped her and muttered, "Sorry."

I tugged a stool over and sat, motioning for her to do the same. She didn't. "Why'd you come back?"

"I almost didn't."

"I know. I've been where you are."

Her gaze skirted past mine. "What do you mean?"

I turned my hands palms up. "I have magic too. Surely, you sense it."

"No." She shook her head. "I can't. You shroud yourself."

"How about if you take my word for it. Why'd you come back?" I tried again.

She pinched the bridge of her nose between thumb and forefinger. "This is my last chance."

"For?" I prodded. She had to talk about her fears. Keeping them bottled up would be a death knell. Power finds expression, whether we will it or not. If we fight it the whole time, it turns us into bitter shells of whom we might have become.

Breath hissed from between her teeth. She retrieved a stool and dropped onto it, but not too close to me. Her hands had been curled into fists. She spread her fingers and laced them together.

"I'm, erm, different. But I can't talk about it. With anyone. So I pretend everything is normal."

"And?" I spun one hand in a come-along gesture to encourage her.

"When I saw the ad for this retreat on the dark web, I hoped..."

A minute passed, and then one more. "What did you hope?" I asked softly.

"That all this would become manageable."

"Or go away?" I supplied.

"I wish, but it's never going to happen."

"No," I agreed. "It's not."

"I'm still different," she murmured.

"From?"

"Everyone here. No one has much magical ability. I guess I'd hoped…"

Another long silence. This time, I didn't insert my own words.

Finally, she added, "Hoped I'd find others like me."

"In a way, you have. Everyone supported you when you returned. Nobody rebuked you or turned away."

The corners of her mouth twitched into half a smile. "You're saying my expectations are too high."

"Yes, and no. I can teach you, but it will take far longer than a few weeks in these mountains."

Alia drew back. Her knuckles whitened where she clasped her hands together. "What are you saying?"

"There are no coincidences. I organized these retreats to locate others with strong ability. Until now, no one has crossed my path. This is the last year I planned to do this, and here you are."

"Not seeing the connection."

"Because you're looking through a twenty-first century lens. I am not trying to seduce you or turn you into anything beyond my student. I can teach you to control your power, how not to be afraid of it. How to accept it."

"But what about university?"

I shut my eyes for a moment and beat back annoyance. She didn't get it. Not yet. I switched gears. "Tell me about yourself."

Her eyes widened. "I did. On the application."

"Bare bones minimum. Some wrote paragraphs."

Alia shook her head. "I'm not going to argue. What do you want to know?"

"Who were your parents?"

"No idea who my father was. Mother was younger than me, sixteen, when she got pregnant. When I was around five, she married the man who helped raise me."

"Did they have other children?"

"No."

"When did you realize you were, um, different?"

A rosy tint spread across her cheeks, and she murmured, "When I became a woman."

"Did you have dreams before that? Any hints of power?"

A furrow formed between her blonde brows. "Maybe. Not sure. I've had lots of them since."

"Tell me about them? Is there a theme?"

"Who are you?" she blurted and pushed to her feet.

I caught her gaze and held it. "I'm no one. And everyone. You ended up here so I can help."

"What if I don't..."

When she tried to look away, I added a bit of force to keep her focused on me—and in the room.

"Don't do that." She squirmed, fighting my hold.

I released her. "Figure out what you want, Alia. Nothing in this life, or any other, is free."

"What do you mean?"

"You said it all when you noted you were different. But then you asked about returning to college. You can't dance on two floors."

"Why not? I'll learn how to control whatever this is and

go back to my life. Maybe then I'll be able to have a few friends, and—"

"Doesn't work that way."

She rolled her shoulders back. "Might for me."

Exasperation cut deep, but raising my voice, or my magic, would drive her away. "Our paths crossed for a reason."

"I can always find you again."

"True in the life you're familiar with. Less so in the world you're skirting the edges of."

"What exactly does that mean? I have your email and cell number."

How to respond? "They were necessary to draw participants together for this retreat."

"So?" She turned her hands palms up.

"They aren't essential for me."

"You're talking in riddles. I'm going to bed."

Because I didn't know what to say that wouldn't reveal too much before she made a commitment to me—and her power, I watched while she walked out the door.

It was almost impossible to explain to the "instant" generation that being infinitely available grated. Had I told her both phone and email would vanish at the close of the retreat, she wouldn't have believed me. Or, if she did, she'd have assumed I'd just trade them out for new ones.

Living without the accoutrements of the modern, civilized world was unimaginable.

A long sigh rattled through me. There are no coincidences, but maybe I'd been wrong about Alia being ready to embark on the shaman's path. From the looks of things, she might never be.

I blew out candles and shuttered the building for the night. A shot of power cleared spilled wax from the floor. The only thing I felt certain of was she had to come to me. Any pressure I exerted would bounce back and slap me.

I passed the bunkhouse where retreat participants slept. A few earlier groups had filled the place with Bacchanalian revelry. This bunch didn't appear inclined to sleep with one another.

My cabin was close. I stretched tendrils of power, grateful no one had trespassed. Occasionally, those I hosted were curious about me. No one ever crossed beneath the lintel. My wards beat them back.

Sleep isn't particularly important for me. Instead, I mixed herbs into a strong tea and waited for the concoction to produce visions. My cushion beckoned. Stepping over an array of crystals, I settled onto it, shut my eyes, and waited to see what the goddess—my guidance—would gift me this night.

I didn't have to wait long.

Alia rose before me, a medieval-looking bow clutched in one hand. She stood in the midst of rubble that extended as far as I could see. Dust and smoke filled the air. The stench of turmoil permeated everything, burning the insides of my nostrils.

Where was she?

Try as I might, I couldn't piece that part together.

As quickly as it had come, my vision faded.

My heart still pounded from the stimulant herbs and

overly caffeinated tea. What I'd seen boded both well and ill. Alia had jumped in with both feet and claimed her destiny, but the world lay shattered before her.

Was she the instrument of its destruction?

A shudder raced through me. Had she crossed my path for a far darker reason than my initial assumption?

So I could destroy her before it was too late?

Was she the catalyst behind the evil I'd felt suspended in the offing?

Many questions. No answers.

Clasping my hands and bowing my head, I asked my spirit guides to provide direction. Sometimes, it's forthcoming.

In this case, I sat until my ass was numb and was no closer to figuring out the riddle of Alia than I'd been a few hours before.

Dawn was breaking when I left my cushion, stripped off my clothes, and padded to a nearby pool. Even colder than usual, the icy water stole both breath and thought.

No clues anywhere. The retreat had two weeks to go, and the ball was squarely in Alia's court. I'd treat her exactly like the other participants.

Of course, I will. What choice do I have?

More settled, but not any happier, I threaded my way across rocky ground intent on drying off and dressing. Each retreat day began with opening prayers where we called on the goddess and the four directions and four elements to bless our efforts. Once that was done, we'd head for the ruins of a Mayan town in search of more benign spirits than the ones Alia had raised last night.

CHAPTER THREE, ALIA

The hawks stuck with me while I talked with Rhys but flew off as soon as I left the hut. Maybe they sensed I no longer needed moral support.

Except I did. Worse now than before.

Messages come in threes, and I'd heard variations on the same theme twice from Rhys and once from Connor.

Messages to stop running from my magic and embrace it. Except the price would be higher than I expected. Rhys had been clear I couldn't maintain my current life and wield power from the sidelines.

I passed the bunkhouse and kept walking. I'd assumed if I could develop control over my magic—or whatever it was— I'd be home free. I'd just squash it under a haystack when it wasn't convenient.

Except it never would be convenient or have a place in the modern world. Had I come to these Mexican mountains in hopes of permanently squelching it? A rolling sensation behind my solar plexus lacked words, but its meaning was undeniable. Blocking my ability, or tossing a blanket over it, wouldn't work.

Not for very long, anyway.

Blending exercising power with my day-to-day life was a nonstarter. No one would believe me if I told them the truth. Worse, I'd be dragged to psychiatrists and psychologists and other contemporary witch doctors who deal with the mentally deranged.

Except I wasn't.

Isolation carved a jagged channel through me. My hopes for coming here, never mind spending the money, crashed and burned. It had been unrealistic, but I'd expected to be fixed, cured of my abnormalities.

So I could have a life where I wasn't a hermit.

Rhys had asked about my parents. Of course, he'd want to know. Magic was probably like any other inherited trait. It sure hadn't come from Mother. She was as plain vanilla as they came with overlapping circles of friends and lots of activities.

When I was old enough to understand that the man I called Daddy, wasn't, I'd asked her about my real father. All she'd said was she made a mistake, and that she'd never seen him after the night I was conceived. I tested her words when she told me she'd never tried tracking him down. They pinged cleanly, radiating truth.

I'd never understood how she could have been intimate with someone, and then never cared about seeing them again, but it's not the sort of thing you can ask a parent.

I've caught her angling sidelong glances my way on

several occasions. She probably knows more than she's told me, but I haven't exactly been ready to rip the scab off with direct questions.

As long as we danced around the topic, we could both pretend I was just like any other daughter. She'd never had any other children. Was she worried they'd come out like me?

I'd walked quite a way from the building where all of us except Rhys slept. The others should be asleep by now. Once again, I was avoiding connection with my fellow students, but I'd done it for so long, it was tough to know whom to trust. Simpler to keep to myself.

Exhaustion dragged at me. My eyes felt hot and scratchy; a sheen of dried sweat coated my body. Whenever a boatload of magic runs through me, it takes a toll. I feel used, dirty, like I need a shower.

I'd sleep better if I was clean, so I ducked into the bathhouse. Naturally, it was deserted. After stripping my clothes off, I stepped into a shower stall and flipped the taps. The water was never hot enough, so I blitzed it with a shot of power and luxuriated in the spray pummeling my flesh.

Soaped, shampooed, I watched as fragrant bubbles ran down the drain.

Out of excuses to stay, I rooted in the linen chest for a towel and dried myself. The clothes I'd removed didn't smell fresh, so I wrapped my head in one towel and my body in another and covered the short distance to the bunkhouse.

Breathing punctuated by soft snores greeted me. Using magic to muffle any noise, I crept to my bunk, dug pants and a shirt out of my pack, and dressed. The damp towels swung from nearby hooks. I'd do better once the new day arrived. For now, I crawled into my sleeping bag and shut my eyes.

Sleep was elusive. The scene where my power jumped the gate played over and over, pushing me to examine what I'd done wrong. If I solved that mystery, I'd never get any rest. I rolled over and then back again.

Intent on playing a soothing meditation track, I dug in my pack for my phone and earbuds but couldn't locate either item. Cursing the fates, I flopped onto my stomach. I'd stick it out until the retreat was over, but then I was returning to university. Given a choice between being a microbiologist and a sorceress, micro won every time.

I longed for normal, ached for it. All my magical side had done was cause trouble. Tomorrow, I'd ask Rhys if there was some way to excise my ability. He'd be horrified, but he was honest, and he'd tell me if he knew of some pill or potion or incantation to rid me of my burden.

I MUST HAVE FALLEN asleep because the buzz and chime of many cell phones jolted me back to consciousness. Light filtered through the windows; dawn must have broken.

Everyone was diving for their phones. I mirrored their movements. Unlike the previous evening, this time I managed to locate the pesky device. Rhys's instructions were that all electronics were to be shut off for the entirety of the retreat.

No one had complied.

I stared at my screen, uncomprehending.

Moans, sighs, and a chorus of *what-the-fucks* suggested my confusion was universal. Out of bed in a flurry of loose feathers from my sleeping bag and the clothes I'd chosen to sleep in, I joined the circle of people pointing and talking over one another.

"What does all this mean?" I shouted to make myself heard.

My screen held three warnings. One for flooding. One for tornado-force wind. The last for invasion.

Connor slipped in next to me and murmured, "No one knows."

"But the attack part? We're in Mexico. Who in the hell would bother invading them?"

"Maybe it's meant for where you live," he suggested.

"What did your phone say?"

"Eh, never mind. Mine said the same thing, and I'm on the other side of the US from you."

I raked fingers through my tangled hair. Crap. Had Russia lost its mind? Or maybe North Korea. Everybody and their dog had a nuclear arsenal these days.

The bunkhouse door slammed against its stops. Rhys raced inside, his usual composure notably absent. "Get dressed. Grab your things. Just the important ones. Don't take time to pack everything. Meet you in front of the main lodge in ten minutes. We have to get out of here."

He was gone as quickly as he'd come.

Most of us stood frozen, staring at the door.

Connor clapped his hands. "You heard the man. Get moving."

Tossing modesty to the four winds, I scrambled out of

the garments I'd slept in, added underwear, and a pair of tough chino pants. A blue woolen shirt and my favorite denim jacket completed my dressing. I hadn't brought much. Everything was in a backpack, which I hoisted over a shoulder.

Cell phone still clasped in one hand, I loped out the door.

The old green bus Rhys had picked us up with sputtered to life. Whoa. He was serious about leaving. I cleaved through panic engulfing me and spread power in a wide arc.

Something dark and malevolent pressed inward from every side. What the hell was it? I pushed harder. A bank of energy punched me in the gut, leaving me gasping and breathless.

What in the unholy hell? A quick scan identified my own magic directed back at me. Clearly, something didn't appreciate me snooping.

Shaken, I started toward the bus again. No one seemed to notice my momentary disorientation.

It seemed to me we'd be safer here than in Mazatlán. The wind and flooding part of the warning were bound to be worse there. And it was a seaport. Ripe for attack, although I still couldn't fathom anyone would be stupid enough to risk world peace over Mexico. Rhys exited the bus and ran to his little house. When he came out a few minutes later, he was carrying a large black duffel bag.

By now, most of us had congregated near the bus. Its nasty diesel fumes burned my nostrils. Rhys kicked one of the external luggage compartments. It creaked open, and he chucked his duffel inside while motioning for us to toss our packs and suitcases after it.

I kept mine buckled to my body. If we ran into trouble, I wanted it close, not beneath me.

"Come on." Connor gripped my arm.

I followed him to the back of the bus and held my pack in my lap. The screen of my phone flickered in and out. "Do you know any more?" I asked softly while others shuffled into the bus.

"No, but something feels off. Your power is stronger than mine. Go ahead, check for yourself."

I didn't bother to tell him I already had.

Rhys was calling names. Guess he wanted to make certain we were all present and accounted for. We must have passed because he closed the door, slid the transmission into gear, and we rumbled out of the enclosure presumably toward the steep, winding road we'd taken when we'd come here.

Despite its rickety appearance, the bus had a decent PA system. Rhys switched it on and said, "Apologies for the abrupt exit. It was unavoidable."

"Do you know what happened?" one of the wolf-shifter sisters called.

"Not exactly." Rhys paused. Perhaps he was searching for words that wouldn't totally freak us out. Except, he'd never been particularly sparing of anyone's feelings before this morning.

Connor's body tensed where it pressed against my side. I wanted to reach for his hand but didn't. Rhys's hesitation fed into my fear; a bitter taste coated my tongue and throat. My stomach twisted into a knot, making me grateful whatever this shitshow was had happened before breakfast.

Rhys cleared his throat. "I have seen something like this bearing down on Earth for a long while now. I'd hoped it would hold off for a few more years, but conditions must have become more auspicious."

"Something like what?" someone asked.

"Conditions for what?" someone else called.

"It's better if you don't interrupt," Rhys replied.

Beyond twenty phones chirping and buzzing, silence reigned. Rhy didn't tell us to turn them off.

The bus bounced over a couple of potholes. Rhys cursed before continuing. "I've sensed darkness, evil. It's manifested in so many places, from corrupt politics to floods and famines and out-of-control viruses and bacteria. The planet is struggling, so her native protections have weakened, paving the way for malevolent forces to prevail."

He jerked the wheel, probably to avoid another chuckhole. "I have no idea what we'll find once we leave these mountains."

"Why are we leaving?" I cupped my hands around my mouth.

"I said no more interruptions," he thundered.

All right, then. I hadn't seen this side of Rhys. It felt as if I'd been slapped.

"We left because staying was impossible. And because our magic is needed for what is to come."

I still didn't get it. Most of my fellow retreat participants didn't actually have enough magic to make a difference in much of anything. The woods were full of game. We wouldn't have starved, but I kept my thoughts to myself.

"The world that emerges from this maelstrom will be unrecognizable," Rhys went on. "If you're lucky, your friends and families will still be there when you get home. If returning is even possible. Can any of you teleport?"

I could, but I'd be damned if I'd say one more word. Not after his last response to me. No one answered.

"Fuck. I was afraid of that. Alia. Can you teleport?"

A direct question, bearing my name. "Um, yeah. Not very good at it."

"What happened to airplanes?" Connor murmured next to my ear.

I shrugged. Part of me, a big part, felt certain Rhys was overacting. We'd get to the airport and sign up for standby tickets to fly home. All would be well, and I could leave this magic shit behind me.

Forever.

Coming here had been a mistake. I'd been managing, maybe not all that well, but I'd achieved a tenuous balance between the disparate sections of my life. No reason I couldn't resurrect it. Having friends was overrated. I'd get by keeping to myself.

"You're quiet," Connor observed.

"So's everyone else," I countered.

"My hawk is edgy. He's pressing against our bond."

I glanced at Connor. His forehead was furrowed; a muscle danced beneath one eye. "Do you know why?"

"Of course. He believes he's far better suited to dealing with this, erm, problem than I am."

His answer surprised me. Until now, I'd assumed they shared a single consciousness. The hawk apparently thought for himself.

The bus hit another pothole. I'd have bounced off the seat if Connor hadn't grabbed hold of me. No seat belts.

Rhys was taking the hairpin curves far too fast for my taste. If we met anyone driving up, we'd have a head-on collision.

The phones had quieted. When I glanced at my screen, it was just wallpaper. No bars. We must have dropped out of range of a cell tower.

"Does anyone's phone work?" a woman called from the front of the bus.

Rhys's voice rose above a chorus of nos. "I told you, but you didn't listen. Soon there won't be any more towers. No phones. No Wi-Fi. If anyone still has a landline, they'll be the last to go because they're wired."

The rear end of the bus swung outward. For one heart-stopping moment, the rear wheel that remained on asphalt whined as it fought for purchase. A blast of power that nearly flattened me pushed us back into position. We barreled onward, losing elevation fast.

"Not going to have to worry about Armageddon," Connor groused. "We'll end up at the bottom of a ravine."

After battling ambivalence, I gripped his hand, grateful for its warmth. So much for my big words about being content to live out my days in isolation. "Rhys won't let that happen," I said softly.

Five minutes later, the bus skidded, brakes squealing as it came to a halt. "Everybody out. Now," Rhys ordered.

No one budged.

Rhys sprang from the driver's seat and activated something that opened the front and rear doors. "Out. Now." Compulsion drove everyone to their feet and out the nearest exit.

Backpack strap looped over one shoulder, I followed the herd. When I made it to the front of the bus, I saw why we'd stopped. A ten-foot section of roadway had fallen in.

Rhys shooed us across and on down the hillside. "I can do this," he said, "but not with you inside. Stay out of the way." He headed back to the bus.

The rest of us trotted downhill until we found a flat spot off to one side that would accommodate most of us. Connor, the wolf-shifters, and I kept walking.

Behind us, the crash of an undercarriage scraping rocks suggested the bus was underway. Brakes squealed. Metal protested. When I glanced at my companions, the shifters wore their animal forms. Connor flew overhead. The wolves ran down the road making little yipping noises. I picked up discarded clothing figuring they wouldn't want to be naked when they shifted back.

In about a quarter hour, the bus heaved into view. The bunch we'd left at the open spot had made their way back inside. I flattened my body to the side of the road and scrunched through the door. It didn't open all the way. No space.

"Where are the shifters?" Rhys demanded.

I shot him a pained look. "Shifted. Connor's up there, somewhere." I pointed.

"Figures." The door creaked shut; we lurched ever downward.

The trip to the retreat center hadn't taken nearly this long. Or maybe it had. We'd been excited to be starting our journey.

I stumbled to the back of the bus and dropped my pack and armload of garments in Connor's seat. Would I ever see him again?

Hell, would I ever see anyone again?

We finally hit the north-south highway. It was clogged with traffic, so much so we were barely moving. Rhys guided us around stalled vehicles that had presumably run out of fuel. Hordes of people walked or ran on both sides of the highway. We were heading north, but an equal number of people had chosen south.

I grabbed my phone to see how far we were from Mazatlán, but it was just as dead as it had been a while back.

Since the bus wasn't moving anyway, Rhys left his seat, stood, and faced us. "We have a couple hours of fuel remaining. We can stick it out in this mess, or we can leave via magic."

"Leave to go where?" I asked, fully expecting him to direct us back to our respective homes.

"There's a site in Arizona, just north of Sedona. It would be my recommendation since it hosts a deep cave system supportive of Earth magics. Better ones exist in the Old Country, but getting there won't be easy."

I resisted rolling my eyes. Getting to Arizona seemed just as impossible as traveling to the Isle of Skye, or wherever he had in mind.

A sharp tapping snapped my head around. Connor's hawk pounded on a window with his beak. Rhys opened both doors; Connor flew inside, shifting almost as soon as he arrived.

"Thanks," he muttered as he picked his trousers, shirt, shoes, socks, and jacket out of the pile on what had once been his seat.

"Well?" Rhys arched both brows.

"It's surreal," Connor panted. "Something flattened Mazatlán. Only buildings left standing are a few huts on the outskirts of town. Every roadway is jammed with cars. None of them are moving.

The wolves slunk through the still-open doors. They weren't as quick to shift as Connor. Guess they'd decided the bus was safer than wherever they'd been. I handed them the clothing they'd discarded.

"Damn it." Rhys pounded a fist into his open palm. "I had no idea this would unfold so quickly." His gaze homed in on me. "How far have you teleported?"

My cheeks warmed, and I mumbled, "A mile or so. Just to see if I could."

He nodded once, sharply. "Same principles apply. The dark place, the one that surrounds you when you travel. Do not let it suck you in."

Huh? What dark place? When I'd tried teleporting, it had been over so fast, I hadn't noticed a thing. Rhys was droning on. I forced my attention front and center.

Explosions boomed in the distance. They lit a fire under the wolf-shifters, who hurried into their clothes.

"Alia?" Rhys was talking to me again, except I'd missed most of it.

"Um, yeah?"

"You good with transporting one or two and then returning for more? You can probably make two or three trips before you need to rest and replenish your power."

Breath hissed through my clenched teeth. Crap. I had to take a stand right here and right now. Back on my feet, I faced him. "Look. I took myself maybe a mile. There was no 'dark place.' I need to practice before I put someone else at risk."

"In a perfect world, sure."

Strands of compulsion snuck around me. It would be easy to sink into his rich baritone and believe every word. I built a barrier, the same thing I'd used to keep the world at bay.

Something unreadable flickered across his face. Somehow, I ended up next to him with a bubble around us. "You have no choice," he growled. "I can transport four, maybe five, but my magic isn't bottomless. By the time I make enough trips to move everyone out of here, it will be too late."

"Too late, how?" I was talking, but focusing on his meaning remained an uphill struggle.

"You'll have to take my word for it. I'll tell you more of what I know, but we're running out of time. If I'd realized the destruction had already begun, I'd have left from the center and not bothered driving down the mountain."

"We could go back," I ventured.

His grip on my arm tightened until I yelped. "There isn't time," he repeated. "And it would waste magic."

Imagery flooded my mind. Red rocks baking under an Arizona sun. Without asking, I understood this was my destination.

"How do I do this?" I mumbled. Worst case scenario, I'd lose myself and whoever was dumb enough to trust my nascent skill.

Relief sloughed off Rhys, surrounding me in waves. "Hold the vision I sent. Take Connor since your power is complementary. Have him pick one more. Leave as soon as possible."

"What then?"

"If you're successful, return here and do it again." He hesitated. "This will be hard for you, but check your magical reservoir. It has limits. If you're feeling breathless, lightheaded, take time to eat and drink."

If I'm successful, huh.

I plodded back to Connor and buckled my pack in place. "You're coming with me," I said. "Pick one more to teleport with us."

His eyes widened. "Are you certain you—?"

"No," I cut him off, "but we're doing this anyway. Unless you want to stay here."

Connor tapped another man's shoulder. An inch shorter than Connor, Joss was a Druid with ties to the animal world. Hair like living fire was gathered in a queue at the back of his neck. The corners of his eyes were pinched with worry. Levis hugged thin hips. A black nylon windbreaker covered a green T-shirt. Because I thought it might help, I linked arms with them both and sent the same image I'd received from Rhys.

"Here is our destination. Hold it in the forefront of your mind. It might help."

"We believe in you," Joss said softly and brushed loose strands of russet hair out of his face. Blue eyes radiated calm.

I latched onto it, gathered magic to me, and loosed my spell.

CHAPTER FOUR, RHYS

Alia and her two companions took on an incandescent aspect and then faded from view. Talk about baptism by fire. So much could go wrong in the universal travel channels. For all I knew, they'd already been subverted by whatever we faced.

So many things I should have warned Alia about, but if I'd peppered her with everything that could go sideways, she might have lost her nerve. Most of the people in the bus would have killed for her ability. She was ambivalent as hell. Skittish and sullen, she teetered on the brink of shucking everything.

Except power doesn't work like that. If you don't embrace it, it has 900 ways of making you sorry. Sort of like being born tall or short or with freckles. Not much you can do to change those things.

"Do you suppose they're okay?" one of the wolf-shifter sisters asked. Her voice trembled.

I could have said something soothing, but whitewashing truth isn't my style. I'd find out soon enough if the journey channels were intact. "Four volunteers," I barked.

No one hustled to my side. Clearly the devil they knew —being stuck in endless traffic in the bus—was preferable to a leap into the unknown. I inhaled sharply and blew it out to buy thinking time. No matter which way I turned things around, I came up with the same answers.

"Listen up. You can't remain in the bus. Not for long. Situations like these attract unsavory elements. People will break windows to get inside, and then they'll rob you—or worse. If you choose to leave the bus, you'll be on the run. Food and water will pose problems. Safety, too."

"Alia was right. We should have stayed at the center," a woman muttered. Not loud, but my senses are well honed.

I locked gazes with her. Terror sheeted from her brown eyes; she wrapped her arms around her slight form. "Only over the short term. We're not returning. I won't force any of you to accompany me. If you came along against your better judgment, your energy would pervert my spell. Goddess knows where we'd end up."

"Why can't you teleport us back to the retreat center?" another woman asked.

"The place I have in mind is better. We can remain there for a long while."

"But what if we'd rather return to the refuge we're familiar with?" the brown-eyed woman pressed.

"If you wish to return, it will be on foot. If you've learned anything in your time with me, it's that magic has limits. I cannot split my focus. If I do, I'll risk not reaching my goal in

Arizona. Plus, if I change plans, Alia will be dangling in the wind."

"By all means, let's be fair to her," someone snarked.

At least I had everyone's undivided attention—even if they weren't exactly embracing my leadership.

"You have three choices," I went on. "One. Remain in the bus until hunger and thirst drive you outside. If something more sinister doesn't force you out first. Two. Leave the bus now and take your chances with the mob." I flapped a hand toward the window.

A steady stream of humanity flowed on both sides of the highway. Dogs, cats, pigs, and goats trotted next to the crowd.

"Or," I continued, "you can come with me. I have no idea what the journey channels look like. If they've already been undermined, we may never make it to Arizona."

"Where would we end up?" Bob asked. Another weaker-than-weak mage, he nurtured delusions of competence.

"Impossible to say. I'll do my best to bring us out somewhere survival is possible, but there are no guarantees."

"Shouldn't Alia be back by now?" he pressed.

"Not necessarily. She's only been gone about ten minutes. This particular magical endeavor is new to her. She might run into challenges."

"What if you can't get back to us?" a wolf-shifter sister piped up.

It was a good question. "Wait forty-five minutes after I leave. If I'm not back, your best bet is to abandon the bus and make your way back up the mountain. Do your best not to be followed. Many would literally kill for the resources I left at the retreat site."

"So, we shouldn't stay together?" Bob frowned.

I took in the mass of people clotting the roadway. "It won't matter until you reach the side road that leads to where we came from. When you do, use magic to make yourselves as unobtrusive as possible. A mile or two up the road, you can join forces again.

"It's five-and-a-half miles from the junction to the center. Keep your eyes and ears peeled. At the first hint you've been followed, kill whoever's tracking you."

"Kill?" the weak witch squeaked.

I unclenched my jaw. They still didn't get it, but why should they? They'd never lived through anything like what hung over us. I didn't fully grasp it, either. Never mind I'd been catching glimpses of a dystopian hell for the last half century.

"It will be us or them," Bob choked out, aiming his words at the witch.

A low moan ripped from her, and she clasped her hands so tightly the knuckles turned white.

"I'm leaving in the next couple of minutes," I told them. "I can take four with me. Do any of you want to come?" Without waiting, I summoned power and began building my spell. It would be different if I were only transporting myself, but it's simpler to jettison power than to add it.

The witch and the two shifters walked close. After a pause, the brown-eyed woman who'd endorsed Alia's idea about sticking it out in the mountains joined us. I draped corners of the spell around the small group.

"Time us from when we disappear," I told the thirteen people who remained.

"Got it." Terry nodded. A self-styled sorcerer, he was ineffectual as watered-down milk.

I turned to my group. "No matter what happens," I told them. "Do not engage in negative thoughts. Don't let fear rule you. I don't care how you do it. Chant. Pray. Meditate. Sing. Whatever. Hold positive imagery. Imagine red rocks and northern Arizona."

I pegged the last bits into place; weightlessness began in my feet. Probably should have warned my charges, but time was not on our side. The bus walls took on a glittering aspect, and we were off, floating in darkness.

The shifter sisters produced something like a Gregorian chant. The witch hummed tunelessly. The brown-eyed woman quoted scripture and clutched at a cross she'd ferreted out from beneath her cotton top.

Excellent. They were following directions.

It made my life simpler.

I homed in on our destination, keeping it front and center in my mind. Were I by myself, the journey wouldn't have taken more than a few minutes, but carting four people along slowed things down.

I tested the integrity of the channel. So far, it appeared intact. Nothing rushed us from the darkness. I'd met many mythical beasts in places like these over the years.

In an ideal world, I'd have joined magic with my charges, but none of them had enough to be of much use. Untrained power can be worse than nothing. I checked nodes as they flashed by. They're a sophisticated type of longitude and latitude calibrated for the magical realm.

"Not too much longer," I murmured.

"How can you tell?" The woman who'd been mouthing scripture left off for long enough to pose the question.

"The mages who developed these channels added a type of marking system."

"I haven't seen anything."

"Probably you have to know where to look," one of the shifters told her.

The edges of my spell lightened sooner than I expected. "Get ready," I cautioned. "The transition out of this incantation can be rough."

My words were no sooner out than we punched through a jagged hole and began falling. I cobbled power into a net to break our descent. It might have been useful for one or two. For five, it barely made a dent.

I tried harder. No point in getting here if we smashed into the ground at high velocity. My heart pounded in my ears; breath caught in ragged gasps.

Finally, finally, I got a handle on the speed dragging us lower. We touched down rougher than I'd have liked, but nobody broke anything.

"Is it always like that?" the witch asked.

I didn't bother answering. Glancing about, I got my bearings. We were about half a mile from where I'd hoped we'd come out, but the distance wasn't insurmountable.

Everyone scrambled to their feet, dusting themselves off.

"Come on." I set off at a brisk walk. Once everyone was on the move, I broke into a lope. Soon, the rocks that formed a gateway to my original destination—the cave system— heaved into view. The sun was heading toward the western horizon, but the rocks still radiated heat.

I reached outward with magic but couldn't sense Alia or Connor or the Druid.

Damn it.

A few words released warding meant to keep passersby out of the caves. Racing inside, I called Alia's name. And Connor's and Joss's.

Nothing. But then, I hadn't expected them to reply.

One of the sisters had shucked her clothes and shifted, head up, nostrils twitching. In a flash, she was back in her human body. "They haven't been here," she announced.

I'd already ascertained as much.

"You'll be safe in this spot," I said—and hoped to hell it was true. "I'm going to hunt for Alia and her companions. Assuming I find them, my next stop is the thirteen I left in the bus."

"Not all of them will be there," the witch said.

"Some will be." Without waiting to get into a discussion, I turned and left.

What I should do is return to the bus first, but if I ferried three more loads of people, I wouldn't have enough magic left to search for Alia.

Should I trade many for few?

I shut my eyes and sent threads of power outward hoping for guidance from somewhere.

Anywhere.

I'd pressured Alia into using the journey channels. Had I signed her death warrant and that of her companions? Unspoken codes govern those like me. One of the most critical is we take responsibility for those we've chosen to train.

If Alia had run into trouble—and she damn well must have since she wasn't here—I had to prioritize locating her, Connor, and Joss.

Grateful for a clear direction, I formed power into another teleport spell and jumped in.

CHAPTER FIVE, ALIA

My magic, fueled by fire, chased us out of the bus and into a place so dark I couldn't see either man despite them flanking me. The air felt still, heavy, but not exactly oppressive.

I made a grab for calm, but my heart raced and breath seared my throat. The carefully curated image of northern Arizona wavered.

"Breathe." Joss clasped my hand.

"Sorry," I mumbled. "This is all so new."

"It has to be like any other magic," Connor said.

"What do you mean?" At least I had the image front and center once more.

"The first rule is believing you can do something," he reminded me.

My cheeks heated despite the chill permeating wherever the hell we were. "I could have used a few more instructions," I mumbled. "All Rhys said was to hold the image in my mind. Surely, there's more."

"We'll find out soon enough," Joss said.

He was trying to soothe me, but I've always been one of those who likes things buttoned down tight. It was why magic annoyed and scared me. It was part of me, yet it had a mind of its own.

"Wish I knew how long this should take," I murmured, and then I shut up. Conjecture wouldn't help. At least my heart rate had quieted some.

Time passed. Hard to say how much. The men wove their magic in with mine. It heartened me that they trusted me enough to share power. The unyielding blackness was disorienting. I focused on the image of red rocks instead.

"What was that?" Joss asked.

"What was what?" Connor shot back.

"Hang on. Another one should flash by. I've seen several now. There. That." He might have pointed, but I couldn't see his hands.

Something silvery passed by on the right.

"You say there's been more than one?" I asked.

"Yes. That's about the tenth one I've seen."

"Why didn't you say something?" Connor muttered.

"Because I had no idea what they were."

My attention had wavered badly. When I tried to reconstruct the image of red rocks, it eluded me. "Do you still have the image?" I asked in a voice I scarcely recognized as my own.

"Erm, it left," Connor admitted.

"Mine too," Joss concurred.

My heart jolted into overdrive. That image had been our lifeline. Without it, we might float forever in endless night. I'd been to Sedona a couple of years earlier. Maybe I could craft my own image and at least get close.

I had to do something. It wasn't only me counting on my magic this time.

"Odd it vanished like that," Connor mused.

Joss chanted soft and low, making me grateful for his presence. Meanwhile, I dredged another image from my memory banks. This one was of downtown Sedona, a collection of vortex and crystal shops interspersed with restaurants of many persuasions.

"New image," I announced and pushed it into both their minds.

This time, I focused my entire being on that image. I was determined not to lose another, although I was fairly confident I could resurrect this one since it was mine to begin with.

The temperature in our tunnel or channel or whatever it was began dropping. At first, I thought it was my imagination. Until I started shivering.

"Hurry," Connor urged.

I wanted to ask what he sensed, or perhaps it was his hawk, but splitting my attention was a very bad idea. Along with the cold, something was stalking us. I didn't question how I knew. I just did. Maybe the same entity that had stolen Rhys's original imagery was closing in to finish the job.

What that meant scared the bejesus out of me. So much so, my mind shied away from fleshing out possibilities.

Waiting around to find out what was hunting us was

sheer idiocy. I dug deep, poured on magical afterburners. Out of nowhere, we burst from the endless black and tumbled end over end hurtling toward a smoking ruin below.

Connor's magic suffused me, smelling of wet forests and ancient trees. Where he'd been latched to my arm, his hawk took shape, wings cutting through the air. I fashioned a rough weave from air and magic. It prevented Joss and me from being crushed by the fall.

As we got closer, I maneuvered us to a patch of green that had once been someone's lawn and crumpled into a heap. Connor landed next to us, chirping.

"Where are we?" Joss asked as he stretched out his limbs checking for damage.

"If my aim was true, this should be Sedona." My voice shook from an overload of adrenaline. "But it's turned into ruins."

"Just like Mazatlán." Connor was back in his human form, buck naked.

"Something must be left somewhere," Joss protested.

Logic dictated it was true, but so far we were running two for two. I lurched to my feet breathing shallowly to avoid inhaling the smoky air. We needed to locate the original meeting place. Rhys had said it was north of town.

An idea formed. I touched Connor's arm. "You can fly. How about if you head north and try to locate the cave system Rhys mentioned."

"I can do that. Will the two of you wait here?"

"We should start walking in the same direction," Joss said. "Something chased us out of the journey place. Not sure standing still is wise."

I closed my teeth over my lower lip. If we could exit the channels, so could whatever had decided we weren't welcome there.

Maybe.

"Crap. Wish I knew more."

"The sooner we find Rhys and the others, the better," Connor said just before he shifted and winged his way northward. I reached out with magic seeking life of any type. Human, canine, feline, insects, birds. Beyond spiders, beetles, and moths, I came up dry. Even the rodent population had taken a major hit, but a few remained.

"Not much left," Joss said.

"You checked too?"

"Uh-huh. Come on. We need to move."

Something earthy and plantlike surrounded me. It took a second before I understood he'd warded us.

"Thank you."

"That type of thing is simple for me. Finding our way through what's left here won't be."

His words turned out to be prophetic. Parts of dead bodies lay everywhere. The stench was indescribable. Our path was blocked over and over until I led us due west and we skirted what was left of the town before turning north again. Connor could find us, regardless.

"Connor should be back by now," I ventured and avoided what looked like remnants of a brick chimney.

"Not necessarily. Those caves are probably concealed. They'd almost have to be."

"Yeah, but all he has to do is latch onto Rhys's energy."

"He might be hunting for us."

I bit my lower lip until it hurt. Rhys would drop everything to look for us if he arrived at the caves and we were absent, which meant the people remaining in the bus would be left to their own devices.

"We need to move faster," I urged.

"Don't see how we can do much better than we are right now."

"I could try another teleport—"

Joss made a chopping motion with one hand. "Bad idea. The dark place wasn't kind to us."

The dark place. At least he had a name for it. We forged onward. I wasn't exactly used to the stench, but neither was I on the edge of puking up bile. What in the hell had happened? Was my hometown a smoking ruin too?

"You'd think someone would be alive," Joss mumbled.

I hadn't scanned for a while, and I didn't now, either. "Plenty of survivors in Mexico," I pointed out. "Must mean there are here too."

"If so, why can't we sense them?"

I didn't have an answer. Had the epicenter of the disaster been north of Mexico? I tugged my cell phone from a pocket and stared at my wallpaper, a shot of Mt. Hood from a trip I'd taken last spring. Rhys had said the Internet would crash and burn. How could it have happened at the same time in such disparate locales?

Because my attention had strayed from the ground, I caught a foot between a rock and a sharp piece of wood and almost pitched facedown into the dirt.

Joss gripped my upper arm. "Steady."

I tossed the wood to one side and kept going. I'd twisted

something but not too badly. What he hadn't said was medical help might well be a thing of the past too. I've always taken getting patched up for granted, something I'd do well to get over, and damned quickly.

Joss cut right. Curious, I trotted after him. And then I heard why he'd detoured. Weak cries came from the wreckage of an apartment building. It almost sounded like an infant.

Surging forward, I circled the building hunting for a way inside.

Joss jumped over what had once been some kind of table and caught up with me. "Probably a trap."

I stopped in my tracks and stared at him. "But it's a baby."

He spun me to face him, hands on my shoulders. "Lots of things can sound like that."

"We have to find out," I argued.

"Do we?"

"You stopped." I reminded him.

"Only to get near enough to check with magic." Letting go of me, he aimed an arm at the building. Glittery darts passed through walls. He waited, eyebrows knitted into a single thick line.

I started to mirror his actions, but if the crying child was bait, it might not be wise to tip our hand. Joss had revealed his presence; mine was still secret.

I hoped.

A visceral tug told me he'd reeled in his seeking spell. "Well?" I kept my voice low, which was stupid since falling buildings and distant explosions covered up anything as puny as a human voice.

He shook his head. "Don't know. According to my feelers, nothing is alive in there."

The wails escalated in volume, almost as if an independent intelligence had determined we were about to leave. Something cold slithered down my spine. "Doesn't feel right," I mumbled and started to pick my way back to our path. I didn't get half a dozen steps before I stopped.

"Keep moving," Joss urged.

By now the wails were a cacophony. "Can't do it." Spinning, I reached through a spell aimed at where I heard the voice—or whatever it was. Eyes shut, I detached my astral self and traveled through the closest wall. I should have told Joss to hang onto the body I'd left behind.

Should have.

Inside the building was worse than my imaginings. Far worse. Bodies were bent at odd angles and piled on top of one another. Spilled entrails mingled with the sharp stench of blood. The cries grew louder. I pushed toward them while balancing power to pour into a hasty escape if things turned south.

What in the fuck was I doing? My first priority had to be finding the caves and Rhys. Something plucked at me and bounced off. So much for wandering attention. I constructed shielding as best I could. My astral body doesn't exist in a physical plane.

Whatever had jostled me did it again.

Felt like a test of sorts. Would I cut and run or stay the course?

My built-in radar didn't sense anything alive, so what

was making that noise? Walls came and went. I had to be damn near on top of the sound. The wreckage of a living room spread around me. One end was crushed. Smoke wafted from somewhere.

Christ. Hopefully, the building wasn't on the edge of blowing up. I had no idea if my astral self could survive something like that. What I did know was too long a separation between it and my body would spell death.

No hands, so I pushed bits of magic to dig through rubble. The crying thing was inches away. I'd either uncover the source of the illusion—not one of my better ideas—or discover this had been a total wild goose chase.

A shred more digging. With zero warning, dirt and debris exploded around me. Two coal black cats shot through the breach I'd created, yowling mournfully. They ignored me and glommed onto a severed thigh, ripping through flesh with sharp teeth.

"You should come with me," I suggested.

If they heard, there was no indication. Plus, I had no way to drag them through the series of walls I'd passed. If my body had been part of the picture, my heart would have been pounding like a trip-hammer.

After taking a moment to get my bearings so I didn't end up lost in this maze of broken walls, I worked my way toward my body. Its pull was strong. Good thing since I'd never done this for anywhere near as long before.

Son of a bitch. I'd done all this for two feral cats. Why hadn't Joss sensed them? He has an affinity for animals. Hell, why hadn't I figured it out? Somehow I skipped the last couple of walls and slammed into my body so hard I yelped.

The arm Joss had tossed around my shoulders tightened. "Fuck. I thought you were never coming back. I was stuck guarding your body, so I couldn't go after you. Never do that again."

He was on his feet now, voice brusque.

"I didn't tell you to do that," I choked out.

"No, but I know enough about projections to not leave in the middle of one."

Still reeling from the collision of body and essence, I dropped my head into my hands and rubbed my aching temples. "Cats," I muttered.

"Huh? You're not making sense, woman."

"What we heard was two cats." I tried to get my legs under me, but everything wobbled.

"Not possible."

"I saw them." This time, I lurched upright, swaying precariously.

"You only thought you saw them. They had to be something else."

Walking might make things better. It could scarcely make them worse. I started toward the north, assuming he'd follow me. My mouth was dry. My head pounded. I needed water. Food.

Joss caught up. "What did these cats do?"

"Once I freed them from where they'd been buried, they started eating the dead."

He snapped his fingers. "Incubus. Or succubus. Bet they were black."

Lost was a mild term for my current mental state. "Yeah,

they were. But what do spirits of the dead have to do with anything?"

"They'd be drawn to all this carnage. Some of them can shapeshift."

First I'd heard of it. "They're demons, right?"

"Yes. Normally, they're drawn to sleeping mortals, but dead ones are a close second. They have sex with them and leave demon residue."

"Why?" My vision hazed, turning double. I staggered.

"To push the gates to Hell farther open. What's wrong?"

"Used too much magic. Need water and food."

Shading his eyes with a hand, he scanned the skies, presumably looking for Connor. "We should run into Oak Creek soon. Not sure it will be safe, but better than what's left of the public water supply."

"Where?" My throat ached.

Power pulsed briefly. "That way. Maybe a quarter mile. It will take us off course."

An image of people waiting in the bus back in Mexico dogged me. I should be going back for them, but tottering from point A to point B was almost beyond my current ability. Why had I insisted on chasing down the cats that weren't?

Because you have a soft spot, my inner voice whispered.

Clinging to it flew in the face of the new normal, but if I didn't the woman I'd been would be lost. I didn't think I'd like who took her place.

"River."

Part dragging, part guiding, Joss led me down a hill to a

creek. Heedless of what might be in the water, I knelt, cupped my hands, and sucked icy liquid down my throat.

A mangled snort brought my head snapping around. Joss moved closer to me. On the far side of the creek sat two black cats, tails curved around their bodies.

Was it the same ones?

Almost had to be since nothing else alive had made itself known. In the space between seeing them and my next breath, they vanished and rematerialized a few feet away.

The one on the left stretched a paw toward me. The paw turned into a hand as the cat shimmered into a stunning man. Fair hair streamed down his perfect naked form. Desire hit me in the groin, hot, viscous, impossible to deny. I'd never wanted anyone the way I wanted the—

Jerking my gaze away, I grabbed Joss's arm. Words tumbled from my lips. Seconds later, we were back in a journey channel. The ragged sound of our combined breath rasped against my ears.

"Good call," he panted. "Another second, they'd have had us."

They? And then it occurred to me the other cat must have transformed into a woman. I'd been so fixated on the male I hadn't noticed.

Cutting the flow of power, critical since I was running on fumes, we tumbled out into yet one more part of Sedona. We should be farther north, but were we?

At least this time, we didn't fall from hundreds of feet in the air.

"Why target us?" I mumbled.

"We're the only thing that isn't dead," he said dryly.

"Nice work, Alia. We're nearer the northern edge of town than we were."

He didn't ask how I was holding up.

Why would he?

We had a job to do, one I'd failed miserably at so far. After a hasty directional check, I plodded on. Connor would show up. Or not. Joss wasn't any more inclined to talk than I was.

The distant noise from explosions had quieted. In a weird way, it felt like whatever was rolling through was done here. Nothing left to annihilate.

"This way." Josh veered right.

Too weary to question him, I kept walking.

CHAPTER SIX, RHYS

The journey channels didn't yield any clues; neither was there anything malevolent. After wasting a couple of hours, guilt drove me back to the bus. It was where I'd left it, but empty. Either I'd been gone too long, or something had spooked the rest of my students enough to drive them out into the world. The steady stream of refugees had slowed to a trickle.

Fear sheeted from the few pilgrims still on the move. When I looked more closely, they were wending their way around downed bodies. Were they corpses? What the hell had happened here? I wanted to know, but not badly enough to blow still more time asking questions.

Or examining the dead.

I pulled the keys. No reason to make it easy for someone to hijack the rig if the traffic jam ever abated. Didn't seem likely. Every vehicle sat empty, abandoned after people despaired of the snarl ever untangling itself.

Smoke mingled with the unmistakable stench of blood, guts, and death.

Staring at the keys, I grunted and stuffed them back into the ignition. Guilty as the next person, I was still stuck in "old world" thought patterns. The odds of me ever returning to reclaim my bus were nil.

Responsibility weighed heavy. I hated to waste the magic, but I teleported to the retreat center. Half a dozen of my attendees were straggling into the courtyard.

"Where's everyone else?" I asked.

"You don't want to know," a witch rasped.

"Are they where I can help them?"

"No," a man named Damon said brusquely.

All right, then. Something was having a heyday gorging themselves on corpses. I rifled through possibilities. Vampires, except they usually can't tolerate daylight. Demons were my next bet. Had whoever perpetrated this ripped down the gates of Hell?

I collected my thoughts and said, "I cannot remain with you. You're welcome to stay here as long as you'd like. The water should be safe to drink since it comes from glaciers. There's some food in the cookhouse. When it's gone, you'll have to gather plants and hunt."

"Will you ever return?" the witch asked.

I flirted with a kind lie but discarded it. "No. Survival will hang by a thread. My skills are needed elsewhere. I can take a few of you with me to Arizona."

"Don't take this wrong," Damon replied, "but I'll take my chances here."

Maybe the others were playing off his game card,

but no one volunteered. Just as well. I'd reached a point where conserving my ability felt important, and Alia was still missing. I skipped the part about wishing them well—talk was cheap—and slid back into a journey spell.

They'd been fortunate to be well on their way to the retreat center when the shit—whatever it was—had hit the fan. It was the only reason any of them were still alive. But they must know as much since they were aware of what befell their companions.

The velvet darkness of another channel surrounded me. Unlike my last sojourn, warnings jabbed me. If the other side had commandeered this network, I'd be stuck wherever I came out. At least they weren't strong enough to bar my entry.

Not yet anyway.

Breath rattled from me. All my years of semi-preparedness had been a cosmic joke. At some level, I hadn't believed my own hype. Assuming I had infinite time had been a serious miscalculation.

"Stop," I muttered to jostle my mind off the hamster wheel where it had taken up residence. What I'd done to date—or not—mattered little. The critical element was what I did from here on in.

Locating Alia sat at the top of my list. So far, I was batting zero. Once I found her, we'd regroup, assess what we had to work with, and—

Whoa, an inner voice cautioned.

The greenest of reluctant recruits, Alia might not want to sign on with me. For all I knew, she, Connor, and Joss had formed an alliance, one where there wasn't space for another mage.

Darts poked me, a potent reminder to hustle back to the caves. Since it might be my last chance in this space, I sent out feelers tuned to Alia's energy. Every mage has a unique feel; it's true even within types of sorcery. Each witch has an individual signature. Ditto for each Druid, Fae, or Sidhe.

Considering different types of magic wielders reminded me I had no idea what Alia actually was.

The barrage of darts grew thicker. A dark presence rolled toward me, not quickly but edging near in its own time.

Damn it. How much longer until I could leave this infernal channel? Staring to the right, I waited for the next node.

And waited.

Had someone blown up the ancient navigation markings? My guts were tight; I unclenched my hands and flexed the fingers.

Worried and certain I was on my own, I drew on my inner bearing system. It's never worked well in this environment. As I expected, my efforts were sluggish, slow to respond. A welcome silver flash drew my attention.

Breath whooshed from me. I dived on top of the node to make certain I could read it before it vanished.

Not the worst news. At a normal trajectory, I was roughly six minutes from my exit. Another node should appear just before, but I didn't trust it would, so I began counting: one-one thousand, two-one thousand...

Somewhere between the third and fourth minute, my

attention wavered. Blood flowed from places darts had skewered me. The bad thing was closer. Much closer. Did I have two minutes left?

Determined to stick this out until I couldn't, I gathered power to launch myself out of the channel and balanced it between my fingertips. The glow of my working lit the endless dark but didn't soothe my worries. The node that should have been here by now hadn't made an appearance.

Since I'd quit counting, I wasn't certain of my precise location. Distant booming jostled with claps of what sounded like thunder. The temperature plummeted.

Worse, the light from my fledgling spell dimmed. Someone wanted me right where I was.

We'll see about that.

Wherever I was, it was close enough. Reaching for my spell, I ignited it. What usually happens is the colors explode. Mine barely flickered.

Shit.

I ground my teeth in frustration and poured enchantment into my exit. One chance. If I didn't escape, I'd truly be stuck here with no way to replenish my power.

Moldering in these channels until something siphoned what was left of my magic before sucking the marrow from my bones was unsettling. As if to punctuate my prediction, darkness rolled ever nearer. Malevolent laughter joined it.

"Come on, goddammit," I urged.

Nothing but wide open would do. I gave it everything I had. My heart pounded; my throat was dry. The lightheaded, nauseous feeling I get when I've shot my wad descended.

I kept on pushing. At this point, I didn't give a shit where I emerged, so long as I was out of the journey channel. Consciousness flickered. I made a grab for it and hung on tight.

A bolt of light cut through the black. I dove through, not trusting it to remain open. It didn't. Clanging as it snapped shut, it caught one of my ankles. I felt backdraft and searing pain as I jerked my leg free.

And then I was falling. No magic left to form a cushion.

Had I done all this for nothing?

It was like slogging through quicksand, but I wove a sloppy mesh canopy. Not much protection, but enough to save me from broken bones. I slammed into dirt hard enough to knock the wind out of me. My ankle ached, but it was minor.

Shaking, I rolled onto my knees and vomited onto a pile of rocks. Sour-smelling sweat dripped down my sides. I forced myself upright and took stock of where I was.

Sagebrush stretched on all sides. A pathetic creek was a few hundred yards away. I made my way to it, fell onto my belly, and washed sickness out of my mouth and off my chin. Once it was gone, I drank. Sometimes water in the desert is poison, but this smelled all right.

Bits of power returned, not exactly in a rush, but at least I wasn't scratching bedrock. As soon as I had enough juice, I triangulated my location against the setting sun.

Not too bad. I was only a few miles from where I'd hoped. When I was a bit closer to the caves, I could initiate a jump spell. Teleporting over short distances doesn't require the channel I'd narrowly escaped from.

As I trudged toward the caves, I did my best to reconstruct what had been gunning for me. Nothing about my recall was clean. I'd have loved it if my memory screamed demon, or one of the denizens from the Mexican underworld.

Anything clear-cut would be an improvement over my total lack of answers. I needed to return to the Old Country, confer with others like me.

Yeah, like that was about to happen anytime soon. Hell would freeze over before I'd engage in a long teleport again.

At least the desert still had rodents and insects. Somehow, they'd escaped destruction. If I'd had time, I'd have stopped to talk with them, hear what happened to turn their world upside down.

A hawk crested the horizon. The sight lifted my heavy heart. Perhaps this small geographic section had escaped unscathed. It took a moment before I realized the bird was flying toward me. Shading my eyes with a hand, I took a closer look.

Connor.

Relief beat a path through me. If he was all right, Alia and Joss had to be too.

Not had to be, but the odds just improved. I broke into a run.

He did a mid-air flip, landing on his feet in his human body. "Thought I felt your presence," he panted.

A cut marred one cheekbone. His usual devil-may-care persona had taken a hike.

"Tell me," I urged. "Everything."

A shrug. "Not much to tell. Sedona looks a lot like Mazatlán did. Nothing left but a nasty ruin."

I spun one hand in a get-on-with-it gesture.

He nodded. "Sorry. Not firing on all cylinders. Something had it in for us in the tunnels. We lost the image of our destination. Alia had been to Sedona, so she dialed in her own. We ended up in the center of the city. Shops. Restaurants. Corpses. I don't get it. At least there were still living people in Mexico."

"They're thinning out fast," I informed him. "I was just there."

A shudder racked him. I took off my jacket and handed it over. No more sunlight to warm the desert.

"We split up," Connor went on and shrugged into my coat. "Since I can fly, my job was to find those caves of yours. I looked and looked." Another shrug. "Nada. I was on my way back to locate Alia and Joss when something pinged off a corner of my energy field. My hawk thought it might be you."

Thank the goddess for small favors. "Kudos to your hawk. We're maybe two miles from the caves on this trajectory." I pointed southwest. "When you find Alia and Joss—"

I regrouped. Better for us to stick together. "Would your hawk mind riding on my shoulder?"

Connor shut his eyes for a moment before answering. "Yes, but he says he'll do it."

He got out of my jacket and shifted. Amber avian eyes regarded me sternly. I didn't blame him. So far, I'd made a botch of an event I should have been far better prepared for.

Jacket on, hawk on my shoulder, I set off at a lope angling toward town with magical antennae extended. I'd find Alia no matter what.

"What happened here?" the hawk—or maybe it was Connor—asked. *"Has to be related to whatever chased us out of the journey channel. And everything else too."*

"It is," I replied. "Just not certain of any of the ramifications."

"Do you have a plan?"

I could have lied, but what was the percentage? "No. Not really. Other than to ferry us to a safe spot to buy us breathing space so we can figure out what to do next."

"Who's doing this?" Connor's mind voice cracked, revealing how pressured he felt.

"We'll talk about it once we're together. There are hints in lore I read back in the 1700s, and—"

The hawk cawed raucously. *"Impossible. No one is that old."*

Oops. "Yes, many are. We're quiet about it, though."

I'd reached the distant eastern edges of Sedona, a residential district. Smoke singed my nostrils; distant booming drilled into the pit of my stomach. I reached to stroke the hawk's plumage. He shied away.

"I bet one of these houses has clothes that will fit your partner," I suggested to offer him an out from such close proximity to me.

Connor didn't wait to be asked a second time. He vaulted from my shoulder. After shifting in midair again, he hurried into the nearest house. One side had caved in, hopefully not the bedroom wing. A minute later, he ran out with clothing slung over one arm and jetted into the next house.

The hunt was good. When he emerged a second time, shoes dangled from one hand. He dropped his bounty on the ground and proceeded to step into tan chinos, a stretchy blue shirt, socks and beat-up running shoes. The last item was a black fleece jacket.

"That was a good idea," he mumbled. "Let's go."

During the few minutes he'd been dressing, I'd upped the ante on my search for Alia and Joss. Actually, I was only hunting Alia with the assumption Joss would be with her.

"They're not far," I told him. "Half a mile or so and heading our way."

He shot me an odd look from beneath hooded lids. Probably, my disclosure about my age still festered. I'd come across long-lived shifters before, but Connor had been on his own for years. Shifters tended not to band together like they used to a hundred years ago.

"Tell me again how you discovered you were a shifter," I prodded.

"I visualized the hawk from when I was a child. He was in all my dreams, day and night. I tried to talk about him with my parents, but they told me all children had imaginary friends.

"One day when I was fourteen, I was walking alone by a lake. It was nighttime, and I was heading home from football practice." He stopped walking, head bowed and hands curled into fists. For a time, the only sound was the rasp of his breathing.

We needed to get going, but I'd broached the question.

He could have shut me down, but he was doing his best to reconstruct his first shift.

"You're safe here. I won't let anything hurt you or your familiar."

He scrunched his eyes tight. "Pain. So much pain. A knife jabbed into my guts, ripped me from breastbone to pelvis. When it cleared, the world looked different. My clothes lay on the ground in a tattered heap. I'd catch hell for that, but it was the least of my concerns.

"My body wasn't mine any longer. I'd turned into the hawk from my dreams. Before I knew it, we were airborne, scribing circles in the still, night air. It was the start of everything. The hawk didn't talk with me for many months afterward, but we'd sneak out almost every night to fly."

He opened his eyes and raked a hand through his tangled hair. "It was my secret. Mine and his. I knew not to tell anyone."

"Have you known any other shifters?"

He shook his head. "Not until I arrived at your retreat. It's why I signed up. Not to find others like me, but to learn about that part of myself."

I started walking again. The beacon of Alia's magic pulsed weakly.

"Things didn't used to be like this," I murmured.

"Like what?"

"Where magic is dirty, something to be hidden away. Long ago, mortals revered those like us."

He snorted. "Times have changed."

Given the wreckage scattered around us, it was a major understatement.

Timbers and stucco blocked our way over and over. The reek of decaying flesh grew stronger as we passed parts of the city that had been densely populated.

Alia's unique signature beat a tattoo against my magical center. Why couldn't I see her?

Heedless of attracting unwanted attention, I raised my mind voice. *"Alia! Joss!"*

Movement from a block away could be them—or not. Defensive magic crackled weakly between my palms. Damn. Would it be enough to repel a sand flea, let alone a dark mage?

Two figures shambled toward us. Joss had his arm around Alia, supporting her. Crap. Had she been injured?

Connor shot forward and wrapped his arms around them both.

By the time they reached me, I had a mini-teleport spell at the ready. If luck was with me, it would be sufficient to move us to the caves.

"Tap into our energy," Joss suggested. With his Druid's intuition dialed in, he'd sensed my deep weariness.

Shamelessly borrowing power, I added it to my fledgling casting and visualized the area in front of the caves. Scant hours had passed since I'd left, yet it felt like days.

Worse, I'd wasted years when I could have prepared for—

"Rhys?" Alia's hazel gaze bored into me.

"We've got this," I growled and kindled my casting. A million and one things could intercept us, force us off course. We'd be helpless during the seconds before my spell spit us out.

The street strewn with body parts, broken timber, and masonry shimmered to nothing. I counted to five before the edges of my casting lightened. As it dissipated, red rocks splashed the horizon catching the last of the day's light. Or perhaps it was the newly risen moon.

I hustled everyone past the barrier shielding the cave entrance from casual exploration.

"I was here and didn't even know it," Connor muttered and drove a fist into a wall.

"Encouraging." I tried for a positive note. "Means others will waltz right past too."

We hadn't covered fifty feet before Joss called, "Wait."

When I turned back, Alia was swaying on her feet, babbling incoherently. After sweeping her into my arms, I kept walking. We needed a break. Where were the four I'd left here?

I'd told them to stay put. Hopefully, they'd done just that. Unauthorized exploration could bring the wrong kind of company to our very doorstep. Suddenly cautious, I pushed power, what little I had left, all around me and breathed a little easier when nothing feral or foul tangled in its webbing.

CHAPTER SEVEN, ALIA

I should have been happier to be reunited with Connor and Rhys. Exhaustion dogged me. Ever since I'd spirited us away from the incubus/succubus duo, I hadn't felt like myself.

At all.

Maybe it was because I'd run through so much power so quickly. For the millionth time I wished I knew more about my own abilities, the same ones I'd been running from since they first reared their pesky heads.

Waves of dizziness rippled through me. My knees wobbled; breathing required attention. Would I simply stop sucking in oxygen if I didn't stay on top of this?

Had the incubus done something? I didn't see how. He hadn't laid a hand on me. Still, a weight pressed on my chest. Each breath cost me. Rhys held me against him as he hurried along dirt corridors muttering in a language I'd never heard.

How had I ended up in his arms? My memory was just as fragmented as the rest of me. Consciousness ebbed and flowed. Some moments everything was clear, others I gazed through viscous mud.

"Lay her down," Connor said.

"Planning on it," Rhys growled and placed me on something soft and fragrant. Lilacs, maybe, or some other kind of spring flower. How did flowers grow underground?

"Be still," Rhys instructed and ran his hands down my body stopping here and there. His touch was far too familiar, but I was too disoriented to protest. Besides, he was seeking information. My prudish twenty-first century morals had no place in this setting.

I'd never had a boyfriend, not an intimate one. Always been terrified of letting anyone get close enough to ferret out my secret. Conversation buzzed against my ears. With great effort I snatched a phrase here, another there.

"Tell me everything," Rhys demanded, but he wasn't talking to me.

Joss rambled on. I heard cats and demons before Rhys held up a hand. Crap, my eyes were closed. How was I seeing anything?

"Hold her," Rhys said in a tone sharp enough to etch granite.

Hands closed around my ankles. Another set raised my hands over my head and circled my wrists. If my body was still within my control, I'd have writhed, but paralysis was setting in.

Rhys bent close and placed a hand on my cheek.

Warmth seared me; it was when I understood my body temperature had dropped to freezer temperature.

"This will not be pleasant," he said, "but you must remain still."

I struggled to form words and failed. Moving my mouth, my lips was beyond me. Panic surged. My heart beat wildly, flailing against my ribs.

"I'll be as quick as I can," he went on.

The hand moved from my cheek to my abdomen. His other hand settled on my forehead. He chanted in the same language from earlier. Heat began in my head and shot through my body. A fiery brand wouldn't have hurt worse, except this one scoured my insides. I waited for smoke, for flames to erupt from my mouth.

Nada.

Screams crowded my throat, but my petrified muscles couldn't let them out. The effect was suffocating. Another hand squeezed the sides of my jaw forcing it open. It helped a little.

Scenes played out behind my closed lids. Horrific images of death and destruction. Cities exploded and caught fire. Unspeakable monsters ripped humans from stem to stern extracting organs and treating them as hors d'oeuvres. Flashes of the University of Oregon campus intruded from time to time. Nothing left there, either.

It flattened hope I'd held that perhaps points north had somehow been spared.

The intense heat turned into sharp jabs. I was being sliced into ribbons from the inside out. Squeals and groans battered me. It took a moment for me to recognize they were coming from me. I tested my mouth.

It moved again.

Rhys had said he'd be quick. It felt like I'd been here, skewered as a vestal sacrifice, for hours.

Freed from the cage of my throat, screams reverberated. Holding back from writhing was the hardest thing I've ever done. The acrid stench of blood burned my nostrils.

"Got it," Rhys shouted.

The pain receded as quickly as it had come, leaving me panting and shaken. He rocked back on his heels. Joss made a choking sound. Connor muttered, "Holy godhead."

Wrenching my eyes open, I struggled to sit. No one held me back.

Rhys was on his feet moving fast.

"I need to see it," I rasped. He'd extracted something from my body. I had to know what it was.

"Better if you don't," he said.

I rolled onto all fours and levered myself upright. My head spun, my vision hazed. I stuck it out by sheer will. "Better if I do," I wheezed.

He turned. A clear, gelatinous ball was between his hands. Within its depths lay a creature with a cat's hindquarters and a demon's head complete with horns. The abomination was black. Its mouth was open as it bit and tore at the enclosure.

"It must be destroyed," Rhys growled and left the room at a dead run.

I glanced around. We were in a smallish cavern. A pallet

was pushed against one wall. The floor was dirt with a few rocks. Water dribbled in several spots.

My head pounded. I rubbed my temples and looked from Joss to Connor. "That, that thing," I croaked. "Was it really inside me?"

Both men nodded.

"How come the succubus didn't invade you?" I stared at Joss.

He turned his hands palms up. "First off, we don't know if that thing inside you was an incubus. Need to ask Rhys. Maybe I'd have had problems with the succubus if we'd stuck around. Anyway, I'm relieved you're all right. You've seemed off ever since you spirited us away from them."

"I've felt off too." As a reminder to my muscles that they had a job to do, I walked in small circles. My insides felt raw, tender. Would there be long-term consequences from my unwelcome visitor?

"And now?" Connor arched a dark brow.

I turned my attention inward, taking stock. "Far from 100 percent, but better."

"That's a relief. I was worried."

"Me as well," Joss said.

I raked my fingers through my hair. "Did Rhys bring anyone from the bus here? Don't we need to go back? It's been hours. They could all be dead for all we know."

Joss touched my arm. "You're not thinking. The teleport channels hold danger."

"They do, indeed," Rhys boomed from the corridor. "That thing I pulled from Alia inveigled its way in while you were traveling. It had naught to do with your run-in with demons."

"Then why did it look like a cat?" I asked.

"It didn't. Not really. It had hind legs and a tail, but that description could be applied to many entities." Breath hissed through his even teeth. "I brought four others from the bus with me. They're not here. I must find them. Meanwhile, stay put. It's a waste of time and magic to be constantly chasing after you."

"Not us," I corrected him.

He flapped a hand my way. "Technicalities. You understood my point."

"What about the others from the bus? Are we just going to leave them there?" I asked.

"Already been back," he informed me. "About half of them returned to the retreat center. The others…"

I opened my mouth to press for details but changed my mind.

"Of course we'll wait," Connor cut in. "Is there any possibility of food or water?"

Rhys clamped his jaws together. A muscle danced beneath one eye. If he hadn't wanted to saddle himself with us, why were we even here?

"It's not unreasonable," I pointed out. None of us have eaten since dinner last night."

"We drank out of a sketchy creek," Joss added.

"Follow me," Rhys growled and led the way down a maze of branching tunnels. After the third turn, I gave up keeping track. At least I was feeling stronger. The half-dead sense was gone.

Our next stop was in a much larger cavern with a pool in its center. Small, luminous, wall-clinging lichen provided pale illumination throughout the tunnels and caverns.

"There should be dried grains and other foodstuffs in those cabinets." Rhys pointed. "Pots too. You'll have to conjure heat, but it's a simple enough affair. I will return as soon as I can."

Before we could question him further, he was gone.

My stomach growled. Joss was already pawing through cloth bags in one of the cupboards. I knelt by the pool and scooped handfuls of water into my mouth. It was fresh, sweet, and refreshing. Joss dipped a pot into the water and returned to the far side of the room. I didn't ask what he was making. Didn't matter. I'd have eaten grasshoppers at this point.

"How are you feeling?" Connor asked again.

I raised my streaming face. "Better."

He scrubbed the heels of his hands down his face. "Still struggling to wrap my mind around all of this. Less than twenty-four hours ago..."

"Everything was still normal," I supplied.

He nodded.

"Cornmeal and dried beans okay?" Joss asked.

"Whatever you make will be wonderful," I replied.

Connor crouched and drank from the pool. When he raised his head, he murmured, "Do you suppose anything is left anywhere?"

"Trying not to think about that," Joss called over his shoulder. He'd crafted a makeshift hearth out of a few stones. It appeared he was directing magic to heat them, which then warmed the contents of his pot likely speeding the cooking process.

"We'll find out soon enough," I said, "but we should be prepared for the worst. While Rhys was working on me, one of my visions was the University of Oregon campus. It was just as trashed as everything else we've seen."

"What could have done this?" Connor was on his feet again.

"What I want to know is why," Joss said.

I kept my mouth shut. The "why" didn't make much difference. I was more worried about where they'd strike next and what they—whoever they were—planned to do with us.

"The worst of this," Connor went on, "is if we hadn't gone to that retreat, we'd probably be dead right now."

"Has to be a reason we're not," I murmured.

"Not really," Joss cut in. "Might be pure, blind luck. Or maybe our magic has a protective aspect. How about if one of you looks for bowls and spoons. This is almost cooked."

I crossed the cavern and began rooting through trunks and cupboards. "Quite a bit of food here. Wonder who stocked the place."

"Guessing it was Rhys since he knew about it," Connor said.

I pulled dusty glazed ceramic bowls from a trunk and rinsed them in the pool. My next find was badly tarnished silver spoons. Holding one up, I turned it over. "This is old. I suspect the bowls are too."

"Doesn't mean they ended up here when they were new," Joss said. "Regardless, bring them over. I'll dish us up."

We sat cross-legged on the floor close enough to the pool to wash the polenta bean mixture down with spring water. At least we weren't going to starve. If it was only the four of us, there was enough food to last a few months.

Well, perhaps two.

"Wonder what happened to Rhys," Joss said.

"Does it matter?" I shot back. The unnatural weariness had departed, but I was walking a tightrope between being an ostrich and running out of the cave system weeping and tearing my hair. I've always been mildly claustrophobic, and I'd been siphoning magic to keep from bolting.

"Yeah, it does," Joss countered. "It isn't as if we're going to wait for him forever."

"We don't know enough to strike out on our own," Connor muttered.

"This conversation is premature," I announced. "We have to give Rhys latitude. A few days before we develop our own plans."

"We should stick together," Connor said.

"No one said we weren't going to," I retorted. My spoon scraped the bowl; I levered myself upright and strode to where Joss had left the cookpot. In the interest of "we're all in this together," I ferried it back to where we'd been eating, helped myself, and sat down.

For a time, the only sounds in the cave were the clink of implements on ceramic and the gently flowing inlet stream into the pool.

"Do you think we should save some?" Connor held the cookpot, gazing into its depths.

"Nah." Joss rolled his shoulders back. "Plenty more where that came from."

An idea blasted me, so elemental I felt stupid for not thinking about it before. "We need to find supermarkets," I told the men.

Two sets of eyes bored into me. "Why?" Connor asked.

"They'll just be closed," Joss said.

I nodded. "Exactly. The food won't have gone bad yet. We can add to our stocks here by a good big bunch."

"It's a good idea," Connor said.

"Except we promised Rhys we'd wait," Joss tossed out.

"Not indefinitely," I told him. "We have another day or so before the fresh food starts to turn. Canned and boxed shit won't spoil."

"Anyone mind if I finish this?" Connor's spoon hovered above the cookpot.

"Go ahead," Joss said.

I echoed the sentiment.

Footsteps pounding along the corridor drove all of us to our feet. The pot clattered to the ground as we rushed toward the door. Not that I'm proficient, but I crafted a hasty defensive spell, holding it between my hands. My palms stung. The monstrosity my body housed had damaged it. One of Rhys's many lessons had covered self-healing, but I'd be damned if I recalled the basics.

I stared down the tunnel outside the cavern. Forms moved toward us, but it was too dark to identify them.

I called Rhys's name about the time two wolves coalesced from the darkness. Their muzzles were coated with blood, which suggested they'd been fighting or feeding —perhaps both.

"It's me," he yelled back.

I released my magic and rubbed my hands together working to get circulation back into my fingers. The freezing-from-the-inside-out sensation wasn't totally gone after all.

The wolves shifted, turning into the sisters from the retreat. Okay, so that was two. Rhys had indicated he'd transported four. Who were the others? More pertinently, where were they?

Rhys caught up with us and shooed everyone into the room where we'd eaten.

"What happened to the others?" I asked.

"Smells good in here," he said. "How about making more of whatever you just ate?"

"I can do that," Joss said.

The sisters sat next to the pool, slurping water.

"I have to go back out and try to find the witch and the brown-eyed woman with her crucifix," Rhys said.

I made a grunting noise and blurted, "She had absolutely zero magic."

"Exactly why I have to make an effort to find her," Rhys explained. He looked tired. Dark circles rode beneath his eyes; his shoulders slumped.

"We told you," one of the sisters said, "she's probably dead."

"Yeah, last we saw, something with two sets of arms was dragging her into that broken-up house near where you found us. The witch should still be in the grocery store one building over," the other sister added.

"Maybe they mean to save Teresa for later." Rhys named the woman with no magic. "Set some of whatever you're making aside for me," he told Joss and hurried out the door.

"Why'd you leave when Rhys told you not to?" Connor stood over the shifters, arms crossed over his chest.

"Look at the Boy Scout," the sister with dark hair sneered.

I joined Connor. "We're on the same side," I reminded them. "What are your names?" I'd known at some point, but the part of my brain that stored data had been affected by my uninvited visitor.

"You were really out of it through the retreat if you don't remember," the other sister said.

"Stop. Just stop." Connor spread his hands in front of him. "Hasn't been easy for any of us. One of you is Karen and the other Moriah, but I don't recall which is which."

"I'm Karen," the dark-haired one replied sullenly. Her tresses were greasy and fell to shoulder level.

It meant Moriah had to be the one with red-gray, shoulder-length hair. Both sisters had dark brown eyes with inky pupils.

"You still haven't told us why you left," Joss prodded.

"We were hungry. Figured we'd hunt," Moriah said.

"We told the witch and whatever the other gal is to stay here, but they didn't want to be alone, so we all went," Karen added.

"The witch wormed her way into what was left of a Safeway." Moriah picked up the tale. When Teresa—that's the one with no magic—tried to follow her, this thing rose up out of nowhere and snatched her."

"What did it look like?" Connor asked.

Moriah made a choking sound. "A werewolf. Except they're not supposed to be able to shift in broad daylight except during the full moon."

"Nah," Karen chimed in. "It had at least four arms."

"We took our wolf forms, but then Rhys showed up." Karen dusted her hands down her nude body. "Of course, now we have no clothes."

I didn't bother to point out they hadn't had them in the bus, either, until they'd picked up what I'd salvaged from the winding mountain road.

"Bet there's something around here somewhere," I told them.

Joss retreated to his cookpot, presumably to make another batch of beans and polenta.

I continued my exploration of the trunks and cupboards because it beat slapping Karen and Moriah silly. I wanted to strike out on my own, but I owed it to Rhys to at least be here when he returned. Maybe he had a plan.

Or not.

How could anyone have plans for the end of the world?

Nervous energy jabbed me from all sides. "I'm not leaving this cave system," I told everyone, "but I am going to see what's in the other caverns."

"I'll go with you." Connor was by my side in a flash.

No one tried to stop us as we walked into the dirt-floored corridor.

"Right or left?" Connor asked.

I shrugged. "Let's be methodical about this and leave markers so we don't get lost."

We worked a pattern. Closest grotto on the right then closest on the left. We moved out from there. Most of the mini-caves were empty. "Why do you suppose no one protested when we left?" I asked.

"Ha. That's an easy one, Alia."

I entered the third cave down on the left. "If it's so easy, tell me."

"Two less mouths to feed."

"But it's not as if..." His words sank in. Breath whooshed from me. Was this my new reality where no one mourned if you came up missing?

"Sometimes the truth hurts." He crossed to a large armoire. "Wonder what's in here?"

The fine hairs on the back of my neck shot to attention. I screamed, "Don't touch it."

"But it wants me to." A dreamy quality entered Connor's deep voice.

Launching myself at him, I grabbed his arm. "Come on. We have to leave." It was like pulling on a boulder. I drilled into his mind, seeking the hawk. *"Help me."*

Connor shook himself, but at least he followed me out of the cavern. "Not fair to recruit my hawk," he protested.

"Leaving you for whatever's locked in that cabinet wouldn't have been, either." I chewed my lower lip. "We need to get back to the others."

"But we've barely begun."

A creeping sense of something ancient, something we'd disturbed, washed through me. Perhaps it wasn't evil, but it was eager for fresh magic.

"We can do more later." I adopted a placating tone and

led the way to the place we'd left. Relief sloughed through me when I heard voices. Rhys had reasons for his instructions. These caverns were riddled with power, not all of which was benign.

Connor shook himself from head to foot. "What just happened? I can't remember any of it."

"We'll talk about it soon. Come on. We're nearly back to where we started."

CHAPTER EIGHT, RHYS

The shifter sisters had found me. Their wolf bodies offered protection to some extent, but they'd been quick to follow when I ordered them to return. I'd have sent them on their own, except I didn't trust they wouldn't run into trouble. They might not sense it, but energy poured through Sedona's ruins.

The New Agers had labeled it a vortex and with good reason. It masked a major gateway to other worlds. I hadn't taken the time to examine the precise spot, but I felt certain the barrier had fallen.

Was that what had happened? Was every portal all over the world gone? Machu Pichu had housed another. It might account for the wreckage in southwestern Mexico. Or perhaps Mayan ruins in the Sierra Madre mountains held their own gateway, one I hadn't stumbled across.

For the first time in a long while I longed for my guild house on the Isle of Skye off the Scottish coast. We'd had a comprehensive library, one cultivated for centuries. Surely within its dusty tomes I'd find a map of every gateway worldwide.

I pulled shadows around me as I loped to where I'd found Karen and Moriah. If they were correct, the witch could still be in wreckage that had a Safeway sign dangling from one post. I sent seeking magic in a 360 degree arc. No reason to belly crawl into the place if she wasn't there.

Twenty-twenty hindsight stabbed me. What on earth had driven me to load everyone into the bus and hurtle down the mountainside? The Sedona location was better, but not that much. At the time, I hadn't realized the extent of...of whatever. I lacked a name for it.

So far, my energies had been devoted to moving us. In doing so, I'd lost half my charges.

They wouldn't have survived this, anyway.

My inner voice was brutally honest. Out of the group, the ones with any magical ability at all were here. Some would probably strike out for where their homes had been. Nothing I could do about that.

A weak ping drew me forward. Nola was inside, after all. *"Come on out,"* I told her.

Minutes ticked past, followed by more. No answer and no witch.

I examined a space between masonry and fallen timbers. She'd passed through here, but so had others. I squeezed my eyes shut. Damn it. I wasn't thinking. The store had food. It would be a draw, except I hadn't found anyone alive beyond my crew.

I was tired, but it was a piss-poor excuse. I sent one more

beam of seeking power into the store. This time, I paid close attention and sought anything moving. Not necessarily anything with a heartbeat.

An entirely different picture bloomed in my mind. Lots of activity in the grocery, none of it human. I took stock of my power. It was depleted because I was. Did I have enough mojo to take on the collection of werewolves and vampires I'd sensed within? The darkened interior provided a perfect hunting ground for the undead.

Undead. How had they even gotten here? Last I checked, vamps hated water. Crossing oceans should be beyond them. Sure, there was sort of a land bridge from eastern Russia to Alaska, but it also required touching water. Plus, I couldn't imagine any vampire being determined enough to go to all that work.

Not when there were plenty of food sources nearby.

Geography aside, I considered vampires' feeding habits. If they hadn't turned Nola yet, they would soon. Intervening might be a fool's errand. Still, I couldn't simply leave her. Feverishly thumbing through my mental file on vampires, I found inconsistencies, but if she hadn't yet drunk from their wrists, I could save her.

Vampires, even the old ones, don't do much during daylight hours. They're sluggish, lethargic.

The more I turned it over in my head, the surer I was a quick in and equally quick exit was doable. I'd pinpoint Nola's location, ride a jump spell to it, grab her, and leave the same way.

No one would be expecting me. In the time it took them to react, we'd be gone.

I hoped.

I rolled my shoulders back, hearing small bones crack, and glanced at the sky. Maybe another hour until dusk. Should be plenty of time. To hedge my bets, I hustled down the street to what had been one of Sedona's many jewelry stores. Since no one was alive to guard the spoils, I forced my way past a precariously leaning wall and found what I sought.

Silver daggers. The first two might be labeled silver, but they weren't. Digging through a rubble heap, I unearthed one that was truly a silver alloy and tucked it into my jacket pocket. Riding on a hunch, I shouldered my way to the back and found a small kitchen. It had salt.

Holy water would have been useful, but I didn't have time to locate a Catholic church. Besides, most of the vials had probably burst open during the worst of the explosions.

As ready as I was likely to be, I returned to the grocery store. A quick scan verified Nola was still within. She probably hadn't answered me because a vamp had sent her into a twilight sleep. They like to immobilize their food sources to ensure they don't run off.

Breath hissed from me. I hadn't seen a vampire in centuries. How they'd traveled across the Atlantic—or the Pacific—remained a mystery. With the gateways down, new pathways might have emerged. Like a shortcut through Hell.

At least I was remotely familiar with their methods.

The devil you know...danced through my mind as I got a bead on Nola's location and filled one pocket with salt. That way I could throw handfuls rather than sprinkling it. With the dagger clutched in one hand, I launched a mini jump spell. Short distances don't utilize the teleport channels.

Eventually, I'd need them again, but not today.

The wreckage vanished, replaced by broken display cases and food scattered every which way. A pack of werewolves growled at me and went back to ripping at a side of beef. Why were they in wolf form? It wasn't anywhere near the full moon.

Where was Nola? She should be under my nose, but she wasn't. I reached for her again. Same data, so I knelt and tossed boards and plastic partitions aside. The debris was deep. At least the incessant booming and muted explosions I'd heard outside weren't audible from in here.

"Looking for someone?" A tinny voice shot me upright.

When I spun, a youngster not much more than twelve faced me. She held the unnatural beauty all vampires possess. Red hair tumbled to waist level. Green eyes scrunched at the corners. When she smiled, the tips of her fangs peeked out. Vampires remain the same age they were when they were turned, which meant this one hadn't had much of a human life.

"I am," I told her.

"May as well leave. She's ours." The vampire edged nearer, a neat trick given the welter of debris.

Time to take a stand. "No. She's mine." I raised my voice and stood tall. With one hand, I tossed salt in a circle around me.

Her smile, which hadn't been much of one to start with, withered. Had I foiled her plans to add me to the night's menu? Or merely slowed them down.

A muted groan from beneath my feet suggested my triangulation had been correct. I wanted to toss things aside until I dug down to Nola, but it would have meant taking my eyes off the vampire. Not the best idea.

My predicament had drawn attention. A semicircle of werewolves formed behind the vampire. Ears pricked, amber eyes gleaming, they regarded me as if I was an exotic appetizer.

Vamps aren't the only ones who turn their victims.

"Fight this," I said, aiming my words at Nola. If she could claw her way through the wreckage, we'd be gone in a heartbeat.

I hoped.

The vampire's bare feet brushed against my salt circle. She hissed and took half a step backward.

Where were the rest of them? I'd sensed several. "Where are your friends?" I asked.

"Close," she sneered.

A jagged piece of pressboard moved aside, followed by broken bits of shelving. A hand closed around one of the sharp edges. Blood trickled. The vampire made a beeline to where Nola was attempting to free herself. Worse, the werewolves swarmed after her.

Blood was a universal calling card, its lure undeniable. Every monster reacts to its presence.

Two forearms were visible.

The vampire was close.

Sprinkling salt as I went—although it's not nearly as effective in a straight line—I grabbed my dagger. The vamp's attention was focused on Nola's emerging body. From what I could see, they'd divested her of her clothing, leaving only a bra and panties on her tall, emaciated form. Long golden-brown hair was matted, and her green eyes pinched with panic. Scabbed-over scrapes ran down her torso and arms.

Growls and yips filled the broken building as the werewolves jockeyed for better positions.

Was there about to be a pitched battle for the spoils?

I checked the transport spell I'd never let go of. Still there. Still ready.

The vamp was nearer to Nola than me. With her unnatural speed, there'd be no contest. Rather than trying to beat her to Nola, I imbued a tracking spell into the dagger, tossed it, and added speed to its trajectory.

The vampire finally saw it sailing toward her and jumped sideways. Nice try. Driven by my casting, the dagger altered course. The vampire's eyes narrowed. She ducked and wove, but nothing she did would make the slightest difference. Eventually, the blade would impale her.

While she was occupied, I vaulted over a damaged shelf and grabbed Nola's waist, yanking her out of the hole where the vamps had stuffed her.

Sensing the endgame was near, werewolves closed around us, tongues lolling. They're a lot like cats in that they enjoy playing with their victims.

The vampire was screeching, calling for reinforcements.

I didn't hang around to see my dagger catch up with her. A quick word, and we were back outside the wrecked store.

Nola's hands gripped mine. "Farther. We have to get farther away," she shrieked.

"Can you run?"

"I'll figure it out."

To her credit, even though she was barefoot she kept up for the most part. I only had to stop and wait once.

"Why didn't we teleport?" she panted. The glazed look had left her eyes.

"The channels aren't safe. Ready to go? It's not far now?"

She glanced behind us. "Why aren't they following?"

"Vampires can't go outside in daylight."

"Fuck. I knew that."

I started running again, but at a more moderate pace.

"What about the weres?" she asked.

"Eh, they were in it for sport. More than enough meat in that store to hold them for months. Why in the hell did the four of you leave the caves?"

There. I'd finally asked the question. Hadn't had time to grill the shifter sisters.

"It was stupid."

"On that, we agree. But why did you?"

"You were gone for a long time. Who knew if you'd come back? We wanted to see if anything was left."

I got hold of my temper before I grabbed her and slapped her. None of this was her fault. She was a product of her culture; the twenty-first century had spawned independent thinkers.

Following orders was yesterday's news.

"I feel bad about Teresa," she murmured as we came within sight of the caves.

"Don't. She never had a chance."

Nola stopped running. "That's cold."

I grabbed her arm and sent power arcing behind us to

ensure we hadn't been followed. "None of the old rules apply. When the four of you ignored my instructions, you signed her death warrant."

Nola tried to jerk away, but I held onto her. "I can't force any of you to do anything, but when you don't listen to me…"

I left it at that. Sometimes too many words get in the way.

"How do you know about any of this?" She waved her free arm sideways.

"I don't. Not specifically. But I was forewarned something like this would happen. I didn't know when or exactly how it would unfold."

"Are we all going to die?" She focused on me; a weak truth spell clanked into place. I left her dignity intact by not slicing through it.

"Not necessarily, but we'll have to feel our way until the full extent of the changes manifests. Then we can plan our next moves."

"You won't abandon us?"

I almost choked. "Christ, woman. I came after you. If I hadn't—"

"I'd be one of *them* the second the sun set." A shudder racked her thin frame.

She'd brought it up. "Did you drink any of their blood?"

Nola shook her head. "They pushed me into a hole under a bunch of broken planks and bound me with a spell. A man told me I'd be part of a ceremony later tonight, and they'd welcome me into their ranks."

"A man? Not the young woman?"

"Nope. I'd never seen her until you yanked me to safety."

"Any idea how many of them there are?" I let go of her arm.

She scrunched her forehead. "Lots. Maybe twenty or more."

I filed it away. That was enough for a full-on seethe. "Come on. Let's go inside."

I led the way and beefed up the illusion concealing the entry point. Vampires are exceptional trackers. Werewolves are as well. It wouldn't take much for them to follow us, but I ensured they couldn't enter.

As we traversed corridors toward the cavern where I'd left everyone, weariness washed through me. I needed food and rest before I'd be capable of so much as a simple conversation about what came next.

CHAPTER NINE, ALIA

Rhys looked trashed when he and Nola staggered into the cavern where the rest of us waited.

"Any food left?" he rasped.

Joss ladled some of the corn meal mixture into a bowl and handed it to him along with a spoon. Rhys sank into a crouch and ate quickly, methodically.

I walked to him. "Which of these caves contains clothing? Or do any of them?"

He glanced up at me, blue eyes scrunched at the corners. "I'm surprised you didn't do a spot of exploring."

My cheeks heated. Not much got by him. "Erm, we did, but there are...things in these caves."

He patted the ground next to him. "What kinds of things?"

I took the hint and sat.

"Not sure." I lowered my voice. "Something set its sights on Connor."

Rhys arched a fair brow. "How'd you extricate him?"

"Probably because I was on top of the problem and noticed before it sank its claws into him."

He nodded and cleaned the rest of the polenta mixture out of his bowl. "Magic calls to its own. These caves attract many who wield power. Most mean well, but others are out for themselves."

"Is there clothing in here somewhere?" I returned to my initial query. Moriah, Karen, and Nola were mostly naked, and it wasn't overly warm in here.

"Used to be." He set his bowl aside without offering details about where clothing chests might be located.

"Do you want more?"

When he nodded, I rose and refilled his bowl. Meanwhile, he made his way to the pool, cupped his hands, and drank. I set the bowl nearby and waited. Nola was curled in a ball next to the shifter sisters. All three appeared to be asleep. Joss and Connor conversed in low tones near Joss's cooking area.

The air around us shimmered as a bubble formed. Rhys had crafted a sound shield. "Do you have specific plans?" he asked pointblank.

"Like what?" I turned my hands palms upward.

"Will you stick with the group? Or will you work your way back to Oregon, or elsewhere."

His bluntness caught me by surprise. "Well, uh, sure I'd like to try to go home. See if anyone is left alive."

"If you do, it will be a difficult journey. No guarantees you could return."

I dropped my arms to my sides. "Okay. I get that you

don't want me to strike out on my own. After what happened with the demons earlier, I'm not especially keen on solo adventuring. Not until I know a whole lot more about how to focus my power."

"There are alternate paths."

"Huh?" I shook my head as I worked to interpret what he meant.

"For getting from point A to point B. Nola was in a grocery store—with a pack of werewolves and an entire seethe of vampires."

My mouth fell open. I took a step back. "You— You're joking, right?"

"Wish I was. They can't teleport but got here somehow." He massaged his temples.

I could relate since mine throbbed too. "Is that why teleporting became dangerous?"

He shook his head. "You're not listening. They've always been barred from using the journey channels. Sedona is a power point. So is Mount Shasta, Machu Pichu, and many other spots scattered around Earth. The reason these spots are critical is they house gateways."

"To where?" I blurted.

"Shortcuts to spots on Earth and borderworlds too."

"Border what?"

His features softened; the faraway look departed. "There are many other worlds, Alia. Earth is far from the only one."

I squeezed my eyes shut for a moment. When I opened them, I muttered, "Feels like a bad episode of the *Twilight Zone.*"

He ignored my comment. "The reason I'm talking with

you is because I'm working out what to do next. Your presence—or absence—makes a difference. A big one."

"Because I'm the only other one with significant ability?"

"Something like that."

Joss and Connor glanced our way occasionally but made no move to come closer.

How did I get stuck in this mess?

"If you hadn't come to the retreat, you'd be in much worse shape, alone and with few clues how to marshal your power."

I took one more step back. "Christ. You read my mind."

"What else is new? My bet is whoever your real father was is alive and kicking, although goddess only knows where. There is a slim chance you inherited your magic from your mother. If that's the case, she might still be around."

"But then I have to go look, don't I? Maybe not right away, but in a few days or weeks."

"Up to you. We'll know more as time passes."

I pinched the bridge of my nose between my thumb and forefinger. Whatever this was, it was permanent. Not going away. Ever.

"This is the new normal," I mumbled.

"Yes. Forever."

I needed to be done talking, so I carved through the bubble. It floated away, turning to motes of white light.

Rhys's speculative gaze bored right through me. I did my best to clear my mind, but failed miserably. He must have sensed my ambivalence, my angst, my fears about being trapped.

"I'm going to rest for a short while," he said. "After I'm up, we'll find clothes for the wolf-shifters and the witch."

"Surely, there are abandoned stores in town—"

"Sure, along with the vampires and werewolves. We'll check them tomorrow if we don't find anything here." He turned away and headed for a declination in one wall.

I joined Joss and Connor. "What was that all about?" Connor asked.

"Yeah. He really should talk with all of us, not just you," Joss chimed in.

"Mostly, he wanted to know if I planned to stick with you or leave."

"What'd you tell him?" Joss arched both brows.

"That I'd be here, at least for now."

Connor clapped me across the shoulders. "Good choice."

Bitterness shriveled my soul. "That's just it," I said. "We're flat out of choices." Before I stuffed my foot further into my mouth, I walked toward the entry and sat next to it. If I closed my eyes for a while, it might mend my attitude.

Only if I shut down my brain, a sour inner voice snarked.

A cavalcade of the day's events crowded behind my lids, beginning from everyone's now useless cell phones jangling as if they'd been hooked to high-voltage electricity. Too bad we hadn't remained in Mexico, but if we had, we'd never have recognized the full extent of the cataclysm.

Fat, dumb, and happy...

Hell, it wouldn't have lasted. When everyone's phones died, we'd have figured it out soon enough. Or Rhys would have.

Rhys. Enigmatic, charismatic. Either his energy or his

sheer physical presence made my chest tight. I'd ignored my reaction to him when we were at the retreat center. After all, I was there to learn how to bury my magic, not to have an affair with my teacher.

Not that I knew much about affairs—or sex. Beyond a few fumbling kisses when I was sixteen, I'd held men at arm's length. I had enough problems without compounding them. Girlfriends had confided in me forever, sharing plenty for me to recognize relationships were a two-edged sword.

Rhys had said something about magic calling to its own. Was that why I was so drawn to him? I'd rather have it be that than my hormones finally going on a rampage. Mercifully, they'd left me alone. If I'd had to contend with them and my unwanted magic, my life would have been a lot tougher.

I curled into a ball, arms around my knees. If I'd thought life was difficult before, it was child's play compared with what stretched before us.

The cavern spread around me. I saw it clearly despite my eyes being closed. Must be that third eye thing Rhys had lectured about back in Mexico...

Damn it.

My thoughts were all over the map. Part of me—a pretty big one—wanted to bolt and run until sweat coursed down my sides and my lungs strained for breath. At least it would burn off the adrenaline coating my tongue with a sour taste.

What a bunch of unlikely bedfellows we were. Three shifters, a witch, a Druid, Rhys, and me. He'd mentioned vampires and werewolves. Was anything good left alive? Or were the seven of us all that was left of humanity? I winced.

Why was it so hard for me to remember—or accept—none of us were exactly human?

Try as I might, I couldn't wrap my mind around it. There had to be others who'd been spared. We couldn't be the only ones. Humans were a canny lot. Plus, the fact twenty of us had gathered in the Sierra Madre mountains argued more mages were scattered about.

If mage versus purely human was the deciding factor for survival...

I sucked in a breath, held it, blew it out, and did it a few more times to quiet my restless thoughts. They were getting me nowhere. Answers would crop up in their own time.

This was the first opportunity I'd had to think rather than react since all the phones died. My attempts to soothe myself failed. The more I thought about things, the worse I felt. Before my thoughts entered a death spiral, I began to chant softly. A meditation Rhys had taught us as a centering exercise.

Whenever my overburdened mind wanted to dive back into problem solving, I refocused on my breath. The process wasn't all that different from when I used to play hide-and-seek with my magical ability.

Emphasis on the hide part. If I'd sought anything, it was peace.

Yeah, I can kiss that goodbye.

Not helpful.

Great. I'd sunk to answering myself.

Clearly, rest wasn't in the cards. Never mind I was so tired my eyes ached, and my body felt as if I'd been run over by a train. When I looked around, everyone else appeared to be sleeping. At least they were prone with closed eyes.

Making as little nose as possible, I got to my feet and walked through the curved entry and into a tunnel connecting the various caverns. Hesitant after what had happened to Connor, I stopped after a few feet and pushed power in an arc, aiming it in front of me.

Not sure quite what I hunted, I changed frequencies a few times. The higher ones pinged weakly. What were they picking up on? I glanced over my shoulder. All I had to do was walk back into the cavern. Probably no one had missed me, or, if they did, maybe they assumed I was taking a restroom break.

A prickling sensation surrounded my forehead. I warded my thoughts. It was simple. I'd taught myself how years before the retreat. My shoulders rolled back of their own accord, pushing my spine ramrod straight. Along with the action came a welcome rush of anger. I refused to spend the rest of whatever my life had turned into skulking in corners for fear some abomination would nab me.

I'd finish what Connor and I had begun. I'd map these caverns so we'd know what was where. Grateful to have an outlet for panicky energy that lit my nerve endings on fire, I started with the grotto across the central tunnel.

Smaller than the one we'd taken refuge in, it contained half a dozen ornately carved wooden chests. They were beautiful, the carving intricate. I've never been an expert on various woods, but these appeared to be teak. Dark, grainy, shiny.

Intrigued but wary, I sidled toward the closest one. It

smelled vaguely of camphor. Or was it ozone? My nostrils twitched as I sorted it out. In the end, I voted for camphor despite it not being entirely accurate.

I stretched a hand toward the latch, drew it back, and extended it once more. What in the hell was wrong with me? I was acting like a ninny. Either step up and pull the damned thing open—or scuttle back to the place I'd left everyone else.

My heart beat too quickly. I reverted to long, deep breaths. Feeling like an idiot, I fanned power, aiming it at the armoire. It pinged back cleanly. Why didn't that make me feel better, more settled?

Because I've never trusted any magic, let alone my own.

What in the fuck happened to the bravery I'd glommed onto a few moments before? Nails cut into my palms where my hands had balled into fists. I had no business here.

I was an outsider. An interloper.

"Go ahead, little mage, open my prison. You will be richly rewarded."

My head snapped around. My casting crashed to the dirt. "W-who said that?" I blurted.

"Open the door and find out."

Not the Twilight Zone. Alice in Wonderland. For all my bigshot thoughts about bravery, I twirled and fled, running headlong into Rhys the moment I cleared the grotto.

He grabbed my shoulders tight enough to make me yelp. "Watch what you awaken," he growled.

"What do you mean?"

His grip bit deep. "I already told you. Many entities live in these caves. It's best not to disturb them."

"But I was only cataloguing what's here," I protested, feeling like a third grader caught stealing cookies.

"I already know."

"You've been sparing with that information." Irritation clawed up my spine. "Let go of me."

He did.

I took a few steps pack. "So what's in all those dressers?"

"A couple contain clothes, but my bet is many of the pieces are unwearable after sitting here for centuries."

"And the others?"

A shrug. "Not sure, but one was luring you."

My gaze homed in on him. "You know this how?"

"Because I'm always listening."

"You were asleep," I protested.

"Not that asleep."

Fine. This was going nowhere fast. I clasped my hands behind me to avoid either hitting him or hurtling into his arms.

"What did I, erm, waken?"

"A Watcher."

I shook my head. "Please. I feel like I'm playing twenty questions. What is a Watcher?"

"We covered that topic—" he began.

"Tell me again," I broke in.

"Angels who have sinned and been cast out of their home is one theory. Another is they're part of the Anunnaki."

I unclenched my jaw before I shattered my teeth. "But there is no god. Certainly no heaven. That's a myth. Weren't the Anunnaki Sumerian?"

He cast an unreadable glance my way, forehead creased into horizontal lines. "When did I say anything about god or heaven? Angels exist. The good ones. And Watchers do too. Yes to your Sumerian question."

I jerked a thumb toward the grotto. "What is a Watcher doing in that cabinet?"

Rhys shrugged. "Hard to say. He must have annoyed someone enough for them to trap him. Or her."

Damn. I was grinding my teeth again. "What would they have done to me?"

Another shrug. "Maybe nothing. Maybe a lot. You never know until you free one."

"Have you?"

He nodded. "It could have gone better, but it also could have gone worse. I'm still here." After a pause, he added, "Demons and angels are cut from the same cloth. If a Watcher exists long enough, they sometimes transition into demons."

A long-forgotten tale about Satan beginning his existence as an angel rattled around in my head. I wasn't about to pry the lid off the Sumerian can of worms.

"Any chance they'd be useful to us?"

A corner of his mouth twitched downward. "We'll have to be in a lot worse shape than we are now to rattle that cage. Besides, most Watchers aren't imprisoned. Odds are we'll run into several along the way. Wait here. I'll try to find garments for the shifters and the witch."

Weariness rippled through me, making me wish I'd been able to sleep. I rocked from foot to foot to keep my eyes from shutting where I stood. Rhys wasn't gone long. When he rejoined me, several articles of clothing were slung over one arm.

"Why didn't the Watcher bother you?"

"The armoire I opened didn't contain one. Think before you ask questions."

His rebuke stung. I swallowed a flood of defensive words. What I settled on was, "I never asked for this."

"None of us did."

Touché.

"What happens next?" I started toward the larger cavern.

"Long as we're out here and curiosity is driving you, come along." He crooked a finger.

I held back, suddenly wary. "Where are we going?"

"You want to know what's here. I'm going to show you."

When I didn't trot obediently to his side, he tilted his head, blue eyes drilling into me. "Have I given you cause to distrust me?"

My cheeks warmed. "Uh, no."

"Then don't start now. Keep up." He started off at a brisk pace, leaving me where I stood.

Two choices. Either I followed, or I didn't. Rhys was nearly out of sight before I took off at a dead run, pushing my weary limbs into action. It might have been my imagination, but laughter floated after me. Was it the Watcher who'd invited me to free him?

I didn't want to find out.

What I wanted was to howl my misery to the skies—or the top of this cave system. A lifetime, short though it had been, of stuffing my true feelings kept my mouth shut. I caught up with Rhys.

"We'll begin at this end," he said and led the way into yet one more grotto. It contained a central fire-pit with blackened stones and not much else. "Long ago, this place hosted human sacrifices. Animal too."

My heart thudded hard. Sweat trickled down my sides. "S-sacrifice?" I blurted.

"Mortals sacrificed their own for many purposes. Didn't you study history?"

"Not that kind."

He laid the clothing on the ground, came to me, and wrapped his arms around me. The beat of his heart against my ear was reassuring. "You cannot run away. There's nowhere to go." His deep voice vibrated in my chest.

"But I want to."

He smoothed tangled hair away from the side of my face, his touch gentle, tender. I snaked my arms around his back. It felt like cheating, but the small respite from reality fed my soul.

I turned my face up, but he didn't try to kiss me. His eyes were shut, and he swayed easily on his feet. After a time, he let go and collected the garment pile. "Ready for the next cave?"

"Yes." My answer surprised me, mostly because it was true. When I'd stood near the Watchers' abode, all I'd wanted was to run for an exit. Vampires and werewolves be damned.

He walked across the tunnel. "This one has additional food—" he began.

"Did you do something to me?" I demanded.

He aimed a soft smile my way. "What do you think?"

"You did."

"Guilty as charged. Are you complaining?"

I shook my head. "Thank you. Nothing's changed, but I feel better."

He turned to face me. "You'll have many meltdowns before you get around to acceptance, and—"

"I will never accept any of this. Never." My newfound sense of peace fragmented. Determined to put distance between myself and Rhys—and his ensorcellment—I pelted down the tunnel and stepped on a rock that threatened to sprain my ankle. After an awkward recovery, I hurried into the place where I'd begun. Everyone sprawled on the floor asleep.

Rhys was powerful. He could make me believe black was white.

Who was he, really? Which side was he on? Had he somehow had a hand in orchestrating this mess?

Those questions and more crowded into my mind. Seeking the simple animal warmth of other bodies, I tucked myself between Connor and Joss and pretended to be asleep.

Rhys walked into the cavern. His energy settled on me, probed me, and stuck around for an uncomfortably long while before he crossed to the far side of the cave.

I still felt his arms around me, the press of his muscled body against mine.

Careful, my inner voice warned.

It could have saved itself the energy. I needed him to strengthen my ability. Beyond that, I'd steer well clear. Or as clear as I could. We were so few, distance from any one of us would be a rare commodity.

Connor rolled over, pinning me against his side.

Rhys's essence, soft and soothing, surrounded me. What had he done?

My safest bet would be to play dumb, say nothing, and hope he never brought it up again, either.

CHAPTER TEN, RHYS

I picked up the garments and followed Alia's retreating form but at a much slower pace. The calming spell I'd infused should have lasted at least twenty-four hours. She'd shaken it off in minutes. Plus, she'd resented what I'd hoped she'd view as a gift.

Her magic—and her cooperation—would make a difference, but she was so rattled by everything that had happened, adrenaline ruled the day. I needed her to have a cool head to marshal her power. So long as she flitted from fear to fear, longing for the impossible, nothing I said or taught or did would sink in.

As I walked, I combed my memory for everything I knew about Watchers. Had this batch always been here? Or were they newly arrived and part of the cataclysmic change that had Earth in a death grip?

Offspring of Ah and his consort, the Earth goddess Ki, the Anunnaki had ruled the world for a long while. Until

Enlil was born, heaven and earth were inseparable, but Enlil split them in two. He carried Earth away, and his father, An, snatched the sky.

Details after that were hazy, but I'd been taught the other five Sumerian gods—Enki, Ninhursag, Nanna, Utu, and Inanna—had stepped in and corralled Enlil and An, imprisoning them on a distant borderworld.

All that happened long before my birth. Had they escaped? Was this retribution for their long imprisonment? If so, where were the others? The ones who'd taken them to task so long ago.

I wished I knew more, but the only way I'd fill in the gaps was to leave the group. If I did, I might be gone for a while. Would they remain here?

Ha. Not likely. They hadn't managed to follow my instructions when I'd been absent less than twenty-four hours. If I left for weeks, I'd return to an empty nest. The logical move would be to leave Alia in charge, but it held two major drawbacks. She'd be loath to accept that level of responsibility. Further, the others might not accept her since they viewed her as a peer.

I stopped into the space with the armoires and probed with magic. No one spoke to me. If entities dwelt within, they weren't in a mood to show themselves.

Not to me.

Meant they picked on those they perceived as vulnerable. So far, they'd zeroed in on Connor and Alia, which meant the entire group was at risk.

I returned to my charges and laid the garments next to the shifters and witch. Alia was pretending to be asleep sandwiched between Joss and Connor. A tiny thread of jealousy pricked. She'd felt amazing pressed against me. I'd aimed to comfort, smooth away her distress, but the sheer nearness of her had been unsettling.

I've never gotten involved with any of my students for many reasons, the primary one being a lack of professionalism. Plus, there hadn't been anyone who'd had enough magic to bother with. Saddling myself with a mortal for anything beyond a casual tryst never held appeal.

My goal for summer retreats had been to identify possible recruits, not bed partners. I sat in the dirt, back leaned against a wall, and mapped out where to go next. I had to tell everyone about the Watchers, so they'd be alert. We also should scrounge what we could from supermarkets before all the produce rotted.

First off, though, I needed to determine if the group was committed to remaining together. They'd be fools to strike out on their own, or even in twos and threes. I could envision the shifter sisters doing just that. They'd been two against the world for a long while.

Of course, if the majority were committed to leaving, it solved one of my problems and freed me to seek information.

Breath hissed from between my teeth. Others like us must have survived. Locating them would be a neat trick, though. My mind was jumping from topic to topic. I couldn't rein it in.

Should we remain here?

I hadn't counted on sharing these caverns with Watchers. I didn't believe they posed a threat, but their masters were another matter. Were the Sumerian gods nearby? I started to reach out with magic but reeled it in. No point in poking a bee's hive before I needed to.

Maybe I should hustle this whole group back to Mexico. They could join forces with their fellows who were already there, and—

I shook my head. The journey channels weren't secure. Meant travel over any distance was off the table. For now, at least. While I was willing to risk myself, it wasn't reasonable to drag everyone along since I wasn't at all certain I could keep them safe.

Hell, keeping them safe here was turning into a far bigger crapshoot than I'd imagined.

I've never been much of a list maker, but one took shape. Come dawn, which couldn't be that far off, we'd hit a couple of markets. Once we returned, I'd determine who was going to stay and build a plan to hone skills. Magic requires dedication and practice. If this group weren't motivated by the turn of events, I had no idea what would light a fire under them.

Once housekeeping items were out of the way, we'd have a chat about the Watchers and how to remain safe from their influence. Relieved I had the bones of a strategy nailed down, I let myself drift. I needed rest to top off my magical reservoir in case we ran into problems as we culled through Sedona's wreckage.

Sleep was a nice idea.

I conjured calming spells, but my overactive mind wouldn't give me a break. When my internal clock struck dawn, I heaved to my feet and tiptoed through the room of sleeping bodies. A cursory search of the food cupboards didn't turn up the tea I'd hoped for, so I broadened my search.

Outside the cavern, the tunnel held an eerie feel, but I didn't waste time tracking it down. Two grottos later, I found a cloth sack with ancient tea leaves. Breathing life into them, I returned to the spot where Joss had cooked the night before, grabbed a pot, and scooped water from the pool. A jot of magic set it to heating, and I tossed a handful of tea into the bubbling water.

Why wasn't anyone stirring?

Other than leaving the cavern, I hadn't been especially quiet.

I started with Joss, Connor, and Alia and called their names softly. When that didn't work, I sent power into Alia's mind.

"Time to waken."

She didn't budge. Alarm sluiced through me. I traded standing over the trio for crouching and laying my hands on her forehead and Connor's. A sharp, bitter sensation jammed cold along my spine. The fine hairs on the back of my neck quivered.

What in the hell had happened? I'd been here literally the whole time. How had something snuck in and cast a sleeping spell over my charges? My mind tracked back to the wrongness I'd sensed in the tunnel.

The two had to be related.

Taking my time, since many malevolent spells are booby trapped, I felt my way forward and focused my third eye on Connor and Alia. His hawk flew across my visual field, flapping and squawking.

"Free him," the bird demanded. *"You must free him."*

"I'm trying." Of course, the bird would be frantic. He was as trapped as his bondmate and would remain so unless I could fix this.

Black gummy webbing formed, vanished, and took shape again. I'd have to move quickly to snip the strands since they wouldn't cooperate and remain visible. The next time they wavered into corporeality, I was ready with laser jabs of pulsed light. My first effort was disappointing. The strands reconnected as soon as I severed them.

Fine. New strategy. My palms slicked with sweat where they rested on Alia's and Connor's foreheads. Breath rasped from me as I waited.

And waited.

What the fuck? Now that whoever knew I was after it, would the webbing remain hidden? If that happened—

There it was again.

This time I surrounded the whole web with magic of my own and ignited it. Alia yelped. Connor bellowed. Both shot to their feet.

"Christ! What are you doing?" Alia batted at places where her hair smoldered.

"Freeing you from evil, you ungrateful twit." Without looking at her, I transferred my attention to Joss. Now that I knew what I was doing, liberating him was simple and not as painful. With far less fanfare, he rolled away from me and slowly rose.

"What's wrong with them?" Connor, whose hawk hovered behind him, pointed at the shifters and witch.

"Same thing that was wrong with you." I made a come-along motion with two fingers. "Follow me so you'll know what to do if this ever happens again."

"Define *this*." Alia's voice was strained.

"Let's wake them first," Joss told her. Worry shrilled his voice.

Druids are guardians of the natural world. Violence isn't part of their wheelhouse. He'd have a harder road than the rest of this batch. Maybe.

We'd reached Nola and the shifters. I crouched and extended bits of magic. "See the webbing?" I asked.

"No," Connor and Joss said almost in unison.

Alia knelt next to me, her attention glued on the three women. "There. Is that it?" She pointed at empty air.

"Maybe. To the left of Nola. It comes and goes. We have to be fast."

Howls ricocheted through the cavern. The shifters' bondmates weren't any happier than Connor's hawk had been.

"Settle down. We're on this," Connor muttered, but the wailing continued.

"W-what do I do if I see it again?" Alia's voice quavered.

"Surround it with your power and squelch it." My tone was sharper than I'd have liked, but I was on edge as I focused enchantment and waited. Keeping magic fresh isn't as simple as one might think. Concentrating on two fronts was about all I could manage.

With zero warning, slimy black threads wavered. I dove after them with a full dose of destructive energy. Alia joined in. Together, we herded the strands into a tight ball before we crushed them.

Nola moaned. In silhouette, the wolves pressed next to each shifter sister, nudging and licking. At least they'd quit howling.

"What happened?" Moriah rolled to a sit looking dazed.

So much for my plans where hitting the shops took center stage.

"Go wash your faces and have some of the tea I made. Then we'll talk."

To my surprise, no one balked. Perhaps they were coming to terms with me being their best chance of survival. I winced inwardly, not at all sure any of us would make it through this.

A few moments later when everyone had tea in a motley collection of cups and bowls, I walked to a spot near the pool and faced them.

"Do any of you know about the Watchers?"

Joss nodded. "Aren't they fallen angels, kind of like Satan?"

"That's one explanation," I agreed. "Another is linked to the Anunnaki."

"Sumerians?" Nola's brows shot up.

"What do you know about them?" I prodded.

"Hecate, our goddess, has ties with their gods."

Huh. First I'd heard of it, but I wasn't about to say so.

"The important part," I went on, "is they came in here and spelled all of you to sleep. If I hadn't been here, you'd have slept for eons until your bodies turned to dust."

"But why?" Alia demanded. "What's in it for them?"

"Thins the competition," Connor mumbled.

"If they're spirits, what in the hell are we competing for?" she demanded.

I chopped a hand downward to silence them. "From now on, we sleep in shifts, and we sleep warded. Their next attempt will be stronger since they saw how I defeated this one."

"Yeah. I didn't help at all," Alia snarked.

I resisted an urge to correct her. She'd assisted, but only once I'd told her what to look for. Nothing to be gained by hammering that point home.

"Why are they targeting us?" Moriah asked.

I shrugged. "Impossible to know, but they won't give up. They'll regroup and try again. Meanwhile, we need to gather forces and go into town."

"Agreed," Joss said. "We need food. Not that much here."

"It will be a problem sooner rather than later," I agreed. "Canned goods keep a long while; the rest of it is perishable. That's our goal for today. The stuff that won't keep."

"What about the vampires and werewolves?" Nola's voice shook.

I flirted with telling her she could remain behind, but that held its own set of dangers. "Vamps are pretty tame in daylight. Weres should only be a threat during the full moon."

"That's not for a week," Karen cut in.

"The werewolves looked plenty menacing," Nola muttered.

"We'll deal with whatever we find. Finish the tea. Get dressed, and we'll be on our way."

We could stand around debating pros and cons all day. Now was a time for action. The longer we stayed inside, the more fearful everyone would become.

The shifters and witch retreated to the piles of garments I'd left for them. Joss and Connor walked to the quadrant Joss had staked out as a kitchen and began a flurry of breakfast preparations. Alia hung back.

I draped a sound shield around us. "What is it?"

She squeezed her eyes shut. When she opened them, they'd shaded to violet in the muted light of the cavern. "What isn't it?" she shot back. "How could anyone have trapped me in a spell without me sensing it?"

"Easily, but now that we know—"

"What good is knowing?" she cut in. "When we can't do shit about it."

"Why don't you grab something to eat."

"Not hungry." She wrapped her arms around herself and shivered. "I don't want to be here, but there's nowhere to go."

"If I took a poll, I bet no one in this cave wants to be here," I reminded her and refrained from adding none of this was about her.

"But I should be doing something." She dropped her arms to her sides.

"Like what?"

"Going home. See if anyone's left alive. Check out campus. I can't believe everyone's..."

She stopped before supplying the word *dead*.

"Maybe they aren't, but given what we've seen so far..."

Tears welled in the corners of her eyes. She blinked them

away. I kicked myself for being honest, but blinders wouldn't help her or anyone else, either.

"So I just do nothing?" Her voice was strained.

"I never said that. Your magic has untapped potential, but you'll never find out how much until you embrace it. We have a task this morning. If it goes well, we'll have another this afternoon."

"What about the future?"

I locked gazes with her, bent, and kissed her forehead lightly. "Each moment beyond this one is the future."

A tear tracked down one cheek. She ignored it. My heart ached for her, but she needed a dose of reality more than coddling.

"You're stronger than you realize." I cracked the shielding around us. Once it clattered to the dirt, she turned and walked unsteadily toward where Joss was filling cups and bowls that had held tea with some concoction he'd made.

Good thing one of us was a cook.

Weariness spilled through me, but I couldn't afford to give into it. Instead, I joined the others intent on eating and leaving here as soon as possible. Goddess only knew what we'd find outside these caves.

On the flip side, who in the fuck knew what the Watchers would do in our absence. We might not have caves to return to.

Ha! I was doing just the thing I'd cautioned Alia about: pole vaulting ahead of the curve. Joss handed me a cracked mug with a spoon sticking out of it. After making a concerted effort to wipe everything but now off my slate, I thanked him, took it, and ate a surprisingly tasty porridge.

"Ready," the shifter sisters informed me from a spot next to the doorway.

"Me too." Alia set down her dish.

I swallowed the last of breakfast and joined them. Once the others drew near, I crafted a ward around us. Another mage could see through it, but maybe, just maybe, we'd make it in and out of Sedona unnoticed.

CHAPTER ELEVEN, ALIA

Untapped power, huh? The stuff I'd spent the last five years hiding from. And now I sounded like a broken record. Rhys led the way to the cave entry point and motioned for us to stop.

I bolted to his side. "Let me do it."

His head whipped around. "Let you do what, exactly?"

I huffed out a frustrated breath. "Every other second, you harp about shoring up my power. How can I if you do everything for us? I'll remove the barrier, check if it's safe out there, and do my damnedest to shield us."

"Like hell," Nola sneered. "Rhys knows what—"

"It's a good idea." Rhys cut her off and stepped to one side to clear a space for me.

Alrighty, then. Big words. Did I have big actions to back them up?

Guess I was about to find out. Rhys would bail me out if

I fucked up. Better to practice with him present than on my own.

I shut my eyes, gathered my thoughts, and sent power zinging outward to check for intruders in the flat, sandy area in front of the caves. I'd said I was going to remove the barrier first, but I'd rethought my strategy.

The muted hum of conversations played out behind me. Feet shuffled. I kept my focus forward. Everything felt okay except for one spot to the far right. I kept returning to it and pushed harder.

Rhys slotted his magic in with mine. It felt weird, such an intimate thing to share. Yet, it also felt right. Not much in my life had since my moon blood brought an unwelcome guest along with it.

"Good catch," he murmured.

I cast a sidelong glance his way. "What is it?"

"Take down the barrier. Let's find out."

If he was inviting me to remove the shielding, whatever lurked outside couldn't be all that daunting.

"What's out there?" Karen demanded.

"Yeah, we want to know," Moriah chimed in.

Rhys twisted to face the group. "I'm not totally positive, but it doesn't mean us ill."

"How can you know that?" Nola asked.

Meanwhile, I hunted for the lynchpin Rhys had built into his casting. It took longer than I would have liked before I gave it a brisk tug. The veil hovering before me dissipated. Light flooded inside, temporarily blinding me. Defensive power surged.

Eh, I was more on edge than I'd assumed. Light crackled

from my fingertips as I headed for where I'd sensed something living. Rhys was still lecturing about trust and shoring up power they'd either taken for granted or neglected.

Glad I wasn't the only one on the receiving end of his rebukes.

A few brisk steps took me to a rock pile. Edgy but taking care not to crush the lifeforce I felt beating within, I moved one rock and then another. Faint mewling suggested the creature was more frightened than me. Two rocks later, shiny brown feathers came into view.

Rhys joined me and reached into the hole I'd made. When he withdrew, a large owl perched beneath his hands.

"How'd an owl bury itself?" Joss asked.

"Look closer," Rhys urged.

The owl focused beady amber eyes on me and clacked its sharp, hooked beak. Was it a warning not to heed Rhys's suggestion?

The bird squirmed. Rhys held fast. I felt rather than saw strands of power he wove around it. Was he having second thoughts about it not being a threat?

"Why, I'll be damned," Connor murmured.

"I'll be damned, what?" I asked never moving my gaze from the owl. It had stopped struggling. Instead, it twisted its head, trying to bite Rhys's hands.

"Not an owl, a skinwalker," Connor said.

"I should have seen it," Joss exclaimed. "They're common in the Southwest, but I never met up with one before."

I shook my head. "What? It shapeshifts?"

Connor nodded.

Feeling bold, I reached for its mind. *"We won't hurt you —"* I began.

"You already are," a gravelly voice shot back. *"Tell him to let go of me."*

"Like I can't hear you," Rhys said. "I'll let you go if you promise to tell us what happened here and if there are more like you."

The owl transferred its gaze from me to Rhys, who bent to set it on the ground. As he did so, he loosed the bonds he'd set in place. "There, this is the honor system, and—"

In a flare of multihued light that damn near blinded me, the owl shot skyward hooting like a mad thing.

Rhys shaded his eyes with a hand as he followed its trajectory.

I readied power to stun him, but Rhys shook his head. "Let him go."

"But you said—"

"I know what I said," Rhys cut in, "but that one would rather die than talk with us. Skinwalkers are an independent group. There aren't many of them left, and they've never played well with other mages."

"Maybe because they're not," Joss tossed out.

"Their only magic used to be altering their form," Connor added. "Wonder what happened? That one burned through power the second he was free."

"The important piece here," Rhys clarified, "is my suspicion mages were spared from the cataclysm appears solid."

"Are skinwalkers good guys or bad guys?" I asked and

cursed all the years I'd wasted when I could have been learning things like that.

"Neither," Rhys said. "They just are."

"Well, they've never joined forces with Satan's crew," Joss pointed out

Rhys returned to the entrance of the cave system and spoke a few words. The barrier resurrected itself. Clearly, it had been sufficient to keep the skinwalker out. Had he been waiting for us to leave to try harder to get inside?

"Why do all of you think it was male?" I asked.

"The owl was," Joss explained. "There are no cross-sex pairings."

Alrighty, one more bit of data I lacked. How to sex an owl.

Rhys trotted back to us and clapped his hands. "Onward. We're going in search of food. Keep your eyes open and your guard up. Stick close. We're not splintering into smaller groups." After a pointed glance that took in Nola and the shifter sisters, he took off at an easy lope.

He hadn't bound his pale hair into braids today. It floated around his head, framing his face and streaming down his shoulders. When I realized I was staring, I dragged my gaze away and fell in between Joss and Connor. Nola, Karen, and Moriah jogged a few paces behind. I caught the odd mutter suggesting they resented Rhys's warning.

The muted booming from the day before was gone, but the air still held tinges of smoke. Out of long habit, I dragged my phone from a pocket. Sheesh. Why was I still even carrying it?

I'd been about to tap into my navigation program to map out nearby supermarkets.

Good luck with that, a sour inner voice mumbled.

We made our way toward what was left of Sedona. The caves were maybe half a mile out of town. Above us, blue skies reflected innocence. If anything had happened here, they hadn't borne witness to it.

How could anything still look normal when my life had twisted inside out?

Not about me. The same voice was back at it. If it hadn't been part of me, I'd have shut it down fast.

My nose twitched as I caught whiffs of the many dead. Yesterday, they hadn't had a chance to begin the decomposition process. Today, a sickish-sweet stench was noticeable. By tomorrow, it would be far worse. After a few days baking in the northern Arizona sunshine, the town would become unbearable.

How long would it take the bodies to fully rot? I had no idea. Would predators take care of some of them?

Again, I was clueless. Coyotes would eat carrion. Maybe wolves, but were there any here? Perhaps they hadn't done much better on the survival front that mortals. I hadn't seen so much as an insect since we arrived.

Rhys guided our group down a side street and came to a stop in front of the wreckage of a Whole Foods Market. Power shimmered around him as he presumably scanned within for danger.

He dropped his arms to his sides. "Think it's okay."

"But there's no way in," Nola protested.

"Come close." He crooked a finger. "I'll jump us inside. Looks as if that rear corner didn't fare as badly."

"I don't like it," Nola muttered.

She wouldn't. Not after being trapped by vampires. "Is, um, anything else inside?" I asked, aiming for a neutral tone.

"I don't believe so," Rhys replied.

Mmph. Not exactly a *no*. The touch of his power was familiar as strands settled around me. Sunlight faded, replaced by the dim, dusty interior of the store. As luck would have it, we ended up near a checkout. I grabbed a few bags. So did everyone else.

"Collect what you can," Rhys instructed. "Stick to perishables. Be quick about it. Meet back here in ten minutes."

He'd cautioned us about sticking close, but we all struck out in different directions. Perhaps he'd only been concerned about it when we were outside. Regardless, I wove over and through downed display cases aiming for the outer perimeter where perishables usually lived.

The reek of death was strong, concentrated. Short, panting breaths through my mouth helped. I kept expecting to trip over bodies, but there weren't any.

Why not?

The answer that came when I was stuffing vegetables into my sacks was unsettling. Someone must have beaten us here.

Or something.

I'd stepped through plenty of bloodstains, but the accompanying bodies weren't here. Something cold clawed its way down my spine. I slapped up warding, kicking myself for not doing it sooner.

I also instituted a scan, checking for the others. I couldn't see anyone, but it didn't mean they weren't here. My first effort came up dry, so I tried again, extending my range to encompass the entire store.

Still nothing.

I froze and let go of the turnip I'd been about to add to a sack.

"Rhys!"

No reply. Not out loud or in my head.

I rocked from foot to foot, bags hanging off my arms. Food gathering forgotten, I retraced my steps to where we'd begun. It was just as empty as the rest of the store. I shouted for Rhys again. This time out loud.

I didn't expect an answer, and I didn't get one.

Turning in a circle, I blinked stupidly. Where had everyone gone? Had I been transported to a parallel universe?

No reason to remain here. Still clutching the bags I'd filled, I gathered power, visualized the street outside, and stopped. What if the area outside Whole Foods contained something evil? Better to reshape my spell to land in front of the caves. A few seconds later, I loosed it.

And waited.

Nothing.

Had I done something wrong?

Walking back to the beginning of a very basic casting, I started over careful with every step. I wanted to avoid the journey channels, since they were polluted with something. Jump spells are quick and basic.

Once I was certain I'd done everything right, I tried again.

With the same non-result.

My heart rate accelerated. Sweat slicked my palms and dripped down my sides. Before panic took over, I closed my eyes and recalled how the store had appeared from the outside. This area next to the registers had sustained the least damage. I walked toward what had been the store's front doors, crunching over broken glass.

The door on the far left looked as if I might be able to squeeze through, but not with all my grocery bags. I dropped them and edged toward a slender opening hoping to hell the structure wouldn't fall on my head if I bumped into something that was hanging by a thread, or a board as it were.

Where the fuck was everyone?

For that matter, where was I?

Rhys wouldn't have allowed himself to be captured.

Maybe he hadn't had a choice.

I stopped a foot from my potential escape route. Mental turmoil wasn't doing me a damned bit of good. My thoughts were a jumble, and I was reacting, not thinking.

What if this was a trap and a whole seethe of vampires was waiting in the street...

Stop. Just stop. Vampires can't be out in daylight.

Yeah, but werewolves can, and god knows what else.

My imagination jumped the gate visualizing what could have dragged all the dead from the store.

I'd frozen in place, an untenable position. I couldn't remain here. Well, I could, but it wasn't wise. No place to maneuver if something came after me.

I took a deep breath, followed by several more.

As settled as I was likely to be, I turned sideways and crouched in an attempt to slip through the narrow opening. My foot caught on something. I yanked it free amidst ominous creaking.

Moving as fast as I dared, I crawled forward intent on separating myself from the unstable structure. Creaks and groans intensified. Something ripped into my knee, maybe a hunk of broken glass. I smelled blood and crawled faster.

Finally, I was able to get my feet under me and waddle forward. Blood gushed down my right leg. Nothing like a dinner gong for vampires, but there wasn't a thing I could do about it.

A sliver of daylight drew me forward. I threw myself through the last batch of sagging timbers standing between me and freedom and shot to my feet. My heart hammered against my ribcage. My throat was so dry, the sides scraped against each other.

No one rushed me. Nothing was here except me.

I turned in a circle, dazed. This wasn't the same place we'd begun. Nothing looked familiar. Behind me, the place I'd snuck through collapsed in a dusty cacophony of cracking beams.

I turned my attention to my leg. At least the blood was slowing, clotting. I didn't want to leave a trail.

Which way to go?

Did it even matter?

Sedona had hills. They were still here, but they felt different.

"Rhys!" I tried once more for all the good it did.

Confused, despondent, I set off in the direction the caves should be.

Would I ever see my group again?

If my magic didn't work—except it had. Maybe. My telepathic attempt to call Rhys hadn't boomeranged back at me.

Visualizing the area in front of the caves, I set one more spell in motion not expecting much. Shock ratcheted through me when the broken asphalt vanished, catapulting me into darkness.

CHAPTER TWELVE, RHYS

Rummaging through the eastern edge of the store, I'd given up on fish; it was already too rotten to salvage. I was standing near the butcher counter when the fine hairs on the back of my neck prickled. At first, I chalked it up to nerves and kept on dropping steaks into a plastic bag.

The next time it happened, I left off what I was doing and picked my way back to our entry point as quickly as I could, which wasn't very fast given everything I had to crawl over.

Joss and Connor had beaten me there. Connor was in hawk form, which probably meant he was uneasy. I didn't see a shredded pile of clothing, so he must have taken the time to disrobe. Closer inspection revealed garments draped over Joss's arm along with shopping bags.

"Did you feel that?" Joss demanded. He doesn't spook easily, but his voice was higher pitched than usual.

I waved him to silence and stretched feelers hunting

for Nola, Karen, and Moriah. They saved me the trouble as they barreled toward us, knocking things over in their wake.

"We need to get out of here. Now." Nola yelped as if she'd been burned.

"Did any of you see anything?" I pressed and switched gears looking for Alia.

"It feels wrong. Let's leave," Nola shrilled.

Meanwhile, the shifter sisters' wolves hovered behind them, demanding ascendency.

"We're not leaving without Alia," I said.

"She can find her own way out," Moriah muttered.

While it was true, leaving without her was unthinkable. I dropped my sacks on the floor and instructed, "Wait here. Do not leave without me." Since it wasn't up for discussion, I gathered power and tracked the dregs of Alia's energy. It led to the produce aisle.

Of course, she wasn't there. Sprinkling a tracking spell meant to be visible, I followed its trajectory.

And ended up right where I'd begun. At the front of the store.

What in the hell?

"Did you search the whole store?" Joss demanded.

"If he did, it was damned quick," Moriah muttered.

Too concerned to explain my strategy, I grabbed my bags, draped a spell around everyone, and moved us into a mercifully empty street. Vamps wouldn't be an issue, but goddess knew what else might be out here.

"Connor, stay with me. The rest of you return to the caves."

"How will we get inside?" Nola whimpered, so frightened the whites of her eyes showed.

Fuck. "Do any of you know how to dismantle beta spells?" A sea of head shakes met my query.

Since the casting I'd used to move us out of the store was still intact, I goosed it. The caves came into view; I shouted a few words to break the barrier. "In with you." I made shooing motions.

The second they crossed beneath the lintel, I resurrected protections around the caves and started toward town. They could break out if they were determined. They'd already done it once with disastrous consequences. I suspected this time they'd stay put.

Connor wheeled above me, wings beating slowly. *"Where are we going?"* he asked. *"My hawk says she's gone."*

I slowed to a stop and held out my arm for the hawk to light. "Did you see her leave?"

"No, but I felt her energy, frantic at first, and then gone."

"Gone, how?"

"Not sure. One minute I felt her, and then I didn't."

Oh-oh. Not good. "Did you sense anyone but us in the store?"

The hawk keened mournfully and shook his head.

I pinched the bridge of my nose between my thumb and forefinger hard enough to hurt. Had Alia decided she was done with us and struck out on her own? It seemed unlikely, but other than my brief bout of nerves at the meat counter, I hadn't sensed anything evil.

She couldn't have simply disappeared.

Except she had.

For once, I was stymied. Did I return to the caves and make certain the others didn't fall prey to whatever had claimed Alia? Or did I hunt for her?

If the latter, where and how since I had no idea which way to go. My tracking spell hit a dead end at the checkout counter. The glowing green line had simply quit. It meant my magic could no longer pinpoint where she was.

The hawk jumped from my arm. In a flare of light, Connor shifted. "Simpler to talk this way," he explained. "Do you have any idea where she is?"

I shook my head. "Unfortunately, no."

"She might have left. She wasn't very happy."

"She'd have told us..."

Would she have, knowing I'd try to talk her out of it?

"Willing to help." Connor wrapped his arms around his naked torso. "Just tell me how."

That was the bitch of it. I had no idea. Connor's hawk was useful to search from the air, but if Alia wasn't here, he may as well rejoin the others.

"Talk with me," he demanded. "I can feel you thinking."

I pushed out a breath, followed by one more. "The only thing I can figure, since I can't sense her energy, is she's moved out of range or to a neighboring world."

His dark brows shot up. "Does she even know how to leave Earth?"

"Not on her own," I agreed.

"But no one else is here."

"No one we're aware of," I corrected. "Unless you count the Watchers and that skinwalker."

He turned his hands palms up. "Don't forget the

vampires and werewolves. So is there a way to search on other worlds?"

Another breath, sour with defeat. "Sure, but there are hundreds of them. Maybe thousands. We could search for decades with no success."

Connor dropped his arms to his sides. "You're telling me what we can't do. How about what we can."

I shut my eyes, collecting scattered thoughts. I hadn't sensed Nola, either. Presumably because the vampires had sequestered her beneath enchantment. Something could have done that to Alia.

Connor's shifter magic drilled into the corners of my mind. He must be sick of me not talking with him.

"Stop that." My tone was sharper than I'd meant.

"If you don't tell me what's rolling around in that brain of yours, I may as well return to the caves and help the others put food away."

I raked a hand through my dirty, tangled hair. "Okay. When I went after Nola yesterday, I couldn't sense her, either. Not until I was right on top of her."

"So, Alia could be here?" Connor persisted.

I nodded.

"I'm going to do an aerial reconnaissance. See if I detect anything alive."

He wasn't asking permission because he shifted and vaulted skyward. I started to call after him to report in, but he'd do that without me suggesting it.

I cobbled a spell together with Alia's unique magical signature at its core, deployed it, and set off at a lope. Sedona wasn't all that big. I'd cover all the streets in the wrecked downtown, the ones that were still navigable. If my spell got a positive hit, it would alert me.

As I ran, I searched for signs of life. It might have been my imagination, but fewer corpses riddled the landscape than I'd seen the day before. Who was moving them?

Or eating them.

Or sucking their blood and then disposing of them.

Vampires might come out at night, but their main interest is the living. I'd heard rumors of them breaking into slaughterhouses and drinking animal blood as a stopgap, but dead human blood is toxic to them.

A flash of light near my right foot caught my attention. I scooped up a multi-faceted crystal and kept on running. The stone's energy was soothing, so I dropped it into a pocket.

A few minutes later, I'd covered maybe half the town and was no closer to locating Alia. My temples throbbed; my throat was dry. The constant drain on my magic was taking a toll.

My attention flagged. The broken chips of asphalt beneath my feet swirled into a vortex, blinding me. Too late, I tossed up a ward, but it wasn't very robust since most of my power was tied up in hunting Alia.

The vortex spun, hauling me off my feet.

Too late, I remembered the crystal that had conveniently landed near me. When I reached into that pocket, fighting the drag of the vortex, the stone was so hot I couldn't touch it.

Double fuck.

I know better.

Someone had tossed the hellish thing right at me in

hopes I'd pick it up. Now that I had, they'd hobbled my magic and were dragging me goddess only knew where.

"Return to the caves," I shouted to Connor, but he didn't respond. Or maybe I was already too far removed for him to have heard me.

I had to rid myself of the marking stone—or whatever it was. Not an easy task. I spun like a Dervish. Just getting my hand back into that pocket challenged me. When I managed it and grabbed the crystal, it singed my fingers. The reek of burning flesh hit my nostrils. Pain made my eyes water.

I'd come this far. No going back.

With a yank, I upended my pocket. The crystal plummeted near me, attaching itself to the vortex.

Great. Here I'd thought I'd be rid of it.

I loosed the threads with Alia's energy in case whoever targeted me could somehow locate her through my spell. Sedona's twisted streets had disappeared, leaving me twirling in blackness.

Who in the fuck had this kind of power?

Had I been right about the Sumerians? It seemed so unlikely as to be ludicrous. Why would they return to Earth after all these years.

Not expecting much, but willing to face whatever lurked in the journey channels if it extricated me from my current mess, I assembled a teleport spell. Nothing half-assed here. I took care with each step and made certain it built on the one before.

When it was as solid as I could make it, I drew on fire to kindle the nascent casting. For the barest moment, the vortex wavered. Hope soared. I poured power into my escape hatch only to have the vortex slap me from all sides. Asphalt ripped my clothing and made cuts in exposed flesh. At least the cursed stone became dislodged in the struggle. It might be there, but I could no longer see it.

Blood gives enemies the upper hand. They can draw on it to control you, so I switched things up and patched my wounds as quickly as I could.

No escape. Whatever this was, I'd have to ride it out.

"Rhys," brushed the corners of my mind.

Were they mocking me? Whoever they were.

It pissed me off. "Show yourselves," I bellowed, not bothering with telepathy.

As if in answer, the vortex expanded, its bits rolling outward. Once it was a couple of feet from me, I stopped spinning and began to fall, gathering momentum fast.

Mage or no, I'm not immune from broken bones, but I require magic to heal myself. Depending on where I ended up, I might not have the ability to replenish mine. Blackness surrounded me. Was I 200 feet from the bottom or twenty? Was there even a bottom, or would I fall forever?

Lot of unknowns.

I didn't expect it to work, but I snagged air currents and wove a cushion beneath me. I couldn't see it, but I felt it, and it held together.

Finally, a point for my side.

The darkness fragmented in my peripheral vision. Slivers of light illuminated a vertical channel. If this worked like teleporting, the presence of light meant I was nearing the finish line of this portion of my trials.

Where would I end up?

Would I be stuck there forever?

I shut down my thoughts and concentrated on keeping the thicker air beneath me. Quicker than I'd thought possible, Light flooded from all sides; the ground rose up to meet me. Contact was jarring, but far easier than I'd anticipated.

Rolling to my feet in a single motion, I turned in a circle taking in what might have been a city. Hell, it could be Sedona, but years down the road from the cataclysm. Remnants of broken buildings lined a nearby street. Pavement had given way to potholes a foot deep. A few cars and trucks sat on flat tires, clearly long since abandoned.

Time travel has never been one of my skills. I went on autopilot, checking my internal map and compass to determine where I was.

Halfway through the process, a muted yelp escaped my throat. Whatever had held my magic hostage was gone. Not that I was anywhere near full capacity, but neither was I hobbled any longer.

I tapped down my elation—no time for it, not yet—and returned to my internal geographic exploration.

Ha. This was Sedona. A Sedona of the future. I couldn't tell how many years I'd been pushed forward. Maybe not more than fifty, or there'd have been more degradation.

Could I get back?

Yes, the sixty-four-thousand-dollar question. As I noted, time travel has never been part of my training or ability.

Thirst dogged me. I walked toward where a creek ran through the town. Any city water system would be defunct by now. A pack of feral dogs ran when they saw me. Hawks wheeled overhead. Life had returned, presumably everywhere, which meant I could hunt for food once I'd slaked my thirst.

A quarter of an hour later, I slid down a steep muddy bank. Once an RV park had sat near the bottom. Sure enough, I spied rusting hulks of what had been motorhomes. Some had cars near them.

I felt rather than saw movement before something jumped me from behind and drove me down the bank. Before I could mount a defense, power hemmed me in.

Familiar power. Relief vied with annoyance. Crap, who in the fuck was orchestrating this?

"Alia. It's me," I shouted.

"Bullshit. Nothing is real here." The bands holding me prisoner tightened.

"You were at my retreat in the Sierra Madre mountains," I began, "when—"

"Shut up. Just shut up. They're mind readers. Could have plucked that bit from my head."

I felt her standing over me, but I was facedown and couldn't move. What could I say to convince her?

"Every mage has a unique magical signature," I reminded her. "Reach through and feel me."

"No! It's a trick."

Christ. What had happened to her? She couldn't have been here long. Or perhaps she had. Time travel is tricky that way.

I tried a different tack. "We're in the future—"

"Duh."

"How'd you end up here?"

"I got dragged when the front of the store— Not going to work. Have a good life."

Rustling suggested she was slogging down the bank.

"Don't leave."

The noise of her exit faded, replaced by silence. Should I try more words? Before I decided, she said, "Why not?"

"If there's a way back to the others, it will take both of us."

"What others?"

She was being cagey. No matter what I said, she could accuse me of mind reading. "Are you warded?"

"Of course?"

"Then how could I be grabbing data from you?"

"Mmph."

At least she was considering my suggestion. "The others are a hawk shifter, two wolf-shifters, a Druid, and a witch. We were seven in all."

I almost tacked a believability spell onto the end of my sentence, but didn't. If she felt manipulated, she'd leave, and I'd expend the remainder of what was left of my magic extricating myself from her cleverly crafted entrapment.

"What did we find in the cave with the armoires?"

Her question surprised me, but the answer was simple. "Watchers." A thought surfaced. "When I was trapped by the vortex, falling through time, someone called my name. Was that you?"

The invisible bands pinning my arms to my sides and my legs together fell away. I rolled onto my back and thence to a sit.

Alia climbed back up and stood over me, hands on her

hips and an unreadable expression on her dirt-streaked face. "If you're another illusion, I swear, I will burn down the world to destroy you."

"Save your magic. We'll need every scrap and then some to get out of here."

A corner of her mouth twitched. She fell to her knees next to me. "Is it really you? I did call, and hoped. Once I figured out what happened, that no one knew where I was, and that no one would ever come to find me, I—"

Because I didn't know what else to do, I opened my arms. "Yeah, it's me. For some inexplicable reason, we're bound to one another. You got dragged through first, but then they came back for me, and—"

She catapulted into me. When I closed my arms around her back, she started to sob. So strong, yet so fragile. I stroked her tangled hair and held her until the storm passed.

I started to utter reassurances, but they'd have been false.

She wriggled, and I let her go. After rocking back on her heels, she smeared grit around her face when she brushed tears aside. "Can you get us out of here?"

"I have no idea."

"Not the right answer."

"Maybe not, but it's the truth."

She smiled crookedly. "Still not certain about trusting you, or if it truly is you, but I'm fresh out of options."

"Does it feel like me?"

A nod. "But this place is like *Alice in Wonderland.*"

"Tell me about it. The more information I have, the better off we'll be."

"Why were you heading this way? Did you sense me?"

"Nope. I was looking for water and remembered the creek. Originally, back in the other Sedona, I had a tracking beam activated, but I loosed it when the vortex grabbed me."

"Huh. It's how I ended up here too. No tracking magic, but a vortex." Breath whooshed from her, and she got to her feet. "Follow me. I've been purifying the creek water with fire and putting it in bottles I've scrounged."

I stood. "How long have you been here?"

She angled an odd look my way. "At least a month. Didn't start counting days until it sank in I couldn't return to where I'd begun."

We made our way down the bank to a rough lean-to she'd constructed out of aluminum panels and rotten canvas. She ducked inside.

I balanced from foot to foot digesting the information she'd shared. In the world we'd left, she'd been gone for a matter of perhaps a couple of hours. Did the vortex suck up days, weeks, months? Batting down an inane desire to throw every scrap of magic at escape, I forced myself to think rather than react.

"Rhys?" She emerged from the shanty, glass bottle in hand.

Her voice dragged me out of the jumble of my thoughts. I took the carafe she'd thrust my way, uncapped it, and drank deeply.

CHAPTER THIRTEEN, ALIA

I still couldn't believe Rhys found me, even though it appeared to be an accident. Part of me—a big part—still thought it was some kind of sleight of hand. That it wasn't really Rhys. If I dropped my guard the illusion would harm me, although how and for what purpose remained hazy.

Screw it. Until proven otherwise, my working assumption was the man next to me was truly Rhys.

He drained the flask and set it on the ground. "How have you been eating?"

"Hunting. I found canned goods, but they were rotten, and I was afraid of botulism. Now that you've seen this place, how far do you think we time traveled?"

"Does it matter?"

I shrugged. "Probably not. The animals seem to have returned, but I haven't seen any people."

"Mages?"

"No." I did my best to school my voice to neutrality, but probably failed. "This is the longest I've ever been alone. Ever."

He sank to a crouch. "Did you try to escape?"

My face grew warm despite the chill of the day. Somehow, we'd moved from early fall to mid-winter judging from the angle of the sun. "Many times. Scuttled my magic down to bedrock for all the good it did me."

He drew his thick, fair brows together. "What happened?"

I sat next to him, crossing my legs in front of me. "Nothing. This"—I spread my arms wide—"never so much as wavered."

"Are you sure you didn't sense the presence of anyone else holding power?"

I considered his question. "I haven't exactly been looking. At first, I kept expecting something bad to jump me. When it never happened, I focused on building this shelter and finding sustenance. I didn't trust the water, so I've been boiling it."

"What aren't you saying?"

His words were so soft, so inviting, tears burned the insides of my lids. I shook my head. "None of it matters. I haven't been especially proud of myself."

"Why not? You're still here."

I squeezed my eyes tight before opening them. Once I figured out the truth, I contemplated ending things, but lacked the courage. The specter of years stretching into centuries—if I lived that long—alone wasn't appealing.

"I see."

Shock blazed down my spine. "Stay out of my head."

He placed a hand on my knee. "This isn't easy. Give yourself credit."

"If I'd been smarter in the first place, recognized a trap when I couldn't find the rest of you..."

Rhys pressed his mouth into a tight line. "It's not coincidental we ended up here. Someone wanted us gone since the others are sitting ducks without our power."

I turned both hands palms up. "Not seeing the connection."

"Magic is like any other physical commodity. It can be tapped and drained."

"Why wouldn't they want us, then? We have far more than the other five put together."

"They could be saving us for last since they know where they dropped us."

Sitting wasn't working for me. Back on my feet, I paced in a tight circle. "Who is they?"

"Wish I had an answer. Do you have anything to eat? I need strength, so we can work on a plan to return to our own time."

I returned to the interior of my impromptu hut, grabbed a handful of dried raccoon meat, and handed it to Rhys. He bit, chewed, swallowed, and made a wry face. "Not to kick a gift horse in the mouth, but that's truly nasty."

A laugh bubbled from me. It was welcome since I'd thought hell would freeze over before I laughed again. "Never was much of a cook."

A corner of his mouth twisted downward. "If you'd cooked it before you dried it..."

"Thought about that, but I worried the smell of roasting meat would draw predators. Coyotes and wolves prowl damn near every night. A couple of bears have even shown up."

Shudders racked me. I tried to stop them, but couldn't. If I didn't watch it, I'd dissolve into another puddle of tears.

"Why is this so hard?" I muttered.

"Because you've never done anything like it before." He worked his way through the strip of meat.

I refilled the flask and set it next to him. As an afterthought, I retreated into the lean-to and grabbed a patty I'd made out of soaked wild grains and salt I'd scrounged from the ruins of a store.

"This isn't that great, either," I said, "but it's nourishing."

Rhys took the misshapen lump and went to work on it. "Not bad. You'd have had potential as a pioneer."

I sank to a squat near him. "If I'd had any idea, I'd have culled through Google and taught myself stuff."

He chewed and swallowed. "That world is gone."

Damn it. Tears were close to the surface again. I hadn't given two figs for a life I'd largely taken for granted. Until it wasn't there anymore.

Rhys chased the grain mixture with more water. "Feel like showing me around?"

I nodded and stood. "Best for us to do that before it gets dark. How'd you end up here? You never did exactly say beyond getting dragged into the vortex. Sedona used to advertise being on top of one. Did it get loose?"

"Mmph. Hadn't considered that possibility, but it's a good one. We left Whole Foods with everyone except you.

Since the others couldn't defuse the warding I'd placed around the caves, we went back, and then Connor and I went to hunt for you. He was in hawk form. I was on foot. I'd covered maybe a quarter of the main part of the town when the vortex snagged me. I yelled to Connor in mind speech to leave. No idea if he heard me."

Crap. I hoped to hell he was all right. He was resourceful, but he was also alone. "How's he going to get inside—if he makes it back to the caves?"

Rhys grimaced. "Fuck. He can't since I sealed them again. Unless the others batter their way out."

"Bet they won't. Not after what happened last time."

Urgency burned a hole in my guts. We had to get back. Had to, and damned soon. Connor was vulnerable. "How long can shifters stay in their other form?"

"Depends on the shifter. For some, the animal body is primary. They can hold it essentially forever."

"Does that apply to Connor?"

"I don't know. Never explored how he was put together."

Heated words flooded my throat. I checked them at the gate. Cursing Rhys because he hadn't bothered to get to know his students better wouldn't solve anything.

We trotted through empty streets, past rotting hulks of metal that were once cars. Buildings that were partially upright in the previous iteration of Sedona had fallen in. Above us, hawks keened mournfully. The chitter of small rodents filled my ears, an ever-present chorus.

Rhys stopped in the middle of the road and spread his arms wide. His magic tingled as it connected with my skin.

"This way." He pointed.

"To where?"

A crooked grin split his striking features. "The vortex. It's what got us here. If we play our cards right..."

I waited, but he didn't finish his thought.

"Play our cards right, what?"

"Maybe we can leverage its enchantment to return us to our proper time."

Huh. "Do you have any idea how to do that?"

"Nope, but it's our best shot. Time travel isn't included in my wheelhouse because I never studied it."

I half ran to keep up with his long-legged stride. "Can any mages do it?"

"Of course. Some witches are proficient. Mostly ones native to the Highlands."

Not exactly handy. We were a long way from Scotland, plus I hadn't seen anyone even remotely human since my arrival. We'd cleared town. Rhys started up a faint trail that climbed steeply. Questions bounced from one side of my head to the other, but I didn't want to divert him, so I extended a slender slice of power feeling my way.

It lit up like a firecracker, sizzling in reaction to latent energy saturating the area. Closer inspection revealed an actual trail beneath our feet, but it had been unused for so long, it wasn't easy to follow. Red rocks surrounded our ascent. Once we got high enough, they were all around us.

Breath seared my chest as I reached a broad plateau. Rhys stood at the base of a red pinnacle with his hands spread over its base. After a moment, he turned and faced me.

"Feel like taking a chance? A big one."

My heart was already thudding against my ribcage, but fear left a sour taste in the back of my throat.

"You have to say more."

A curt nod. "Your magic is deployed. I feel it. Can you sense the untapped power in that?" He angled a thumb behind him.

I refocused my magic-imbued beam. It blazed even brighter than it had on my way up here. "Um, yeah, but what do we do about it?"

"If I recall correctly, Sedona had four vortex points. This might be the most powerful. Even if it's not, it should support our purposes."

I crossed my arms over my chest. Chills made me shiver. "I didn't have any control when I was transported here."

"And I had precious little, but it's different when you ride on a casting from its inception."

"Are you certain?"

He thinned his lips into a scowl. "Of course not. Magic doesn't work like that. Remember I prefaced this with asking how you felt about taking a risk."

"What's the downside?"

"We jump into the vortex and never find our way out of it."

If he'd punched me in the guts, his words wouldn't have been harder to absorb. I sank to my haunches because my legs weren't overly steady. "But we got here." My voice emerged a high-pitched squeak.

"Because someone was pulling the puppet strings, and this is where they wanted us."

"What's to stop them, whoever they are, from barring us from leaving?"

"Nothing. Except I don't sense anyone else with power nearby."

I bit my lower lip so hard I tasted blood and then hastily licked it up and sent magic to seal the wound.

Rhys walked to where I crouched, settled beside me, and placed a hand on my thigh. "I believe I can bend the energy in our favor. Whether it will bring us out where I aim for is a big unknown." He hesitated. "You can remain here, and—"

"No!" burst from me.

He tightened his grip on my thigh. "You've carved out a life for yourself. My idea could kill us both. Or we might end up in a worse spot."

Breath hissed from between my teeth. He's always been a straight shooter. Pissy of me to be twisted out of shape he wasn't the bearer of better news.

"Any idea of our odds?" My voice only shook a little.

"None."

"Can we get back here if, well, if we can't get anywhere else?"

He sighed. "Also an unknown. The vortex is here. It will want to return to its source. Whether it would be willing to drag us along is anyone's guess."

Rhys snaked an arm around me. I leaned into him wishing this moment in time would last forever.

"I'm going to explore how my power marries with the vortex," he murmured. "While I'm about it, figure out what you want to do."

He was gone before I could lodge a protest. The place

his body had pressed against mine felt cold, barren. My choices were limited. Either I remained here, returned to my solitary existence. Or I went with him.

The thought of being alone again was unbearable.

Wimp. My inner voice burned with derision. It was right. If I ignored flirting with suicide, I'd managed decently. Hadn't starved to death.

Rhys returned to where I still squatted in the dirt. I stood and turned to face him.

"Did you decide?"

Heat seared my cheeks. "Not exactly."

"If this works, I should be able to find my way back to you."

"How?"

"Once I have the feel of the vortex, I can perhaps bend it to my will."

"If you can't?"

He dropped his hands on my shoulders. "No matter how many questions you ask, I cannot offer guarantees. Of anything. But I have to try to get back. Connor is alone and vulnerable. It's not safe outside the caves. Once night falls..."

Rhys didn't have to fill in the blanks. Connor would be easy pickings for the vamps and werewolves.

"How do you know it's the same time back there?"

"I don't. The fact that you've been gone a month and me only a handful of hours argues time flows differently, but it's an even more pressing reason to attempt this. What will it be, Alia?"

"Do you need me to pull this off?"

He frowned. "Not sure, but more magic never hurts. It's not a reason for you to throw your lot in with me, though."

"What is?"

"This is cheating, but—" With no warning, he angled his head and closed his mouth over mine. The touch of his lips sent heat ratcheting through me. I opened my mouth to him, kissing him back as if he were a lifeline in a tumultuous sea.

We ended up with our arms around each other, drinking one another in as if we were anywhere except high above the ruins of a future Sedona.

As abruptly as he'd kissed me, he stepped back. "I shouldn't have done that." His chiseled mouth was swollen from contact with mine.

"But you did. Why did you say it was cheating?"

His gaze sought mine. "Because I want you to come with me. If I leave you here, I might never see you again."

My body was alight from being in his arms. Unfamiliar sensations coursed through me. I'd been kissed before, but never like this.

"Why is that important?"

Light was leaching from the day. I'd found the transitions abrupt, perhaps because of the total lack of lighting once the sun fled.

"It doesn't matter. Are you coming with me? If we go, it must be now. The vortices gather energy from the sun. Once it's down, we'll have to wait for tomorrow."

Something else I'd never have guessed. "Maybe tomorrow is better," I ventured. "We could bring food with us, and—"

"Connor needs us," he prodded. "If we're successful, we

won't need food." A pause. "If we're not, we also won't need food."

His words sank in. The glow from his kiss frittered to nothing.

I squared my shoulders. "I'm coming with you."

"Are you certain?"

I nodded.

He gripped my hand. Together, we walked to the base of the red rock cylinder and stood side by side.

"Lay your left hand on the rock," Rhys instructed as he placed his right hand on it. "Hold my hand with your other one. Whatever you do, don't let go."

Power swirled around us. Rhys's magic mingled with the pull of the vortex. It terrified me since I'd fought it all the way here. Giving in to its draw was hard.

"Open your power to me." His voice was hoarse, distant. My fears this wasn't truly Rhys after all sprang to the forefront. I pushed them aside. Whatever was happening was too far down the road to derail now.

It might have been illusion, but we jumped from our perch under the rock into darkness that surged and pulsed around us. Something pressed in on us from all sides. I clung to Rhys's hand and did my damnedest not to pass out.

Different from my last trip courtesy of the vortex, this one hurt. My nose bled; my eyes teared. Or maybe they were bleeding too. It was so dark, I couldn't see Rhys. Or anything else.

Something large with feathers brushed against my face. It stank of death.

Screams tore from me. I had to run. Get away, but there was nowhere to go.

Through it all, Rhys kept on chanting. Why hadn't I noticed it before?

He was pulling power from me, so much I had very little left. Why hadn't I noticed that, either?

If Rhys wasn't really Rhys. If this had all been a game, a plot to do away with me, I couldn't alter it now. I relinquished my goal of staying awake and let go.

Of everything.

CHAPTER FOURTEEN, RHYS

I was trying to conserve power and doing a piss-poor job. Not even enough left to comfort Alia. When she passed out, it was a blessing. Thank all the gods she'd managed to cling to my hand. If this whirling mess had a bottom, I didn't know where it might be. It was clumsy since my fingers were laced with hers, but I gathered her into my arms to make certain she wouldn't fall.

What enormous hubris to even consider I'd have a chance in hell of manipulating this energy source. So far, all it had done was drain me.

And Alia.

When I'd requested access to her power, she'd trustingly offered it.

Fuck. I would not let her down.

Something big with wings shared this space. What in the hell was it? So far, all it had done was brush up against me. Usually, if creatures mean ill, they don't toy with you.

Eh, some of them do.

My mind was tripping along, oblivious to what I needed it to do.

I shuttered the flow of power to conserve what little I had left. Worst thing that might happen is the vortex would take a hike in search of richer pastures. I waited through two breaths, then five. Nothing changed. I still banged against the sides of the vortex as it traveled through goddess only knew where.

A low growl buzzed against my ears. I tightened my hold on Alia.

Birds don't growl.

Even though I hated to burn through even an angstrom of magic, I risked a burst of light. And wished I hadn't.

I'd known we weren't alone, but our cellmate was a griffon. Handsome fellow with his eagle's head and lionesque body, given what I'd seen in two seconds of illumination from my mage light. Was he our jailer, or a fellow prisoner?

Pressure from every side had been part of things since we jumped into the swirling darkness. It seemed to be increasing, but I wasn't certain. How long had my initial transit taken? Surely, we'd been in motion longer than I expected.

Yesh, but that was when I nurtured the illusion I had any control over the process.

No reason to bother with telepathy. "Can you help?" I shouted to be heard over the noisy rush of air currents. The mythical creature didn't answer. I hadn't expected it to. Had he been why Alia was screaming before she slumped against me?

I slapped my free palm against my forehead. I had to focus, goddammit. Foul energy was afoot, aimed at diverting me from ever leaving. It had been hard at work since the moment we entered this space. The vortex wouldn't give a crap about me once I ran out of magic. I could not allow that to happen.

Why had I been stupid enough to link my magical center with Alia's? If I hadn't done that—

And there I went again.

I clenched my free hand hard enough nails cut into my palm. Pain had a centering effect. Risking another burst of light, I threaded tendrils through holes in the vortex wall to figure out where in the fuck we were.

When the answer came, it took restraint to keep from cheering. I slapped warding around my mind as I examined the weave of time. Not dissimilar to border worlds, time existed in a kind of layering system.

We'd moved from the Sedona where Alia had made a primitive home to perhaps twenty years in the past. Another twenty-ish might bring us close. How to finetune this process was beyond me at the moment, but I'd figure it out.

No choice. Not really.

Alia stirred in my arms. Should I waken her? I'd severed my connection with her magic the moment she passed out.

She saved me the decision when she murmured, "Let go of me. I'm okay."

"Simpler if I hold you."

"Do you know where we are?"

"Yes and no."

My answer must have pissed her off because she wrenched away from my grip and ended up pressed against my right side with an arm hooked beneath mine. "If you know something," she hissed, "spit it out."

"We shouldn't talk about it."

"Then use telepathy."

"Anyone with magic could hear."

She was silent after that, perhaps embarrassed she hadn't recognized as much.

Something about having her awake cleared my muddy thoughts. I kindled a dim light and surveyed our surroundings.

"We're in some kind of tunnel," Alia said, followed by, "What was that?"

"A griffon." My attention was on a series of raised nodes on the far side of the vortex wall.

"No. That." She pointed to what I'd been examining.

Hoping to hell the vortex didn't grab the opportunity and amputate my arm, I reached through a hole in its weave and grasped a knob next to the nodes. It got me close enough to see runes carved into the nodes.

"Can you read what it says?" she asked.

I could, except the choices weren't what I'd have preferred. If they were actually choices and would spit us out in the year indicated by the runes.

"Rhys." Her voice shrilled.

"They're years. But not the right ones. Closest is 2020."

Another growl obscured the tail end of my words.

"What in the fuck was that?" Alia shrieked.

"We have company in here," I explained. "Already told you. It's a griffon."

"They're not real."

"Neither are we," I said dryly and redirected my light so she could see him. "Hush, let me figure this out. These dates are separated by four years. Maybe they're not linear."

"What does that mean?"

"These can't be the only nodes. It could be as simple as finding the year we need and pressing its node."

"I didn't do that on my trip to the future."

"Neither did I," I confirmed, "but perhaps someone else did. Mages have known how to bend time forever. Instructions have to be in some of the eldritch libraries, except we don't have access to them."

"Rhys!" she yelped and pulled on my arm.

I yanked it through the vortex's weave seconds before it slammed shut. I'd been afraid that might happen, but my attention had wandered.

Again.

"It's sentient," Alia muttered.

"Yes, but not quick on the uptake."

We lurched downward, but this time I was on the lookout for more nodes. Sure enough, within a couple of minutes another set came into view. I bent as close as I could get, desperate to read the runes.

With a flurry of wings, the griffon pushed me out of the way and bit through the vortex with his sharp beak. I snaked an arm through and stabilized our descent.

"Bingo," I crowed, my palm hovering over the magical numbers 2022.

"Are you sure this will work?" Alia cried.

"No. Do you have a better idea?"

"Go for it. Can't be any worse than in here."

Rather than a growl, the griffon hooted what might have been laughter. Had it known these were the nodes that would lead back to our own time?

The hole in the vortex was closing. This time, I was on top of it.

Now or never. Releasing a breath I didn't realize I'd been holding, I slammed the node to its stops.

The vortex shattered. So did the tunnel around it. Alia and I plummeted through chilly air toward a city far below. The griffon soared near us. What was his stake in all this? Was he running from something? Or had word gone out Earth was in ruins and free for the taking?

I wove air currents beneath me to break my fall. Presumably Alia was doing the same since she wasn't shrieking with fear. Close enough to recognize Sedona's wreckage, I shut my eyes and prayed my luck, which has always been robust, hadn't deserted me.

We landed about thirty feet apart, tumbling onto dusty bits of asphalt. On my feet in an instant, I ran toward Alia, who was getting up more slowly. When I shaded my eyes to search for the griffon, he was nowhere in sight.

Alia shook herself from head to toe. "This looks right," she ventured.

"Let's test it." Raising my mind voice, I called Connor's name.

Dusk was falling. Night—and vampires—would be here

soon if the nodes ran true. "Come on." I held out a hand for Alia and started in the direction of the caves.

"Aren't we waiting for Connor?"

"He can find us."

If we're in the right place, and if he's still alive...

Alia winced. "I sort of heard that."

"You've told me to stay out of your mind." No need to say more.

We trudged through ruins. The reek of decaying flesh was still strong, but it would linger for months. Or until predators returned to feed on the dead.

The whoosh of wings snapped my head around. A large hawk bore down on us. Relief washed through me. I'd been more worried than I let myself know that my absence had spelled his demise.

"Connor!" Alia squealed.

He reached us, did a somersault midair, and came to rest in his human body. "Where in the fuck did the two of you go off to?" he growled.

"How long were we gone?" I countered.

"You didn't answer me."

I shrugged. "Seems to be going around."

"Two days," he said grudgingly. "Caves were barred to me, but the others can't get out, either." His blue gaze drilled into me. "You have to fix that. Teach us how to manipulate the barrier."

"Agreed. It was a lapse on my part." I didn't add I'd had no way of knowing I'd be snatched forward in time.

"Did you see the griffon?" Alia asked.

His dark brows shot up. "Erm, no. What griffon? They're not real."

"Hurry," I urged. "It will be dark soon."

"Tell me about it," Connor groused. "There's a fucking herd of vampires here."

"Seethe," I corrected.

"Meh. Doesn't matter what you call them. If I didn't have wings, I'd have been dinner."

This time, I didn't bother to correct him. Dinner would have been the kindest, simplest outcome. Others, like being turned, were far worse. Vamps have always been fascinated by shifters. They'd probably have done their damnedest to entice him into their ranks.

We were on the far side of town with the sun sinking quickly behind the red rocks. A cursory scan of my power suggested I had enough to move us to the caves far quicker than our feet could manage it.

"Come close," I instructed, wrapped everyone in a minor jump spell, and transported us to the caves.

Once there, I barked a few words. The barrier fell, and we lurched through.

Joss, Nola, Karen, and Moriah mobbed us.

"Where have you been," echoed off the walls.

I held up both hands. "First," I said, "pay close attention." Turning toward the opening, I made my spell visible as I wove earth and air to create the barrier before locking it into place. "Just do the reverse to dismantle it," I told everyone.

"We tried," Moriah said.

"Lots of things," Karen seconded.

"Connor was outside," Nola explained. "But we couldn't get to him."

Odd they'd been able to defeat the barrier that first time. Perhaps the same someone who'd kidnapped Alia and me wanted them to stay put.

Weariness washed through me. I stumbled down the corridor to the room where Joss had set up an impromptu kitchen. Luckily, bowls of cooling grain sat on a sideboard. I snatched one of them, spooning oatmeal into my mouth mindlessly.

The others crowded behind me. "You never did tell me where you were," Connor pressed as he slithered into trousers and a sweater that sat in a pile next to the pool.

"We got dragged into the future," Alia answered for me.

A collective gasp surged. Between the two of us, we filled in the blanks as I finished my cereal and started on a second bowl. Alia ate too.

"Anyway," I said after I'd filled my empty bowl with water and drunk deeply, "it appears time exists in layers. The vortex is one way to access them, but there must be others."

"Why can't we just go back to before all this happened?" Nola demanded.

"How far before?" I asked.

"We'll just end up here sooner or later," Moriah pointed out.

"Maybe we could stop whatever happened." Karen nudged her sister shifter.

The possibility hadn't occurred to me, but it was

enticing. "First, we need to determine why everything turned to shit," I reminded them.

"Sure, but if we could do that..." Joss dusted his palms together.

"Christ, this is starting to feel like an out-of-control episode of *Star Trek*," Alia muttered. "At least they had the prime directive of not disturbing anything in the future."

"They violated the hell out of it," Connor said. "Many times."

"Get some rest," I told everyone before we ended up rehashing an old television series.

"What happens tomorrow?" Connor asked.

I shook my head. "I have no idea, but we're back together. It's enough for right now."

And it was. My gambit, longshot though it was, had paid off. Somehow, the griffon was mixed in with this, but I was too tired to figure it out.

"I'll be across the corridor," I told everyone and headed for the room with the armoires. After rifling through a couple, I wadded clothing into a makeshift cot and fell onto it. If Watchers were here, I couldn't sense them.

But I didn't try all that hard. They wouldn't bother me.

Eyes shut, I floated, replaying everything that had happened since the vortex snagged me. At some point, I must have drifted off because when I rolled over, Alia lay next to me with one arm tossed over her eyes. The even cadence of her breathing told me she was asleep.

Why was she here and not in the other cavern?

Memories of our kiss stirred sensation, but I resisted covering her mouth with mine. Touched by her trust in me—

trust that had expanded when I invited her to jump into the vortex—I gently draped an arm over her and tucked my body around hers.

She snuggled close, making little mewling noises in her sleep. Poor thing. She must have been terrified when the vortex vomited her into the future. Still, she'd made the best of an untenable situation, creating order out of chaos. Younger than the rest of us by well over a decade, her resourcefulness shone through.

In that moment I vowed to protect her, keep her safe. Between magic and brute strength, I'd do whatever it took to ensure no harm befell her.

Was it a promise I could keep? Only time would tell that tale.

Behind my closed lids, the griffon took shape, snapping his avian beak and flapping his wings.

Nothing in the magical realm is accidental, but I didn't have the bandwidth to figure things out. Why he was here would have to wait for a clearer head. With Alia's vanilla-pine scent soothing my senses, I fell asleep.

CHAPTER FIFTEEN, ALIA

I still couldn't believe I'd escaped the hellish future Sedona. Painful though it was, I'd sort of come to terms with living out my days there—after I slogged through my suicidal phase.

I hadn't filled in the blanks. Maybe I didn't have to. Rhys could have seen everything in my mind if he chose to rifle through it. I'd spent most of the first two weeks alternating between despair and frantic activity to erect a shelter between me and whatever evil sought my destruction.

At first, I'd assumed I could scrounge canned goods from wrecked shops.

Wrong.

The cans that weren't bloated with botulism had been carved open by something with big teeth. How in the fuck could animals recognize which cans held food and which ones would kill them?

I had located blankets. Full of moth holes and rodent

189

rips, they remained warm and useful. I worried about Hanta virus until the unreality of everything sent me on a laughing-crying jag. On the one hand, I was contemplating the least intrusive way to end my life. On the other, I was wasting breath on a virus that could do the job handily.

Maybe.

One thing my travels around Sedona turned up was pharmacies. For the most part, their stock remained untouched. After breaking through rusting locks, I'd secured a sizeable stash of narcotics.

If I decided to check out, I'd just OD.

Going to sleep felt preferable to slicing my wrists or jumping off a red rock and hoping to hell it did the trick. The way my luck had been running, I was just as likely to break enough body parts to die a lingering, pain-filled death.

Eh, not so lingering, after all. The first sunset would bring predators. They'd view me as prime buffet material. A shudder ran through me, followed by several more. Everyone else was asleep, the sound of their easy breathing comforting.

What was wrong with me? I was safe, or as safe as our new normal provided. Before my mind provided a blow-by-blow of being torn to bits by wolves or coyotes, I pushed to my feet and padded out of the cavern to the one across the hall.

Rhys lay on his side, fair hair fanned out around him. Such a beautiful man. I've never taken time to lust after anyone. The fallout would have been too great. Sooner or later, they'd have unearthed just how different I was, and that would have been that.

But Rhys knew me. He'd risked himself to go after me,

although at the time I'm certain he had no idea just how perilous it would be. He'd probably assumed I'd be somewhere in this time, not half a century in the future.

I resisted an urge to kneel and smooth hair away from his face. He was doing his best to watch out for us. Had he not been saddled with retreat refugees, he'd probably be somewhere hobnobbing with fellow mages and working on saving the world from future destruction.

Taking care not to disturb him, I selected more garments to create an impromptu bed and lay next to him. Not touching, but near enough to fill my nostrils with his spicy scent. It reminded me of mulled wine and crackling fires. Something about his presence soothed my inner turmoil. The tightly wound spot deep within me relaxed a notch or two.

Enough so when I shut my eyes, sleep finally transported me to an easier world. Unlike any of my other dreams, this one featured the griffon who'd been our partner in crime in the vortex. At first, it frightened me, but when it didn't reach for me or appear threatening, I took a shot at communicating with it.

"What do you want?"

No answer, so I tried, *"Why are you here?"*

He didn't reply. It was probably a lost cause, but I cycled through a bunch of questions before he flapped his wings and vanished. Was I supposed to follow him? If so, how?

Why was I so sure it was male?

I explored the space he'd occupied but couldn't find any hidden gateways. Was he hiding, playing games, or just one more ephemeral vision? I'd had plenty my first couple of weeks in the other Sedona. Imagery that came and went, most far more threatening than the griffon.

Come to think of it, I hadn't seen any mythical beasts—until we were in the vortex. If the griffon lived there, it hadn't come out to play my first trip. Was it because whoever was manipulating the puppet strings that transported me into the future was a threat to it?

The demarcation between dreams and wakefulness is sometimes hazy, but I'd clearly crossed out of dreamland.

Mmph. I needed to ask Rhys about the griffon; he hadn't mentioned it when we'd recapped our sojourn to the others. Maybe it was a kind of spirit guide for him. I'd read about things like that at the retreat center. One exercise encouraged us to find our totem animals—all but the shifters who already had them. I'd done my best, but nothing had come to me.

Rhys had said something like it can take years.

I stifled a yawn. My overwrought body was finally in relaxation mode, the tension bleeding out of my muscles. The next thing I half remembered was Rhys cradling me in an arm and moving closer. Remembered is relative, since I was still mostly asleep.

Aware, but sleeping as I leaned into his warmth.

Time passed. No idea how much since the caverns retain a perpetual state of twilight courtesy of small light-generating lichen. Rhys still had an arm around me with his body curved against my back.

I heard the murmur of voices from across the hall and turned until I faced Rhys without dislodging his arm. "Time to get up," I murmured and started to move away.

"Not yet." His voice was husky with sleep, and he tightened his grip on me.

"But the others..."

"Can get along nicely on their own for a bit." He cupped the side of my face with a calloused hand. "Why did you come here last night?"

My cheeks warmed. "I was wound tighter than a spring. Your energy holds...peace."

His lips parted in a soft smile. "Thank you. It's quite a compliment."

Before I could respond, he closed his lips over mine. My first instinct was to draw away. Instead, I kissed him back, opening my mouth to his insistent tongue. Unfamiliar sensations buffeted me. Where my breasts were crushed against him, my nipples hardened. The length of his penis jutted into my belly. Curiosity about that hard length, and what it might feel like buried inside me, stole my breath.

I didn't remember reaching for him, but my fingertips traced hard lines of muscle in his shoulders and back. He lowered a hand to cup my ass and pulled me against his erection. While I understood the mechanics of sex, my sole experiences consisted of furtive rubbing under the covers at night.

His breath warmed my mouth. My hips rotated against him in a dance all their own. It was a lot like when I rubbed myself except instead of my fingers, I was using his appendage. Panting, I ground myself against him.

He thrust a hand between my legs.

It was so intimate, I gasped. My eyes flew open.

"I can do this for you," he said into my mind as his fingers scribed circles over my sex.

It had been one thing when my eyes were shut, and I could pretend I was alone. This was too intense, too personal. My face was on fire when I wriggled away from his touch. My entire body pounded with unslaked need, a new experience. I'd always brought myself off and moved on with whatever.

"It's all right," he soothed.

Embarrassment saturated every pore. I rolled over and got to my feet, adjusting my clothing. The room smelled like us, like sex. The others would know—if they hadn't already figured it out from the noises we'd been making.

Somehow, he was standing next to me. Before I could make a break for, well, for somewhere, he wrapped me in his arms, said "I'll be here whenever you're ready," and let go.

"What if I never am?" I mumbled. My sex beat like a second heart.

"I'll take my chances. I was attracted to you at the retreat, but I've made it a policy never to date students."

Interesting. "What changed?" I hadn't planned on saying anything, but the words tore out of me.

His partial smile grew until it lit his entire face. "The world. Or haven't you noticed."

"Still, there's a..." Words failed me.

"A what?" He was still grinning.

"I don't know. A cosmic balance, or something."

"And how is us having sex going to alter it?"

I dropped my gaze to the ground. "Erm. I've never had sex with anyone, so I can't answer that."

"Alia. Look at me."

It took a bit since I was still ashamed of my neediness. At least the urgency around coming was receding. Finally, I met his ice-blue eyes.

"Better. One of the plusses in all of this is you're not alone anymore. You don't have to hide who or what you are. Everyone here understands."

Against my better judgment, I smiled back. "I'd rather have things the way they were, even with me hiding my magic under a barrel."

"You don't get that choice."

"Nope. Guess I don't."

"Hey, you two. Breakfast is almost ready," Joss called.

Crap. Sound traveled even more efficiently than I'd imagined. How could I face the others?

"We did nothing wrong. You'll march across the hall. No one will say anything."

"Fuck. You're in my head again."

He winked. "Best get used to it."

Bending, he began folding the items that had been part of our bed. Since the mess was half mine, I helped. Holding out a hand, he said, "Come on."

I skirted his invitation, walked ahead of him, and joined the others.

Joss had made something with eggs and the vegetables we'd taken from Whole Foods. It smelled divine.

"Don't get too used to this," Joss cautioned. "Once we're out of fresh food, there's unlikely to be more."

"We can hunt," Connor said around a mouthful of food.

"Good luck hunting vegetables," Nola murmured.

"Many edible plants grow wild," Rhys said.

The witch shrugged. "Not like asparagus from the supermarket."

"Some people who lived here must have kept gardens," Karen tossed out.

For a time, we ate in silence and washed down the food with an herbal tea.

"We need to go back out today," Rhys told everyone. "Get the lay of the land. See if any other stores have provisions."

Moriah cleared her throat. "Connor wasn't the only thing trying to get inside."

"I am not a thing," he informed her.

After rolling her eyes, Moriah continued. "It was hard to sense through the barrier, but I'm pretty sure vampires and—"

"I was there," Connor cut in. "Vamps, skinwalkers, and werewolves circled at different times."

"They must have formed an alliance," Joss muttered.

"Unlikely," Rhys told him. "Vampires never join ranks with anyone."

"All right, so at least they agreed not to try to turn the skinwalkers to their ranks."

"We don't know that, either," Rhys said. "Look, people. Assumptions are dangerous. They can get you killed. Absent full and complete information, anything we meet out there is potentially dangerous, which is why we stick together, and—"

"Didn't work very well in Whole Foods," Karen snarked.

"My fault," Rhys shot back. "I never should have

suggested we split up once we were inside. There's that thing about assumptions again. I underestimated, and paid a price."

As he went on talking, I watched him from the corners of my eyes. What he said was well thought out. Given he didn't know any more than we did about our current situation, he was analyzing available bits and pieces.

Why was it so tough to admit I was attracted to him? What would happen if I was honest about my feelings?

The answer wasn't long coming. I'd be vulnerable, in a position where he could hurt me. We might do okay in bed, but would there be a long haul?

Whoa, sister. My inner wise woman cut my thoughts off at their roots. With a phalanx of unknowns, the last thing I needed was further exploration of my nascent sexuality.

We had bigger issues, some of which were being dissected except I hadn't been paying attention. I finished the remains of my breakfast and did my best to catch up.

"Before we break and leave," Rhys was saying, "have any of you seen a griffon?"

"They're not real," Karen said flatly.

"Yes, they are," Rhys corrected her. "One accompanied us here from the future." He turned to Connor. "Did you catch a glimpse, perhaps?"

The hawk shifter shook his head.

"Be on the lookout for him when we're out and about," Rhys said. "He hitched a ride to this point in time for a reason, and I'd like to know what it is."

"He was in my dreams last night," I murmured.

Rhys's head swiveled in my direction. "What did he say?"

"Nothing. He was just there."

"Maybe you're the connection," Joss said.

I looked down at my empty bowl. He might be correct, but it didn't make me feel any better.

"Could be," Rhys agreed. "Alia's magic is an unknown quantity, both where it comes from and its extent."

If I'd been uncomfortable before, I was doubly so now.

"Come on." Rhys rose and motioned to us. "Let's see what the day brings. Nola. Practice opening the barrier."

After shooting an exasperated glance Rhys's way, the witch scurried out of the grotto.

Fighting a sense of impending doom, I took up a position at the tail end of the group. The last time I'd left these caves, I'd ended up years in the future with no ability to intervene.

Sticking close might be an antidote, but not good enough to protect any of us against superior forces wielding goddess only knew what kind of magic. Usually, sunshine brightens my mood. Today, I cringed as it hit me full in the face.

What in the hell was wrong with me?

My situation was so much better than it had been this time yesterday. Why couldn't I accept that and run with it?

"Alia. Keep up," Rhys barked.

The barrier slammed shut behind me, cutting off any possibility of retreat.

I smoothed wrinkles from my troubled soul and trotted after everyone else.

CHAPTER SIXTEEN, RHYS

The scent of Alia's arousal still clung to me, distracting as hell, but I couldn't afford to split my attention. Not for a second. Why hadn't Connor seen the griffon? He'd had an arial view. Was the creature selectively invisible?

The only mythical beasts I knew anything about were dragons. And only because they'd still flown freely above the Old Country several centuries back. I'd run across the occasional Kelpie too. Sorry pieces of work and damned tough to kill.

There went my mind again, off on irrelevant tangents. While keeping a close eye on everyone, I shepherded our small group to a different part of town. Sure enough, what remained of a shopping complex came into view after a couple of miles of brisk walking. This one held a big box pharmacy next to a Safeway. Excellent. We could stock up on antibiotics. Magic is usually better than drugs, but not always. Unless the Druid had healing capacities I wasn't aware of, we lacked a skilled medic.

The reek of the dead, bitter and cloying, persisted; it would take weeks to dissipate.

Nola halted, waiting for instructions.

"We'll try the drug store first," I announced after painting the area with a swath of power and determining we were alone. Probably. Others could be nearby but cloaked. Vamps could be asleep within. I wasn't worried about them. Not at ten in the morning.

Alia finally caught up.

"Everything okay?" I asked her.

A noncommittal shrug. "Don't mind me."

Not the answer I'd hoped for. Still, I was loathe to grill her in front of everyone. It wouldn't help to drag words from her. Had the griffon returned? I hadn't seen him, but it didn't mean much.

Our trip through the pharmacy was productive. All the medications were locked in a large safe, but I drilled through the locking mechanism with a shot of enchantment.

"Whoa." Joss whistled long and low. "Junkie central."

"I worked as a nurse for a while," Moriah informed us and proceeded to fill a plastic bag with various bottles and vials.

We were picking our way over and under wreckage on our way back to the front door when a wave of cold washed through me. It invited me to stop and examine it, but I knew better.

"Hurry," I urged and positioned myself behind Alia. No

way was I about to leave her at the tail end of our queue again.

Daylight was welcome once we emerged from the ruined building. I'd expected company, but the street with its collection of abandoned cars and trucks was empty.

"What was that eerie sensation?" Alia shook from head to toe as if to rid herself of a plague.

"Did any of the rest of you feel anything?" Rather than answering Alia, I glanced around the group.

"Our wolves were edgy," Karen said.

"My hawk too," Connor cut in.

Should we chance the store or cash in our chips and retreat?

A rumble from beneath us clinched things. It grew louder, punctuated by what could have been rocks grinding against one another in a subterranean region. The others drew close without me telling them.

"Get us out of here." Nola's voice was high, shrill.

I cobbled a quick jump spell together, draped it around us all, and visualized the caverns. At first, I thought we'd pulled it off. The street disintegrated, leaving darkness.

Except it didn't go away. These superfast transport spells are over in seconds. No lingering in the in-between place.

"Where are they?" Moriah snarled, her words garbled. Like as not, her wolf was fighting for ascendency.

By "they" she had to mean the caves. I wanted to know too. Courtesy of rest and food, I poured replenished power into my casting. No going back now. If I reeled in my ability, we'd languish wherever we were.

All of us.

Feathers brushed my face. Alia yelped, so it must have touched her too. Pretty much had to be the griffon. My senses reinforced we were descending at a fast clip.

Not much beneath Earth's surface other than Hell, but I didn't perceive demon presence. The griffon's energy didn't ping off my magic at all. Had I not seen him when I left the future, I'd never have guessed who owned the feathers.

A burst of light illuminated our surroundings. Where I'd tried for a stealth approach, Alia was apparently sick of skulking in shadows. We were in a cylinder lined with rocks that had been mortared together. I thought I saw the griffon, but his fur and feathers winked out as soon as light flooded our prison.

I'd been right about one thing, the platform we stood on was traveling downward.

"Where in the hell are we?" Connor muttered.

I lacked an answer.

"Could be part of the vortex system," Joss supplied. He aimed for calm, but his tone betrayed worry. As it should. Something had overridden my magic, not a simple undertaking. Since it wasn't helping us, I withdrew my spell to conserve my ability.

The rickety platform hit bottom hard enough to jam my jaws together. A corridor sprawled before us.

"Not leaving much to chance, are they?" Moriah growled.

Now that I could see. I'd been right about her—and her sister—being partially shifted. Their hands and feet had turned to paws. The drugstore bag hung from a talon.

"May as well play along." I kept my tone light and

started down the dirt corridor. It was surprisingly smooth, as if someone took care to clear rocks out of the way.

"You make it sound as if there's a choice," Joss mumbled. He probably didn't mean for me to hear, but I have sharp ears.

The corridor branched. Interesting. Which way were we supposed to go?

Alia slithered around me. Without a shred of hesitation, she selected the left-hand road. I hustled after her. "Why this one?"

She turned to flash me an undecipherable look but didn't answer. The sight of her face, lips set into a tight line, eyes glazed over gave me pause. Was she in thrall to something?

I lassoed power around her, intent on protecting her from harm.

A low, keening shriek filled my ears. "Stop that," she cried. "It's making things worse."

My spell crackled when I dismantled it. Alia cringed but didn't cry out again.

"What's wrong with her?" Connor switched to telepathy.

I didn't bother to tell him whatever we faced could drill right through his attempt at a private conversation.

"Possessed," I replied.

"By what?" Connor's usually deep baritone turned into a squeak.

"I don't know." The terseness of my reply was a wake-up call to how frantic I was. The situation had spiraled far beyond my ability to control it.

Alia spun, facing us. When she raised her hands, her

mage light was cradled in one. Mini lightning bolts, aimed over our heads, flew from the other. "You must go back."

Damn it. Something had commandeered her vocal cords. The voice wasn't hers.

I pushed forward and ran into a barrier. It carried quite a punch and tossed me a few feet into the air. I scrambled to my feet and walked to where the unseen barrier had barred my way. Now that I knew it was there, subtle alterations in the weave of air alerted me to its presence.

"Go back," Alia repeated in the not-hers voice.

"I'm not leaving you."

"You must. I have been called."

Fuck. This was getting worse and worse. "By whom?"

I didn't expect an answer, so when she said, "the ancients," it caught me by surprise.

"Ancient what?" This time, Connor asked the question.

Same thing I wanted to know.

Disembodied wings folded around the front of Alia's body. Maybe the griffon except I couldn't see the rest of it.

"Fight this," I urged and gathered power into an arc that should drill through the barrier between her and me.

"I belong here," she intoned. "Leave now while your safety is guaranteed."

"Good advice," Moriah muttered. Power flickered around her, weak with a pallid yellow light.

What the hell? Was she trying to leave on her own? That wouldn't end well.

"Stay put," I thundered. "We stand together."

"Sure. But Alia's out of the equation," Karen said.

I drew my hand back but thought better of slapping her. "If you were the one who'd been—"

Alia's light extinguished, leaving us in darkness until I called my own into being. The place Alia had stood was empty. The low rumble of rocks grinding together was punctuated by them falling from above. A warning if I've ever seen one to get the fuck out of here.

"We need to run," Nola keened.

If she'd had sufficient power at her disposal, she'd have been gone without a thought for the rest of us.

Low whizzing made me feint right to avoid being hit by rockfall. "Come on." I started down the path where Alia had stood. The barrier that had tossed me on my ass was gone.

"Why aren't we leaving?" Moriah called after me.

I stopped and turned to look at the group. Moriah's transformation was half complete, the drugstore bag abandoned by her rear feet.

"If one of you had been taken, would you want the rest of us to abandon you?" I inquired. Not bothering to wait for an answer, I sprinted along the tunnel intent on gathering clues about Alia's whereabouts.

The others would follow me since they lacked sufficient magic to extricate themselves from this place. Even if they didn't, they'd be close to where I left them. Retreating to the spot where the platform had spit us out was doable, but the long trek upward to the surface wasn't.

The corridor stretched before me. As I ran, I opened my senses seeking clues. Alia had alluded to ancients. It narrowed things down, but not enough. Because my power was fanned in a circular arc, I missed the same subtle alteration that had signaled the last barrier.

This one burned like the devil when I plowed into it. Hissing with discomfort, I righted myself. No one was behind me. So much for my lectures about sticking together. I cycled through a couple of spells before a combination of fire and air made the barrier visible.

No way around this one. No way through.

Connor hurried to where I stood. "Looks bad. What's next?"

"Jump spell. Are you in?"

He nodded tersely. I didn't ask after the others. Visualizing the far side of the barrier, I loosed a spell that included us both. Prickly heat engulfed me as if I'd fallen into a fire pit. Connor gasped but didn't cry out. I pushed harder, forged a way through before my body morphed into an inferno.

The pain vanished quickly, leaving me sucking air. "You okay?" I asked.

"Barely. Let's hit it."

We ran side by side. Edgy, I waited for the next shoe to fall. It didn't. The path wound downward.

"How do you know they didn't move her?" Connor demanded. "As in out of here."

I didn't. But I lacked clues.

"Do you know who took her?"

"No."

"What happens if we don't find her?"

He was asking all the questions I should have been turning the world inside out to find answers for. We came to a place where the gently sloping track gave way to a precipitous drop-off.

I extended threads of enchantment stamped with Alia's energy. Nothing pinged back. Was it worth jumping into a pit where I couldn't see the bottom? Had whoever captured her set a trap for me, something to throw me off the search?

"Want me to fly down and have a look?" Connor began stripping out of his clothes.

"Be careful. Stay near the opening. I don't want to have to search for you too."

"Thanks for the vote of confidence, boss," he said just before he turned into a hawk and dove through the hole.

I flooded the space with as much light as I could muster and watched the hawk circle lower and lower. Suddenly, he shot upward, wings flapping madly. Despite massive effort, he wasn't gaining enough altitude. Something was trying to drag him downward.

I'd already lost one team member today. I'd be damned if I'd lose another. Fashioning a hasty net, I sent it beneath the hawk's flailing form, tightened the edges of my spell, and gave a mighty heave.

Connor's hawk burst through the opening and lay on his side at my feet, beak opening and closing as he gasped for air. I gathered the bird into my arms, testing for broken places in his mind.

Mercifully, it was still Connor and still whole. Squawking weakly, the bird wriggled against my grip. I set him next to me. The shift took a while, but Connor emerged and made a grab for his trousers and sweater.

"Thanks," he mumbled.

"Any idea what's in there?"

"None. Never felt anything like it, but it was strong. And it spoke to me. Sort of a resistance-is-futile theme."

"Come on." Extending a hand, I hauled him upright.

"Where are we going?"

"To collect the others."

Connor stopped dead. "We can't give up on Alia."

"I'm not, but we can't get to her this way. Let's get moving."

The griffon flew into my mind, wings fanning imaginary air. *"Alia is ours. She has a purpose to fulfill."*

"Not going to happen," I growled.

"What's not going to happen?" Connor sounded mystified and still shell-shocked from his near miss with death—or imprisonment.

"The griffon, the one you never saw, just told me Alia is his."

"Does that make sense to you?"

"No, but it's because I don't know much about griffons, who they work for, what they represent."

"How can we find out?"

I didn't bother answering. What we needed was an arcane library, one collected by generations of mages. Did Sedona house such a thing? It was a distant possibility. For the millionth time, I kicked myself for my rush to leave the Sierra Madre mountains. I had a decent collection of books and scrolls there, for all the good they were doing me.

Long before we reached the split in the pathway, the others found us. Joss was in the lead. "Sorry we weren't there to help," he said. "We've rethought this."

"Wouldn't have mattered," Connor reassured him.

"Where's Alia?" Nola asked.

"Still working on it," I muttered, grateful the group had a change of heart. Their lack of cohesiveness was a problem, one that could easily sabotage not just my efforts to locate Alia but our very survival.

A lecture died unspoken. No number of words would make a difference. Instead, I shepherded us back to where my jump spell had gone awry. This time, we ended up in front of the caves as if the side journey had been a time warp, a diversion to capture Alia.

"Go on—" I flapped a hand at the entry.

"Where are you going?" Joss asked.

"To unearth information. Stay put till I get back."

I hadn't unpackaged my spell, so I rode its coattails to the same vortex energy spot where we'd emerged from the future, under the red rock pinnacles. Alia was probably getting farther away by the minute, but I needed information. Breath burned in my lungs and throat as I ran up the steep track. When I located the hotspot, I instructed it to allow me entry.

Everything was uncharted territory. When the vortex opened to my plea, I dove inside. Not my smartest move, but I was a desperate man. The vortex was ancient. Whether it held what I sought remained to be seen, but I had to try.

Alia might be a lynchpin for someone's grand plan, but she was central to my world too. We'd been thrown together for a reason well beyond either of us. To have her snatched away before I figured out why didn't wash.

"*Why have you come?*" echoed through my skull.

"I seek knowledge."

"Knowledge carries a price."

"Name it. If I can, I will pay."

"Your magic will be subsumed."

Shockwaves buffeted me. *"Not all of it,"* I countered and readied myself for a pitched battle as I attempted to retreat.

"We shall see. Do you still wish knowledge?"

I swathed my magical center with warding before I answered, *"Yes."* I'd get through this somehow—with my abilities intact.

The vortex was amazingly accommodating. I found precisely what I'd hoped was there: an arcane library. Tucked into an alcove, it extended in all directions, managed by a cunning space-time continuum. Books and scrolls materialized based on my thoughts, like an eldritch card catalog system. Time was not on my side, so I cheated nine ways from Sunday to find what I sought.

Initially, my goal had been to locate Alia, but I fine-tuned it along the way. First, I had to find out who she was and why the enemy was so interested in her.

CHAPTER SEVENTEEN, ALIA

The fucking griffon was back. What in the hell? Why was he so interested in me? Worse, something was within me, sapping my will, and redirecting my magic for its own purposes. I tried to talk to no avail. What came out of my mouth weren't my words. Hell, it wasn't even my voice.

I should leave, go far away.

You were far away, an inner voice reminded me. Yeah, I could have stayed there, but the lure of being with Rhys and my pathetic weakness and fears had ruled the day.

Next time—if there was a next time—I'd just start walking with my magic shrouded. And keep on going until no one could find me. Might not need to walk. All those abandoned cars had to have gasoline. I'd never directed magic to jump start one, but I was certain it could be done. Ditto for refills at empty gas stations. Any dreams I'd had about a life with Rhys had been just that: dreams. I'd been destined to be alone since my magic first made an appearance.

Nothing about that had changed. May as well get used to it.

My head snapped sideways as if I'd been slapped, except nothing actually touched me. "Stop that," I yelped. This time, my voice worked. Before I got used to it, my vocal chords froze up again.

I was being dragged through the corridor where the griffon had used my voice to tell the others to turn back. Rhys came after me anyway. It touched and worried me both. I'd known he cared. He'd traveled into the future. Even if he had no idea where his path led, he'd been hunting for me.

I heard the griffon tell him to leave off, that I was his.

"I. Am. Not. Anyone's—" I managed to squeeze out, but I felt certain Rhys hadn't heard me. I barely heard myself. This whole thing was surreal. Like it was happening on another plane of existence. Somehow the griffon was inside me pushing us forward. Or maybe I was inside him. We were separate, yet blended. He definitely had the upper hand.

"Why are you doing this?" I tried again.

No answer.

The tunnel ended abruptly, and then we were falling. Panic engulfed me. I reached for my magic, but the same thing happened. It was there. I could sense it, smell it, but it wasn't under my control.

Fury trumped fear. When the griffon nabbed me, I'd been too shocked to put up much of a fight, but that was then. Sticking around to see what happened when we hit bottom wasn't happening.

Not today.

Not in this universe.

I summoned fire like a madwoman, all the fire I could lay my hands on. It ran through me, setting my body ablaze. I didn't give a fuck if it killed me. At least it would drive the griffon out. Smoke filled my nostrils. I sucked it in welcoming the ensuing coughing fit. I'd kill myself before I'd be shanghaied for god only knew what purpose.

Icy water drenched me, snuffing out the flames. It just kept coming.

"You're more trouble than you're worth," the griffon snarled, beak clacking furiously.

"Then let me go." Hey, I was talking again.

Talking and still falling but not as fast. Did it mean we were near the bottom of whatever this was?

I'd given up on my mage light. Before I could kindle it again, light flickered and flared around me. The bottom was close, but we were floating rather than falling. What was this place?

My feet touched down. Rather than dirt, a thick brown rug cushioned my landing. I glanced about, hunting for the griffon, but he was gone. I didn't wait to find out why he'd left. Who knew when I'd have another chance. Not expecting much, I reached for my magic, intent on teleporting the fuck out of here. I'd risk the journey channels if they offered an escape hatch.

For the briefest of moments, I thought I might pull it off. My power was intact and hustled to do my bidding. I didn't try for anything fancy. My spell was basic and built until the space I was in started to fade to nothingness. Hope soared. I punched my casting—and ended up flat on my back with the wind knocked out of me.

"Get up," a harsh female voice ordered.

Instead, I rolled onto one side and buried my head in my hands. A flurry of wings followed by sharp pecks jabbing my arms and shoulders suggested the griffon had returned. Clearly, he'd brought someone with him.

Before he upped the ante and drew blood, something that truly would offer them power over me, I bolted to my feet, stood tall, and set my hands on my hips. "Leave me the fuck alone. I didn't ask for any of this. If you're going to kill me, get it over with. Otherwise, let me go."

I'd been right about the griffon. He perched on his lion's haunches next to me. The rough female voice came from a tall, haughty presence wearing a long, white robe sashed in dark blue. Silver hair cascaded down her shoulders to the middle of her back. A bronze torc circled her throat, and rings graced most of her fingers. She carried an old-fashioned lantern. Silver eyes matched her hair.

"Impressive words from a captive," she smirked.

In a distant corner of my brain, it registered she wasn't speaking English, but I didn't have any trouble understanding her.

"I've gone to a lot of trouble to find you," she went on.

"Why?" I cut in. Even though I aimed for English, the odd foreign syllables rolled off my tongue.

"This is your time."

I huffed out a frustrated breath. "You're speaking in riddles, woman."

She narrowed her eyes. It might have been my imagination, but silvery sparks shot from them like tiny darts. "How could you know nothing?"

"She doesn't. Checked her mind," the griffon squawked sounding more like a large chicken than a mythical beast.

Great. The griffon was speaking that other language too. Maybe he always had.

"What is that?" I asked.

"What is what?" Both of them stared at me.

"That language."

The woman made a face as if she'd tasted something rotten. "An old version of Sumerian. Of course you speak it."

"Why of course?"

"Told you," the griffon squawked smugly. Heated words ensued between him and the woman.

This was too *Alice-in-Wonderland* for words. Except she woke up. The travel spell I'd drawn together was still mostly whole. I focused on it, intent on leaving this sideshow behind.

Eh, no such luck. The halves of my spell flopped open as if I'd cleaved it in two with a machete.

"Stop trying to escape," the woman shouted.

Undaunted, I started over. My magic was still in decent shape. Hands grabbed my shoulders from behind. The woman shook me until my teeth clattered together.

"This is our era, our time. Mortals made a botch of things. We got rid of them. Finally. You carry our blood. It's why you're still here. Do not fight this."

I blinked stupidly as her words sank in. "That's bullshit. Others beyond me are still alive. Let go."

She did. I rubbed the places her fingers had bruised my flesh.

"Come to your senses, have you?" she inquired as if naturally I'd make the right choice.

"You're behind what happened?" I sought clarification. In case I'd missed something.

"Us. And others. Why does it matter? We've finally cleared the way for—"

I drew back a few steps. "I want nothing to do with you. I will not work for you or be associated with you. You ruined life as I know it."

"To make way for something better. You'll change your mind."

"No. I will not. I will never cooperate. Either kill me or let me go." I'd already said that, but I didn't care.

I girded myself for being struck dead on the spot. The two of them stared at me as if I'd lost my mind.

"This is an honor," the griffon protested.

"You've finally come home," the woman said.

"To what?" Bitterness lined my tone. "My family and friends are dead."

"We're your family," the woman insisted.

"Yeah, right. If this is how you treat family, count me out. I have no idea who you are. You admitted to wrecking the modern world. Christ, you murdered billions. Why would I want to be associated with you?" Fury displaced fear. No matter what I said, they'd never understand. No doubt, the feeling was mutual.

I turned and walked away. Certain it couldn't be this simple, I kept on walking anyway. Once I got some distance away—if I did—I'd set a course for the caves. How could I possibly be related to Sumerians. They'd died out millennia ago, before the start of the Christian era if I remembered correctly.

They had to be lying to me. But why? My magic was strong, but theirs ran rings around it. I'd been lost in thought. When I glanced around to get my bearings, I was in the same space with the same brown rug.

What the hell? Had I been walking in circles?

I stopped and shook my head. I'd set a straight course. How was I still here?

"Are you quite finished?" the woman inquired in the same tone she would have used with a recalcitrant five-year-old. It might have been the tone or her patronizing attitude, but something inside me snapped. Fury boiled over. I didn't have to reach for power. It bled from every pore.

Snapping noises suggested something unseen was disintegrating. I was beyond caring. I'd offered myself up to death, been ready to be the instrument of my own destruction. Anything was better than being roped in by this duo and god knew how many others waiting in the wings.

What had the woman said? *Us and others.* Meant they weren't working alone. In a distant corner of my mind, a small sliver of rationality said I should gather every shred of information I could. A far bigger part didn't care.

I pointed a finger at the woman and imagined her immobilized. The griffon had vanished. Maybe his self-preservation instinct was stronger than hers. My magical center expanded, doubling every few moments until I expected my body to explode, annihilated by its own power. And by fire, my strongest element.

The odd part was I didn't mind. Drunk on magic, I luxuriated in infinite power. It might not have been, but it was so much more potent than anything I'd experienced before, it may as well have lacked boundaries. The woman had sunk to her knees, head bowed.

Before she could summon reinforcements, I held a vision of the caves in my mind and instructed the enchantment burning a path through me to take me there. The transition was instantaneous. I stormed inside, not bothering to seal the entry behind me. I was more than a match for whatever dared darken our doorway.

Connor met me in the corridor. Whatever he'd been about to say died unspoken. The expression in his eyes—amazement mingled with horror—brought me up short.

"What?" I demanded. "Did I grow an extra head?"

By now, the others had joined us.

"Not an extra head," Moriah said, "but you're glowing."

"It's like you're alight from within," Karen added in a hushed tone.

"What happened to you?" Joss's voice cracked with strain.

I scanned the group. "Never mind me. Where's Rhys?"

"He went to find some sort of library to help him figure out how to locate you," Connor said.

What kind of library would have that kind of information? "So, is he somewhere in town?" I pressed.

A loud crash from down the corridor brought me at a

dead run. Rhys was here after all. He had to be. The others were hiding him from me. When I got done with them—

Spectral figures oozed from the cavern across from the main one where we'd taken up residence. They surrounded me, bowing. Were these the Watchers from the armoires? How had they gotten loose? My mind reeled with unknowns until a wave of dizziness threatened to fell me.

Things couldn't get any stranger, but they were about to.

With a rush of feathers, the griffon swooped in from nowhere and positioned himself next to me. A collective gasp from the others—or maybe it was the Watchers—rang in my ears.

"Oh, get lost," I sputtered. Last thing I wanted was more of the griffon or his handmaiden. I'd paralyzed her, but nothing magical lasts without the maker there to renew it.

"I'd love to"—the griffon clacked his sharp, hooked beak—"but you and I are linked. So are they." He spread a wing to encompass the ghostly entities still hovering.

"Unlink yourself." I made a chopping motion to expedite things. I wanted to find Rhys, and I never would saddled with this bizarre entourage.

Connor, Joss, and the others were nowhere in sight. I didn't blame them. The weirdness element had expanded by a factor of ten.

"I already told you. I cannot do that." The griffon sounded annoyed.

I spun to face him, hands on my hips. "Explain."

"I expected you would be different. Nonetheless, you are still my queen."

His statement was so preposterous, I burst out laughing.

I was still laughing when I ran out of the caves intent on finding Rhys. The day was fast ceding to night. It gave me pause. Vampires and werewolves were a problem.

The griffon was back, dogging me. Maybe the ghouls were too, but I couldn't see them.

Ignoring everything, I stretched power outward hunting Rhys's unique feel. It was there, but so faint I double-checked to make certain I wasn't deluding myself. Power is a funny thing. I hadn't fully acclimated to mine before. What I dealt with now was a whole different animal.

Before I'd had a poky old Volkswagen. The new version was more like a souped-up Porsche where if I tapped the accelerator, it almost got away from me. No matter how I sliced things, Rhys popped up in the same spot: the red rocks soaring above the town's ruins. I should check for vampires, but I didn't bother. Nothing would stop me until I located Rhys.

Holding an image of my destination front and center, I engaged a jump spell. If the griffon tagged along, not much I could do to dissuade him. Rhys's energy pulsed strongly where I emerged high on a precipice. An opening gaped below. Had he jumped into it?

I hesitated. Maybe I'd been trapped by one too many places today, but leaping blindly held zero appeal. Stretching my mind voice, I called, *"Rhys."*

A minute ticked by, and then one more. I sent power spiraling into the chasm, seeking information while the griffon perched mutely on a nearby boulder. Its presence was eerie, unsettling. Was he spying on me for some conglomerate? Seemed more likely than his cockamamie tale about us being bound.

"Rhys!" I tried again.

Light bloomed from the rift. Rhys burst through in a blaze of brilliance and landed next to me. I launched myself into his arms, holding on as if he was the only solid thing in a world disintegrating around me.

So much for my decision to walk away from him forever.

He didn't hold me for long. Instead, he untangled my arms and stared hard at me, probing with magic. I flinched. "Stop that."

"Sorry. I had to find out for sure." His gaze landed on the griffon. "Located her, eh?"

"For all the good it did," the griffon groused.

Huh?

"What do you know that I don't?" I demanded.

"Probably not enough." Rhys's reply was uncharacteristically cryptic.

"You have to say more." I resisted an inane urge to stamp my foot.

"We'll talk in the caves," he said. "Safer there."

A long, mournful howl reverberated off the red rocks. Wolf, but whether it was natural or from a were was hard to tell.

"Vamps won't be far behind." Rhys snapped his fingers.

The hillside and precipice crumbled, replaced by the open area in front of the caverns. It answered one question. The ghouls twisted this way and that, perhaps awaiting my return. Why hadn't they come with me?

"They can't teleport," Rhys explained and barked a few words to open the barrier.

Fuck me. He was in my head again.

"Inside," he said and gave me a small push.

I stumbled through, ready to be done with today. Maybe when I woke up, everything would be relegated to a macabre dream.

This time, no one hurried to greet us, but they stood when we walked into the cavern with the pool. I hadn't seen the griffon since leaving the red rocks, but he popped into view once we were inside.

"What's going on?" Connor asked.

"It's what we're going to talk about." Rhys's deep voice wasn't as reassuring as usual.

I crossed to the pool, intent on getting a drink.

The griffon shrilled a warning, positioning itself between me and the entry.

Damn. Double damn. None of us had sealed the cave system. Three vampires sashayed into the room. Gorgeous, enticing, reeking of death and rotten blood, their smiles displayed a lot of fang.

Too late, Rhys shouted the words to seal the gates.

Silver stakes flew to my command. Armed as well as I could be, I piled into the nearest vamp, a stately dark-haired male, and drove both stakes into his heart.

Putrid blood geysered, coating me with noxious fluid.

The griffon flew between me and the other two. "Not safe, mistress," he squawked.

"Either help or get out of my fucking way," I shouted, spitting out blood.

This time, silver daggers heeded my call. Stakes. Daggers. Silver is silver. Undaunted, I raced after a female who'd targeted Rhys and Connor.

Intuiting my intent, the griffon flew across the cavern and dug his spiked talons into the Vampire's neck, opening several large vessels. My aim, augmented with magic, ran true as I chucked daggers into the creature's ruined neck.

Two down, one to go. I wiped blood out of my eyes and stared hunting for the last one. He wasn't there.

A pathetic squeal led me into the tunnel at a dead run.

Rhys pelted after me.

CHAPTER EIGHTEEN, RHYS

Vampires. Slipshod of me not to bar the entry, but I'd been preoccupied by what I'd discovered in the library housed deep within a wing of the vortex. I'd have read more except Alia's mind voice told me she was close. Not that she couldn't take care of herself. Quite the contrary. Descended from Innana, queen of heaven who ruled both sky and Earth, and her sister Erishkigel who ruled the underworld, Alia had been in stasis for millennia before her birth.

A long-ago Sumerian mystic scryed enough of the future to decide someone like Alia, aligned with the modern world yet carrying ancient bloodlines, would be elemental to their plans.

How those plans had unfolded in the seeming absence of Sumerian royalty remained an unknown. I'd moved from scroll to scroll in my search for relevant pieces stopping when something caught my eye. It wasn't my normal methodical process at all.

The library let me in this time. Whether it would be so accommodating for future visits remained to be seen. The price, if there was one, had yet to be extracted. Perhaps, my hasty egress forestalled whatever the library's guardians had planned. Not that I'd actually met them, but someone had spoken with me before allowing me access.

Intriguingly, Alia's birth spawned a series of events culminating in the widespread destruction that led to our current mess. I'd recognized a spark in her, but I'd missed so much more.

To be fair, I hadn't been on the lookout for harbingers of disaster. Should have been, given what little I knew, but an innocent teenager would never have ranked high on my list of suspects.

Watching her mow through two vampires was mesmerizing. So much so I missed where the third had gone. High pitched yowls from the corridor suggested vamp number three wasn't sticking around to be staked. Alia was hot on his heels, but I was right behind her.

She didn't need me; I hadn't wrapped my head around that, yet. The griffon shoved past, growling. Did he have control over which part of him dictated his vocalizations? I'd read about him too, albeit briefly. He'd been tasked with watching over Alia, keeping her safe from harm as her power matured. Where the two of them had bided, waiting out millennia, remained shrouded in mystery.

Alia feinted left into a small cavern where additional foodstuffs were stored. I skidded around a corner. Vampire number three held Moriah against him, her back to his front. One arm spanned her shoulders, the other her hips. She hissed and spit and writhed in his grip.

With a twist of her head, she started to sink her teeth into his forearm. Probably a ploy to force him to let go, but it would backfire badly.

"Noooo," I shouted. "No blood contact."

The griffon swung behind the vampire and pecked holes in his back and shoulders. The cloying reek of long dead blood filled my nostrils.

Alia extended an arm. A sword with a gleaming silver blade dropped into her hand. She looked as surprised as I felt. So far, she'd crafted stakes and daggers. If all she did was request silver, whoever was delivering called the shots.

She gripped the handle with both hands as she searched for a spot to strike. The vampire's front was protected by the shifter's body. Why hadn't she shifted? The wolf was far stronger.

My question could wait. I reached for the blade.

Alia handed it over without question.

"But it's yours," the griffon squawked in outrage.

"Maybe he knows how to use it," she told her newly acquired sidekick.

Right she was. I cut my teeth on swordplay. Light on my feet, I positioned myself on the vampire's left side. It was doing its damnedest to sink its fangs into Moriah's neck. So far, the griffon's interventions were keeping it fully occupied.

The undead twisted this way and that to avoid more beak strikes.

I timed my move carefully. I had to slip my blade

between ribs and on into his heart. A near miss to the pancreas wasn't good enough. If I didn't get it right the first time, I'd have to withdraw and try again. By then, the vamp would probably call on teleport powers and leave with Moriah still clutched in his arms.

Or not. If he'd been able to do that, he'd have been gone. Perhaps the white magic barrier around the cave system kept him from breaking through.

Balanced on a precipice, time slowed and then stalled as I took aim, gathered a bit of magic to grease the skids, and drove my blade home. With older vamps, it's never a long wait. This one crumpled into a pile of bones in the space between two breaths.

Moriah pushed the bones aside. They disintegrated into dust. She was breathing hard. Bending, she vomited into the dirt.

Alia ran to her and held her hair out of the way. "How did he nab you? I didn't see anything."

"They're quick," she panted. "Ungodly fast. I tried to shift, but couldn't. And then we were down here. Like a quick teleport."

Alia made cooing sounds and led Moriah away from the stack of vomit-splattered bones.

I bent to scrub the undead's filthy blood from the blade, but it shimmered to nothing. Purpose served, it returned to wherever it had come from. The griffon settled onto his haunches near the door and proceeded to use a rear paw to clean blood off his beak.

Footsteps alerted me before the others stormed into the small cave. Karen sped to Moriah, pried her out of Alia's arms, and held her close. "How in the hell? I never saw you leave. You were just gone. My wolf howled and howled but couldn't find yours. Christ. I was afraid you were dead."

"Water," Moriah croaked. "I need water."

"Come on. I'll make us some tea." Karen started out of the cave with an arm around her sister shifter.

"You were going to talk with us," Connor prodded.

"Still am," I told him.

"When?" He arched a dark brow.

"Soon. Why don't all of you return to the pool. Maybe Joss could come up with something to eat."

"Sure." The Druid turned and left. This cave reeked of decay. No one wanted to stick around.

Connor balanced from foot to foot. Finally, he walked to the pile of bones and nudged it with a boot. "How do they fall apart so fast?"

"Means he was old," I explained. "Even though they look just like they did the day they were turned, their bodies are subject to decay. If you kill a young vamp, his body reflects how long it's been since he died. So if, say, he died a handful of years ago, there'd be little degradation."

"This one could have been a crypt for centuries," Connor muttered.

"And he would have been if the vampire virus wasn't keeping him looking fresh and vital."

"Wait? It's a virus?" Alia sounded shaken; probably an overload of adrenaline wasn't helping.

"Something like that," I replied. "It's contagious, which is why when they bite you they pass it on."

Shudders racked her. Connor draped an arm around her

shoulders and drew her close, murmuring, "It will be all right."

"Easy for you to say," she shot back.

A beak clack from the griffon could have meant anything.

"I need to talk with Alia," I told them. "Once we're done, we'll join you and tell you everything."

Alia's hazel eyes shaded to violet. "Maybe not everything. I'll be the judge of that."

"Then I'm not leaving," Connor announced and walked to a nearby wall where he sank to a squat.

"Will you respect my privacy?" Alia stared at him.

"Of course." Connor nodded. "But if we're going to work together, it's not fair to keep anyone in the dark."

The griffon waddled to Alia. "Come with me. Leave these people in peace."

She rounded on him. "Leave them to die, you mean."

He ruffled his wings.

Before he got pushier, I said, "Alia knows very little. Let me fill her in."

A hiss was followed by, "You don't know all that much, either, mage."

Alia crossed the cave and stood between Connor and me. "I didn't ask for you," she told the griffon. "Fine by me if you go back to wherever you came from."

He opened his beak, apparently thought better of engaging his charge in an argument he couldn't win, and vanished in a swoop of wings and magic.

Alia dropped her head into a hand, massaging her temples. "Good riddance. He makes me nervous."

"Why is he even here?" Connor asked.

I flapped a hand at them both. "Quiet. What I found in the library was this. It's incomplete because I left before I was done reading."

"Sorry about that," Alia mumbled.

"It's okay. My hasty exit meant I didn't end up paying a price for the knowledge I did glean."

"What price?" she asked.

I shook my head. "Not important. Thousands of years ago, before the Christian era, Sumerians held powerful places in the ancient world. Their prophets were superior to those employed by the Greeks, Romans, Norse gods, or Celts. One—or perhaps several—foresaw Earth's problems and engaged in a preemptive strike so they'd have at least one person to span the gap between their time and the current one.

"Toward that end, they crafted Alia's essence from the blood of two queens, placed her in stasis, and waited until she was needed to introduce her into a human womb."

"Ewww, that's just creepy." Alia shuddered.

"Where does the griffon come in?" Connor asked.

"Not certain," I replied. "He was tasked with watching over Alia, but I have no idea how they sequestered him over thousands of years."

"Were they truly behind the destruction?" Alia asked in a small voice.

"I believe so," I replied carefully.

"So, does that mean once I was born, we were headed for disaster?"

"It appears so."

"The woman said much the same. Fuck. This is all my fault," she wailed and grabbed handfuls of her hair.

What woman? Now wasn't the time to ask. I walked behind her and placed a hand on each shoulder. "Hush. You've got the time line wrong. This was not your fault. Whoever's masterminding this didn't waken you until they had a plan that was already unfolding. The years it took to develop are nothing in the grand scheme of time."

"But if I hadn't been born—" she persisted.

"The only way you wouldn't have been was if Earth wasn't already in trouble," Connor said.

"What if I don't want to be tribute, or whatever the hell this is?" she snarled.

"Just keep telling them no. Eventually..." In truth I had no idea what they'd do or not do.

"I should leave. Been telling myself that for a while now." Enchantment glowed as she reached for her power.

I didn't want her to go, but I held no rights over her. While I searched for something, anything, that might stop her, Connor said, "We need you."

The flow of her magic flickered. "All I'll do is bring trouble down on you if I stay."

"Both are true." My voice was surprisingly steady.

She twisted until she faced me. "Then I should go."

"Is that what you want?" I asked.

A reluctant head shake. "But I'm a magnet for problems. Maybe if I wasn't here, you wouldn't be as much of a target."

"Or we could be an even bigger one," Connor tossed out.

I started to tell her I'd have had a rougher go than her defusing the vampires, but she had to find her own reasons for staying. If she couldn't, we'd stand at this crossroads again and again.

Connor pushed upright, his gaze bouncing from Alia to me and back again. "I'm going to see if Joss needs help with lunch. We really should hit up another grocery store or two before all the perishables become inedible."

The clip of his footsteps echoed as he moved down the tunnel.

More to corral the death smell than anything, I layered magic over the vampire's remains and kindled a destruction spell.

"Wish I knew the right path," Alia murmured.

"Who was the woman you alluded to?"

Confusion marred her even features, but then she said, "That's right. I never got an opportunity to tell you. I'm not sure who she was, but she and the griffon know each other. She wore old-fashioned clothing and carried a lantern. And chided me for trying to escape."

"How did you?"

A shrug. "I got mad, imagined her paralyzed, and walked out of there. Do you know who she is?"

"Not really. The lantern suggests Birgit, but it's the wrong pantheon. Maybe someone like Ninshubur."

"Who was she?"

"A Mesopotamian goddess who served as handmaiden to Innana. She was also a messenger between deities, so it would make sense she'd been assigned to welcome you to the fold."

Alia turned away and pounded a fist into the dirt wall. "This gets worse and worse. What fold?"

"The Sumerian hierarchy. Let's join the others. Afterward, if you'd like, we can take another shot at the library."

"I'm not sure I want more information. What I want is for them to leave me alone." After a pause, she added, "I still think I should leave."

"Where would you go?"

"I have no idea. Been considering taking one of those abandoned cars and driving as far as I could get."

I'd contemplated the same but not until we ran through all our options here. It wasn't fair, but I said, "I want you to stay with us."

"Why?"

Did I blunder through some excuse-laden explanation or go for the truth? Sometimes words get in the way. I walked to her and opened my arms, offering a choice.

She froze not moving toward me, but not moving away, either. Her lower lip trembled. "I'm afraid."

"Of what?" I resisted an urge to wrap her in an embrace. I needed her to come to me.

"You. Me. Everything. What if we don't work out? What impact will it have on our group?"

"You're getting way ahead of things. Let's figure out today."

Alia shook her head. "I've never been like that. Plus, I've never been with anyone before, so I don't trust myself. Or the process or much of anything else." Her voice ran down.

She looked so forlorn, I jettisoned waiting for her to approach me and gathered her close. "I can't tell you things will be all right," I murmured, "because I have no idea if we'll even be alive this time tomorrow. But there are no coincidences. We're together in this place for reasons I have yet to fathom."

"I thought we should have stayed in Mexico." Her voice was muffled against my shoulder.

"When the first explosions hit, I consulted my guidance. They were quite clear about Sedona as our preferred destination." I smoothed tangled hair away from her face, angled my head, and kissed her.

At first, I thought she might pull away. Instead, she sank into our kiss, closed her arms around me, and made soft cooing sounds. The taste and scent of her was intoxicating, awakening a yearning so deep it startled me. Was this as simple as her Sumerian blood or something far more complex?

I ran my hands down her back, luxuriating in the feel of her body, until they settled on her rounded rump. My heart beat faster; arousal took hold. Before it drove sentient thought from my mind, I broke our kiss and took a step back.

Spots of pink graced her pale cheekbones. Her eyes were soft with desire. "Why'd you stop?"

It was a fair question. "One day, we won't. But you have decisions facing you. I want you to make them with a clear head."

"Thank you. I think. Maybe I'm on the hunt for excuses to put off any kind of decision-making." She smiled and held out a hand. I grasped it.

We walked out of the cave and along the tunnel. The sound of voices and smells of food beckoned. When we entered the cavern with the pool, everyone was settled eating except the shifter sisters.

"Where are Karen and Moriah?" I asked.

"They left," Joss said.

"What do you mean left?" Alia's voice was shrill.

"We tried to talk them out of it," Connor said.

"They nattered on about not being safe," Nola added. "The vampire deal kind of kicked them into high gear. We tried to stop them, but they shifted and ran out of here." She pointed at two piles of discarded clothing.

Alia started out of the cave.

"They said not to hunt them down. If you do, they'll just leave again." Connor called her back.

The griffon popped through a glowing gateway. "I can find them, mistress."

From her spot next to the entry, Alia turned and stared at her unwanted companion. "Let's get a few things clear. I am not your mistress. Next time, stay gone. If I have need of you, I'll let you know."

"As you will." With an awkward bow, he retreated through the same portal.

I didn't bother telling her if what I'd read was accurate— and I had no reason to disbelieve it—she was stuck with him from here on out.

"Are any of the rest of you considering jumping ship?" I asked as I spooned some kind of grain into a bowl.

"Nowhere to go," Joss mumbled.

"Unfortunately, true," Connor said.

Alia still looked as if she were on the verge of taking flight. Finally, Connor's words must have sunk in because she filled a mug with the grain mixture and leaned against a wall while she ate.

For now, we were still a group. Who knew what tomorrow would bring? Since it would be pointless to get too far ahead of the game, I set down my dish. "We're going to make plans."

"Like what?" Nola asked.

"Depends on you," I replied and gathered my thoughts.

CHAPTER NINETEEN, ALIA

Not that my life has been all that long, but I've never been this conflicted about anything except maybe when my magic first showed up. What would have happened if I hadn't gone to the retreat? According to the woman, my life would have been spared, but the anguish of standing by, helpless, while everyone around me was wiped away by the tsunami—or whatever it had been—would have been soul-crushing.

I doubt I'd have had the heart to continue.

I winced. My pity party was turning into a theme. I had managed to make half a life in the future but only by focusing on each moment, and then the next and the next.

The wolf-shifters' defection rattled me. If they thought things were sketchy in these caves, they'd be in for a rough ride on their own. Moriah would have ended up one of the undead had it not been for the griffon—and Rhys.

Watching him with the sword had been hypnotic. Hell,

watching him do anything was mesmerizing. Back to the blade, he knew precisely how to swing it and where to strike. I'd still have been staring at the infernal thing wondering how to deploy it in the time it took him to dispatch the vampire.

Was I wrong to shoo the griffon away? At least it wasn't fighting me. Maybe I should take Rhys up on his invitation to spend time in the metaphysical library reading scrolls that pertained to me.

The clank of metal on ceramic told me my mug was empty. I'd been eating on autopilot. The others were talking. I tuned in to their conversation.

"If we left here, there are no guarantees," Rhys was saying.

"But can't we find a place that at least doesn't have vampires or werewolves?" Nola asked.

"Even if we did," Joss cut in, "they could easily show up. Weres travel in packs. Vampires are mobile too. The lack of fresh blood will drive them to expand their hunting grounds."

"They can survive on animal blood," Rhys said.

Hmph. News to me.

"This time travel thing," I spoke up. "Can you go back as well as forward?"

"In theory," Rhys replied. "What do you have in mind?"

What did I have in mind? Something pretty half-baked. "Erm, if I could travel backward, would I regress age-wise? In other words, if I went back ten years, would I be nine? Or would I be the age I am now?"

Rhys cast a speculative glance my way. "You'd be your current age. What are you thinking of doing?"

"Not sure. Maybe tracking down the griffon and that woman and talking them out of what they did."

"It will never work," Rhys said flatly. So flatly, it irritated me.

"Why not?" I snapped.

"They view you as a tool, a pawn, and not a particularly important one at that."

I stopped leaning against the wall and rounded on him. "Then why bother to make me in the first place?"

"Were you given a rationale?" Connor asked.

I shook my head. "Only that I'd be some kind of bridge between the ancient and modern worlds. Doesn't make any sense since they killed everyone off. Not much need for a cultural interpreter."

"You might be onto something." Excitement lined Rhys's words.

"Like what?"

"Maybe they didn't mean to wipe everyone out, and—"

"Nope." I cut him off. "That woman suggested the opposite. As in they'd cleared the decks, and I needed to get with the program."

"She might have been putting on a good front," Joss said. "Spells, especially powerful ones, have a way of escaping their makers' control."

I was warming to my idea. "So, if I used the vortex to go back to before three days ago, or last week, or whenever, I might have a chance."

"Time travel isn't that precise. The best you could do

would be to return to this date last year. Besides, you'll never find them."

"I'm willing to take that risk."

Was I really? It would be a leap of faith to enter the vortex again, even though I understood the rough node system to home in on a destination. Would it work the same going backward as forward?

No reason it shouldn't.

"Alia." Rhys's voice shook me out of my internal musings. "You cannot do this alone."

"I have to." My voice was surprisingly strong. "If the time warp holds true, I'll only be gone a short while in this time frequency, but my exploration might last weeks."

"We'll get along if you go with her," Connor told Rhys.

A flurry of wings and magic announced the griffon. An idea blossomed. I faced him and said, "You'll come with me since we're bonded or linked or something. Of course, you'd have to remain invisible."

The creature shook his head. "I heard enough to know this is a fool's errand."

I was getting sick and tired of people telling me to shelve it. A second idea blasted through me. "You'll know how to find the ones I must speak with."

"True, but I will not assist with this endeavor."

I focused a beam of power his way. He flinched, but I had to know. "Are you bound to do my bidding?"

He hooted what might have been laughter. My face heated. "Only to watch over you. Your makers wouldn't have been stupid enough to make me mind you."

"Does that mean you'll keep her safe?" Rhys cut into what was fast becoming an embarrassing conversation.

A beak clack and a nod answered him.

"We'll be good for a few days," Connor insisted. "We're only three at this point, so the food will stretch further."

"Karen and Moriah might change their minds," Rhys pointed out.

"If they do, we'll manage," Nola said.

"If you can do something to alter what happened," Joss added, "it's worth whatever it costs on this end."

"Don't know that I can," I murmured. Doubts rose to the fore. How had I ever thought I could make the slightest difference? My magic was like a feral beast, only tangentially under my control. What if I made things worse?

"See?" the griffon hooted. "Not such a grand idea after all."

Fuck. He read my thoughts as easily as Rhys.

"What do you want to do?" Rhys prodded.

Yeah. No kidding. Shit or get off the pot.

"I'm going. Maybe it will be for naught. Maybe I won't be able to get back here, but I have to try."

One more beak clack suggested what the griffon thought of my half-baked plan.

"Given our last traveling junket, I'm reasonably certain I can return us to this place," Rhys said and started for the tunnel leading to the entrance.

"Wait," I called. "I didn't say I wanted you to come."

"No, you didn't. But I am anyway." He didn't even turn around.

"You have a hard time accepting help when it's offered," the griffon observed and waddled after Rhys with his awkward bi-creature gait. It was only then I realized he was speaking English rather than Sumerian. Great. A multilingual mythical beast.

My Praetorian guard was gone. Would they leave without me?

Connor drew close and clapped me across the back. "This was your idea. Don't wimp out now. Actually, Moriah, or perhaps Karen, mentioned something like this after you and Rhys returned from the future."

He was right. One of them had.

I gave him a quick hug, wondered if I'd ever see him or Joss or Nola again, and hurried out of the cavern. The barrier was down when I reached it. Rhys and the griffon stood outside splashed by sunlight. No Watchers. No skinwalkers.

Where did the Watchers go when they weren't watching?

Crap. I was losing it.

"We'll start at the same spot where we returned from the future," Rhys announced.

The griffon took to the air. Clumsy on his feet, he radiated grace with his better than ten-foot wingspan. What would it be like to ride him?

Rhys chuckled. "It would beat walking, but come on. He's not likely to offer his services as a chauffeur."

"Stop that. Stay out of my head."

He shrugged. "Sorry. Second nature."

We cut across the northern edge of town to the track leading upward. Not surprisingly, the griffon was already there. Perched on a large boulder, he'd folded his wings behind him. They gleamed more golden than brown in the sunlight.

"You could have used magic," he groused.

"Might need to conserve it," Rhys pointed out, matching the griffon's Sumerian. How many languages did he speak? Was it all of them?

He pushed around me until he stood on the edge of the hole leading into the vortex's power point. I hustled to his side and stared into the chasm. Colors swirled like thick volcanic mud, creating ever-changing three-dimensional shapes.

Rhys began to chant. The light show below us moved faster but didn't create a path. Was it safe to enter? This wasn't how it had looked fifty years in the future. Back to his owl impersonation, the griffon hooted softly.

Power flared from Rhys's extended fingertips. It flowed into the hole, pushing the colors toward its outside edge. Still chanting, he said, *"Follow my lead. The vortex doesn't want us, so we must be quick."*

I started to ask how he knew but thought better of it. "Coming with us?" I asked the griffon. In answer, he spread his wings and vanished. Interesting. He'd shared the vortex with us coming back from future Sedona, or I thought he had.

Quick as a lynx, Rhys grabbed my hand. Together, we jumped into the breach. The colors burned when they touched me. Or maybe my imagination was working overtime. Rhys's voice ebbed and flowed as foreign words, ones I didn't understand, kept us safe.

Suddenly, a familiar panel of nodes flared to my right.

Reaching across me, Rhys grabbed the handle. This time, the vortex didn't form a barrier. Maybe he was right about it wanting us gone. His breath seared me with heat as he pushed something.

Just like the first time, the vortex shattered around us. Unlike the first time, Rhys's power circled me. "What are you doing?" I shouted and tried to jerk my hand out of his, but he held fast.

"We can't just blip into being. We're invisible until we find the right spot."

Yeah. Right. Of course. Why didn't I think of that?

Because I don't think in those terms.

Desert spread below us. No matter which way I looked, I couldn't see anything resembling a city. Had we come out in the wrong spot?

Seconds later, we touched down more gently than I expected. Rhys's spell dissipated. Since we were alone out here, no need to conceal ourselves.

I turned to him. "Where are we?"

"Good question. Do you still have your phone?"

I did. Hoping it had retained some battery life, I dredged it from a pocket and turned it on. The Verizon logo in the upper right corner flared to life. It was stupid, but my eyes burned with unshed tears at the reminder of a life lost to me. A few key taps logged me into Google maps.

"We're maybe halfway between Flagstaff and Sedona."

The distant hum of motors suggested a highway wasn't far. "What year did you pick?" I asked.

"2020. Figured the pandemic could work in our favor. Fewer people out and about."

I glanced around. "Any idea if the griffon came with us?"

"None."

"Why didn't we stay within the vortex? We're miles away from it."

Rhys shrugged. "Don't know the answer to that one, either."

Suddenly, the hubris of sallying into the recent past and storming the gates of some Sumerian stronghold seemed ridiculous. How in the hell would I ever find anyone, let alone rattle any cages? And why would they listen to me?

"Should have thought about all that before we left the others." Rhys's tone was soft.

"Do you think we should go back?" I asked. It would be a long walk to Sedona, but maybe we could hit the roadway and hitchhike. We looked a little beat up, but not so bad drivers would shun us.

He shook his head. "I'm going to presume the journey channels haven't yet been perverted. Since we're here, let's go to the Old Country. My guild house has an extensive library. It might be our best bet locating your kinsmen."

A shock ran through me. I scarcely thought of Sumerians as family. Never mind blood ties. "Are you certain we can get back to Sedona?"

"No, but there must be other ways to access time travel. It's where the library comes in. Plus, we might find some of my brothers."

I scrunched my nose. "What about sisters?"

He chuckled. "This will run counter to your twenty-first century sensibilities, but my guild was all men."

"Were any all women?"

"Sure. Witches, for one. And circles that worshipped Artemis and Arianrhod. Hecate too, although she was primarily a witch goddess."

I thought about Joss, Connor, and Nola. Even though I'd been delighted when my cell phone flared to life, we shouldn't tarry. "Let's get moving."

The familiar touch of his power settled around me. The griffon could find us. I wasn't concerned about his absence. For that fact, I wasn't at all certain what he added to the equation.

Before I voiced a question, the desert was replaced by the velvety blackness of a journey channel.

"Shouldn't take long," Rhys murmured.

Shouldn't being the operative term. So long as we didn't run into the dark things that had taken over this place, we'd be okay. Who was to say how long they'd been there?

"*Uh-uh.*"

"*Uh-uh*, what?" I countered.

"Nothing negative. It disturbs my enchantment."

I cleared my thoughts. In far less time than I expected, the darkness ceded to bands of light. When it cleared, we were in an old building. It had to be very old from the smells of damp stone and rot.

Rhys grinned. "Excellent. Hit the mark first time out of the box."

"Where exactly are we?"

"The Isle of Skye off the western coast of Scotland in a manor house that's belonged to my guild since before the Middle Ages. I'd show you around, but there's no time for indulgence. Come on. We'll set up shop in the library."

I followed him down many branching corridors. Some parts of the building were better kept than others. A hasty search for other life turned up mice, rats, bats, crows, and insects. Was the place abandoned?

Rhys turned sharp right and pushed tall, double doors with runic markings open. A long rectangular room stretched before us with floor-to-ceiling shelves. The smell of rot was more pervasive here, perhaps an artifact of whatever material the many scrolls were made of.

Books and scrolls plopped from shelves, landing on a scarred wooden table. I ducked to avoid a particularly heavy tome. "Why are they falling?" I asked.

"They're not. I summoned the material I hope will be relevant. Start with the ones nearest you."

"What am I looking for?"

He aimed a pointed look my way. "Sumerians. Remember them? I'll be researching time travel."

My cheeks grew warm, and I hooked a foot into a chair, moving it so I could sit. Two scrolls scuttled close in clear invitation. I shook my head. I've done plenty of library research, but the study materials were never sentient.

Pushing reservations—a whole lot of them—to a distant back burner, I undid a piece of rotten twine and unrolled the first scroll. "Erm. I can't read this."

"Yes, you can. Focus your power. The words will come into focus."

Weariness punched me in the guts. I shut my eyes, called on my power, and tried again. It was far from instantaneous, but after a few minutes, the runes made sense. Perhaps a quarter of an hour passed. I was deep into a scroll detailing the history of my people.

"Rhys! Where'd you come from?" a male voice shouted just before a tall, bearded man wearing what looked like monk's robes skidded into the library.

Rhys shot to his feet, hands extended. "Micah. It's been far too long."

Rather than grasping his hands, Micah focused green eyes on Rhys. "Not so fast, brother."

"Huh." Rhys's forehead crinkled in confusion. "Not so fast, what?"

Micah flapped a hand. "You remember. The prophecy."

"Can't say as I do. Which one. There are many."

Micah fell back a couple of steps and raked his hands through tangled coal-black hair. His features were sharp with a beak of a nose and a squared-off chin. "The one pertaining to you, mate."

Rhys shrugged. "Not sure I ever knew that one."

"Mmph. You have been gone a while." Micah spared a glance my way before saying. "When you darken our halls once more, disaster will follow in your wake. Perhaps best if you gather the knowledge you seek and then leave."

Rhys had said this guild was all men. I risked pissing Micah off, but I didn't care. After pushing to my feet, I stood tall. "Disaster is already here. We returned from the future to try to forestall it."

Micah's eyes widened. I got the feeling not much surprised him, but what I said had.

"Are you the only one here?" Rhys asked him.

After a curt nod, Micah plodded to the head of the table

where we'd taken up residence. He fell into a chair and said, "Tell me everything, but make it quick."

The griffon chose that moment to pop through a glowing portal.

Back on his feet, Micah raised his hands.

I scooted between them. "The beast is with me."

"Of course, he is. What wouldn't I have known as much," Micah muttered in something other than English, except I understood perfectly.

"I'll be as brief as I can," Rhys began. "A few days ago, I was in the Sierra Madre mountains holding a sorcery retreat..."

CHAPTER TWENTY, RHYS

It didn't take long to catch Micah up. I wanted to hear the exact wording of the prophecy concerning me, but our time was limited, and we had bigger irons in the fire.

"You came hunting information on Sumerians?" Micah sounded incredulous. "They haven't had a presence here for better than a thousand years. Closer to two, now I think about it."

"And time travel," I reminded him.

The griffon made a hooting noise, perhaps in response to Micah dismissing the Sumerian gods.

"Not as if we had many choices," Alia cut in.

Micah pushed to his feet looking many years older than when he'd walked into the library. "Apparently, you can take your time, since the apocalypse isn't exactly bearing down in the wake of your appearance."

"Any chance you could summon reinforcements?" I asked.

"For what purpose?" Micah arched a black brow. "Not as if the Sumerians ever had aught to do with us. Hell, they eschewed the other pantheons. Always saw themselves as a cut above."

"They *were* here first," the griffon huffed.

"In their minds," Micah muttered."

"Not useful," I rebuked him. "Since you know what the future holds in a couple of years, perhaps there might be other ways to forestall what happened."

In lieu of a reply, Micah shuffled out the door mumbling to himself.

"Why wasn't he more willing to help?" Alia glanced up from a scroll she was holding open with both hands.

"He might be. What we told him takes some digesting." I returned to a tome with crumbling pages labeled a primer on manipulating time. I'd gotten far enough to understand their approach was more a manipulation than using something like Sedona's vortex.

According to whoever had penned this missive, time exists in parallel bands. Movement between them was simply a matter of bending the weave and slipping through. It sounded simple and too good to be true. Worth a shot, though, as it could save us time on the return trip.

The griffon squatted on his haunches, head tucked beneath a wing.

An audible sigh floated across the table. Alia sank her head into both hands.

Alarm twisted my stomach into a knot. I reached across the table. "You okay?"

She dropped her hands to her sides. "Yeah. No. Erg. I don't know. This"—she flicked a few fingers at a stack of scrolls—"is so hard to understand. Absent it being in a different language, the meaning is obscure."

"Of course. These were all written between perhaps 900 AD and the latter part of the Middle Ages."

"But how will I ever learn anything?" Her hazel eyes shaded to green.

Around us, rush lanterns flared to life. I hadn't requested their services, so they must function on a time circuit some mage had installed.

"You don't need to learn a thing. They won't talk with you," the griffon squawked as he sat straight. "I told you that before we left."

"And why not?" Alia rounded on him.

"Because they haven't yet called upon you to fulfill your part."

On her feet, she stalked to where the griffon was and folded her arms beneath her breasts. "In the future we came from, they sure talked. Let me get this straight." Her tone was sharp, cold. "They pulled me from some psychic stasis, ensured I was born, and now they're running out the clock?"

"Not familiar with that saying," the griffon hooted.

"Fine. I'll rephrase things. They know I've been born. Why in the bloody hell would they be surprised to see me?" A pause. "For that fact, why wouldn't they welcome me?"

A cross between a purr and a roar rumbled from the griffon's beak. "You don't listen well, young mage. I already told you your time hasn't yet arrived. No one expected you to bend time and turn into a nattering wench."

She flapped a hand, waving him to silence. "Never mind. There's a plan. Is it cast in stone?"

"Not helpful." I walked to her offering moral support. "We really should get back to—"

"Why?"

This time, I was in her gunsights. "Would you rather forget about this and return to the others?" May as well lay all the cards faceup on the table.

"Not sure what I want," she mumbled. "He"—she jabbed her index finger at the griffon—"says even if we find them, they won't talk with me."

"You knew that part before we left," I reminded her.

"Whose side are you on?" she demanded.

"Ours. If there's any way we can intervene—"

"There's not." The griffon sounded so smug I wanted to punch him.

"Is there any chance you'll help us find the Sumerians?" Aliz's attention was back on the griffon.

He clacked his beak and shook his head twice.

"Fine. Then you're no good to us. Leave."

I expected him to argue since, according to the lore, he was bound to her, but his fur and feathers shimmered to bits of golden light.

Alia stomped back to the table and took up her post, rolling the scroll she'd been reading as she hunted for where she'd left off. No one who didn't live through earlier times understands what a huge improvement books are. When you turn pages, they stay put.

"I'm going outside," I told her.

Her head snapped up. "I know I'm being bitchy, but why?"

"So I can practice one of the techniques I just read about. Nothing like trial by fire, as it were."

"Is it okay if I stay here alone, what with the no women thing and all?" A corner of her full mouth twisted downward.

I opened my mouth to say *of course*, but shut it. We'd never allowed unaccompanied females in our domain, but many of my order kept clandestine mistresses swathed in spells.

"Good point," I said. "I can check out the incantation from in here."

She drew her brows into a thick line. "Then why say you were going outside?"

"It's easier without all this stone between me and my goals."

"I see." Her tone indicated she didn't, but she returned her attention to the scroll.

I spread magic in an arc and headed for the spot it burned brightest. Not wise to blitz through very much, but I could probably give this a quick once over. Switching to my third eye, I hunted for the layers separating this time from others both before and after it.

They were there, but then not. Deep in trance, I probably missed the first part of what was unfolding in the library. A high-pitched squeal dragged me back to the present post haste.

Alia stood facing a regal woman garbed in a white,

flowing gown. Golden hair shot with silver cascaded down her back. Jet-black eyes lacked visible pupils. Her face was all planes and angles with a full-lipped mouth. Ravens graced each shoulder.

Power flowed around Alia, magic designed to keep the newcomer out of her space. "Who are you?" Alia's voice was shrill as she rocked from foot to foot never taking her eyes off the woman.

"Return to your proper time," the woman thundered. To punctuate her point, both ravens cawed loudly.

Odin had favored ravens, but my bet was this woman was Sumerian.

I joined Alia. The woman didn't spare me so much as a glance.

"Did the griffon find you?" I asked.

"Stay out of this, mage," she barked.

"Almost had to have," Alia said and shook herself from head to toe. It centered her because she turned a saccharine smile on the woman. "You saved us a lot of trouble. Call off your plans to claim Earth for your own. I refuse to be any part of your scheme."

The tongue-lashing I expected didn't materialize. What did was raucous laughter. When the woman, or goddess or whoever she was, got hold of herself, she said, "You overstep yourself."

"In what way?" I demanded. "She is blood of your blood. As such, she deserves—"

"Nothing," the woman screeched. "She deserves nothing from us. We gave her life and are due her undying gratitude."

"Ha! Sorry. Might have worked like that hundreds of years ago, but no more," Alia said.

"If you make too much trouble—"

The griffon hustled through a portal and planted himself between Alia and the woman, wings spread to their fullest extent.

"Leave," the woman screeched.

The griffon fanned his wings and stayed put. "I brought you here to fix this, not make it worse," he chirped.

Interesting. His bond to Alia transcended direct orders from his superiors.

"Thanks, but there is no fixing," Alia informed the griffon. "Not unless they"—she pointed at the woman—"have a change of heart."

"Never happening," the woman fumed.

"Why not?" I jumped into the fray.

"I'm not having this conversation with you."

"Then have it with me," Alia inserted silkily.

I felt proud of her for holding her own. She must be terrified. The power she'd summoned as a shield now encompassed her and the griffon.

"You're deluded, child. You owe us absolute obedience for your life, which could be snuffed out in a moment." She snapped her fingers to demonstrate how fragile Alia's existence was.

Alia gasped and strengthened the shielding around herself. Her eyes bulged; she seemed to be having trouble breathing.

That did it. I wasn't about to stick around while the goddess decided Alia was too big a pain in the rump to continue to live. Still, we needed a moment to extricate ourselves.

Drawing on the building's stone foundations, I wove my power in with that of my order and crafted a barrier between the woman and Alia and the griffon. It wouldn't hold forever, but it should last until we teleported the fuck away from this place.

Alia's breath came in harsh, panting gasps. "Thanks. What'd you do?"

"Won't last long. Come close."

The woman clawed at the barrier before remembering herself and shooting golden darts at it.

No time to waste. I constructed a hasty travel spell, draped it around the three of us, and kindled it. Power reached for us, tracked us into the channel. I angled defensive magic intent on annihilating any loose end that might allow her to follow us.

"I've got this," Alia rasped. Fire shot from her hands, igniting the intrusive strands until they burned to ashes.

"I can never return," the griffon keened.

Alia shot him a pained glance. "Why would you want to?"

"Never mind that," I cut in. "Focus, everyone. If she sends others after us, it will take all our magic to defend ourselves."

Traveling directly back to the States seemed like a bad idea, so I picked eastern Canada as an interim destination. It would give us a neutral playing field and wouldn't lead Alia's kin to the Sedona caves. Before we popped out, I layered invisibility around us.

The channel blew up, leaving us in freefall. Except for the griffon, of course. This time, he flew beneath Alia until she straddled his broad back. I drew air into a cushion beneath me. Concern the griffon would take off with Alia was tempered by understanding he was bound by eldritch magic to protect her.

An ice-crusted beach illuminated by moonlight came into view. I rolled into a landing and trotted to the griffon and Alia a few feet away.

"Brrr." She wrapped her arms around herself. "Where are we?"

"Northern coast of Newfoundland, if I navigated correctly. Come on. We need to get out of the weather."

The griffon took to the air. I gripped Alia's hand and set a course for a deserted shepherd's hut I'd sheltered in before. Built of stones, the structure should last the ages. It was farther than I expected. Alia's teeth were chattering and my feet growing numb when I finally spied the sturdy hut set between three large boulders.

"Here we go," I said. Someone had padlocked the door, but I made short work of it with magic, and we scooted inside.

Before shutting the door, I scanned the skies for the griffon.

"He says he'll find us in the morning," Alia said.

Good to know. The wooden door made a scraping sound as I pulled it into its frame and sealed us in with enchantment.

Alia's mage light brightened the interior of the one-room cabin. A bed piled with furs was pushed into the far corner.

A stove with a tidy stack of wood next to it sat on a stone hearth.

She made her way to the bed, kicked off her shoes, and dove into the furs until only her face was visible.

"I can build a fire," I told her.

"Sure, that would be nice."

While I tossed kindling into the stove and lit it with a thought, she rustled deeper into the furs. "You were right," she said.

"About what?" I'd begun feeding larger pieces into the stove. Whoever owned this place would know someone had broken in, but by then, we'd be long gone.

"This trip being a waste of time." She squeezed her eyes shut for a long moment. "How could I be descended from such a bunch of pricks? Usually, you end up with one or two crappy relatives, but it seems like they're all fucked up."

"I feel bad for the griffon," I said softly. "He took a chance, hoping he'd repair things."

"It blew up in his face," Alia supplied.

Done with the fire for now, I took stock of the cabin. It hadn't changed since my last visit here. A pump handle provided water. I rinsed a glass, filled it, and brought it to her.

"Don't you want any?"

"Go ahead. More where that came from."

She tilted the glass and drank until it was empty. I refilled it and did the same before settling next to her. "Room for two?"

"Sure." She edged toward the wall.

I got under the covers and wadded up a beaver pelt to

make a pillow. Lumpy and hard, the bed felt amazing. Or perhaps it was the simple act of lying down. Turning toward Alia, I opened my arms. After a moment's hesitation, she scooted into them and nestled her head onto my shoulder.

"What do you want to do next?" I asked as I savored the feel of her pressed close against me. The fire was warming the small space, and the bed was downright toasty.

"What do you mean?" she murmured.

"Are we giving up? Do you want to try again?"

A sigh rattled against my neck. "Try, how?"

"We could go to the Mediterranean and hope for luck finding them. Perhaps they wouldn't all be as intransigent as the one in the library."

"Nah. So far, I've met two of them. Both were cut from the same cloth."

"I didn't peg you for a quitter."

"And I didn't peg you as a sucker for lost causes."

I chuckled. "Caught me dead to rights. There has to be a way to do this, though."

"Does there? I mean, all those television shows that dealt with time travel were clear about not tampering."

"Yeah, but they weren't dealing with Armageddon."

She drew closer and tossed a leg over me. "If the world's going to end anyway, I'd rather not die without, without..."

Her mage light hovered off to the side. When I glanced at her, her face was a lovely shade of rose, and she was the most beautiful creature I'd ever laid eyes on.

Words would have been extraneous. Sexual heat suffused my body, and I lowered my mouth to hers.

Instead of kissing me back, she pulled away long enough to ask, "Is it okay that I asked. I mean, you don't have to if—"

I smoothed hair back from her face. "Hush. It's the most alluring offer I've had in centuries."

She smiled. "Really?"

"Test me with a truth spell."

Instead, she rolled me over, lay on top of me, and crushed her mouth atop mine.

CHAPTER TWENTY-ONE, ALIA

My boldness shocked me. I hadn't planned to blurt out what I had, that I wanted to see what sex was like before the apocalypse—or whatever it was—swept us all away.

Rhys should have run for the hills. It wasn't as if I'd said I loved him, or even that I liked him—although I did. Not sure I'd recognize love if it mowed me down. Worse, I'd pinned him under me desperate to feel the chiseled planes of his body pressing against mine.

Thoughts scattered as I experimented with long, deep kisses and little biting ones. His arms were around me. Fingertips left trails of liquid fire as they ran down my back. When his hands gripped my ass, pulling me against the hot, hard length of him, shivers took over. Not from cold but from anticipation of what I'd only imagined.

My nipples turned into exquisite points of desire where they pebbled and pressed into his chest. My hips developed a rhythm of their own as I ground my sex against his shaft. Little moaning sounds were coming from me; I couldn't control them.

Or much of anything else.

My previous furtive attempts at self-stimulation had happened quickly, under my covers when I was certain no one was near enough to figure out what I was doing. This was as different as night and day. My hips bucked and writhed with a mind of their own as my body sought release.

In one fluid motion, Rhys toppled us onto our sides. It interrupted my single-minded drive to come, but opened another avenue. I was shy, my face on fire, but I pushed a hand between us and closed it around his appendage. Thicker than I'd imagined, it jerked in my hand.

Surprised, I let go. "Did I do something wrong?"

He didn't answer with words but took my hand and placed it where it had been atop his throbbing shaft. Next, he closed his fingers around mine showing me the pressure he liked. I squeezed, and his appendage moved again. I'd had no idea it would be...alive.

But then, why should I know anything about sex?

He peeled back the furs. The room was warm from the fire crackling merrily in an old cast-iron stove.

"That feels amazing, but you need to let go long enough for us to undress." His voice was familiar, but not, a husky sensual growl.

My face, which hadn't exactly recovered from my last spate of embarrassment, must have turned crimson. I'm far from a prude, but I'd never shown my body to anyone. Nudity hadn't fazed the shifters or witch. And I'd dressed and undressed in the dormitory at the retreat center along with everyone else. There, I'd been quick and kept myself as covered as possible.

This was different. So different.

He unzipped my jacket and pushed the two halves aside. After tugging me to a sit, he slid it off my shoulders and then removed my stretchy woolen top. I swallowed hard, caught between lust and desperately wanting him to find me beautiful.

Lost in my own need, I'd missed him removing his jacket and shirt. His skin glowed golden in the flickering firelight. Coppery nipples were as puckered as my own. Slabs of muscle began in his shoulders and flowed down his arms.

Reaching a tentative finger, I followed the line of shoulder to biceps to elbow. Why hadn't he touched me?

I reached for a pelt, intent on covering my nakedness.

He batted my hand away. "Do not cover yourself. Your breasts are works of art. Men would have waged war over them, over you."

Fingers fumbled with the fastenings of my trousers. Once he had them undone, He moved to the foot of the bed and pulled them down my legs. Gooseflesh had nothing to do with temperature. My panties came next. After rolling off the bed, he faced away, toed off his boots, and slid his trousers down his legs.

With no underwear in the way, the high tight globes of his ass came into view. Breath caught in my throat. I almost had to remind myself to breathe. Slowly, ever so slowly, he turned around. His cock jutted from a tangle of blond hair, curved proud against his belly. With his broad shoulders, slim hips, and muscled legs he reminded me of statues of the gods I'd seen in museums during my one trip to Europe.

"That's better." He gifted me with a dazzling smile and sat next to me on the bed. "Lie back. Let me pleasure you."

Maybe I was a tad slow following his suggestion because he placed both hands on my shoulders and pushed me onto my back, straddling me. Kisses ran down my neck, out to my shoulders, and back to my breasts. He cupped one with a hand and fastened his mouth on the other, sucking and biting.

Sensation surged. My arms curved around him; I held on tight as he moved from breast to breast. Somewhere along the line, I came once and then again. My eyes must have been shut because it was a surprise when fingers plunged into me.

And an even bigger one when he closed his mouth over my sex. The intensity was beyond my wildest imaginings. My back arched; my hips sank into an age-old dance. Trapped between the fingers inside me and his mouth, pleasure swamped me. Orgasms crowded one atop the other.

When he withdrew his hand and his mouth, my eyes flew open. "Don't stop." Damn. I barely recognized the voice as my own.

"Oh, I don't plan to."

He pushed my legs wider apart. Where his fingers had been, he placed the head of his cock. It felt impossibly big, but I wanted it inside me with an intensity that had no comparison to anything else in my life. I was moaning. My breath came fast. There wasn't enough air in the cabin or the world.

"I'll try to be gentle," he murmured and pushed a tiny bit farther inside.

My hips rose up to meet him. I grabbed his ass and pulled. He didn't want to hurt me, but I didn't want to wait. Virginity can be a curse, and now that I was so close to losing mine I wanted everything all at once.

He held back. "Are you sure?"

"More than sure."

Despite my words, he proceeded at the same glacial pace. Until he didn't. After uttering a low, guttural moan, he sank all the way into me. It might have hurt if I wasn't so deep in lust.

Impatient, I tumbled us until I was on top. The sensation was different. My sex rubbed against his pubic bone. Suddenly, his hands were on my hips as he set a rhythm. At first, I fought being controlled, but then I rather liked letting him establish our cadence. Letting go of everything but sinking and rising over his appendage that was growing larger and harder by the moment, awareness ignited every nerve ending.

Wanton moans filled the cabin, some mine, some his.

Familiar magic wrapped me in a warm cocoon as we drove higher and higher. Maybe he gave me a push with his power, but the climax that ripped through me just kept on coming. A series of waves, each more potent than the last.

Deep within me, his cock jumped. Heat painted my insides as he juddered and came. Our bodies strained together before I collapsed on top of him in a sated, sweaty heap.

He closed his arms around me and murmured in some

language I didn't recognize, but neither was I trying. Despite seeking words, they failed me. None could capture what we'd just done together.

Through the night, we slept, woke, and made love until I was so tender I wondered if I'd be able to walk the next day.

"You can fix that problem with healing power." He chuckled.

"Damn it. You're in my head again."

"Get used to it."

I grinned. "What if I was just using you for your incredible body?"

"You weren't."

"How can you tell?" I was genuinely curious.

He stroked my back and gathered me close. "We were meant to be, darling. You came to that retreat for a reason."

I wasn't so certain, but the concept was appealing, so I didn't ask any more questions. The first rays of light poured through the cabin's only streaked and dirty window as we lay in one another's arms. Time to get up and figure out what to do.

"It probably is, but we held the world at bay for a while."

There he was. In my mind once again. It would take some getting used to.

The expression on his face was so wistful, it caught me off guard. "Yeah, we did," I said softly, followed by, "We need to try to get back to the others. Maybe we can regroup and talk the Sumerians out of their grand plan, but it's not going to happen this time."

"Much as I hate to say it, I agree with you. Hang on. Let me heat a pan of water so we can clean up a bit."

Joy surged as I watched him work near the woodstove. I'd imagined what my first time would be like. Today's events had outstripped my hopes tenfold. No matter what happened from here, I'd always have beautiful memories to sift through.

"You'll have a hell of a lot more than that," he growled. "You'll have me."

I just smiled. It couldn't be that simple, but I didn't want to interrupt my happiness with my usual endless spate of questions.

Half an hour later, we were somewhat cleaner and dressed. I piled the furs back on the bed in a rough approximation of the way we'd found them while Rhys dismantled his spell and opened the door.

We walked outside into pale sunlight that didn't offer much in the way of warmth. Not surprisingly, the griffon squatted in front of the cabin. Had he been there all night? I didn't think so.

Amber avian eyes moved from Rhys to me and back again. He clacked his beak, waiting for something.

"Thanks for keeping the watch," I said.

Another beak clack.

"We're going back," I told him.

"Good choice." He snarled sounding more like his lion half. "I've become a beast without a country."

"I might have learned enough about time travel from the library at my guild house to finesse it from here," Rhys said.

I closed my teeth over my lower lip. "What happens if you, erm, didn't?"

He shrugged. "Tough to say about these things. I should

be able to return us to this spot, or to Sedona in this time frame. From there, we'll ride the vortex."

The incredible gap between his knowledge base and my own was palpable. Why would he, a seasoned mage, want to have anything to do with me?

The spell he'd begun crafting shimmered in the still morning air. If there'd been any wind at all, it would have been unbearably cold.

"Having second thoughts?" He arched a brow and sent a pointed glance my way.

"Erg. Stop reacting to every single nuance that crosses my mind."

He frowned. "That's fair."

A subtle shift in the feel of his power suggested he'd withdrawn. Still, I did my damnedest to cling to neutrality. He returned to his nascent casting. "You can do the same," he murmured.

"Huh? The same what?"

"He means you can take up residence in his head," the griffon squawked.

"Come closer, both of you," Rhys instructed.

The scent of his magic, redolent of wet pine forests this time, surrounded us. I inhaled hungrily, wanting to be as close as I could.

"Ready?" he asked as he wove his hands in a complex pattern.

"*Mm-hum,*" I replied. The griffon made a hooting sound. Damn but he had a score of divergent vocalizations. Was he the only one like him? Had he left friends or family with the

Sumerians? I opened my mouth to ask, but this wasn't the time, and it wasn't any of my business.

In that moment, right before the ice-crusted beach flickered and vanished, it occurred to me I wasn't fighting his presence any longer. The blackness of a travel channel surrounded us. For a while, I watched as walls flashed past. After a time, my chest tightened, and my throat grew dry. The markers I sought were conspicuously absent.

"Where are the nodes?" I choked out.

"There aren't any in this modality," Rhys told me.

"But then, how...?" I shut up, not wanting him to think I doubted him.

"I plugged in coordinates back in Newfoundland. This might work, or it might not. Nothing is irretrievable."

The griffon had tucked its head beneath a wing, oblivious to everything. No help from that quarter. A chill worked its way down my spine. Chalking it up to nerves, I ignored it.

Until it happened again, and then a third time.

"Something isn't right," I muttered.

"What do you mean?" Rhys tightened the arm he'd slung about my shoulders.

"Not sure." I snaked out a few tendrils of seeking magic in an attempt to clarify my misgivings. Rhys blended a strand of his own enchantment, searching in tandem with me.

A sudden intake of breath was followed by an abrupt end to my exploration. "Good instincts," he said. Words tumbled from his mouth, hot, quick, urgent. Their impact on his spell was immediate.

I stroked the griffon's feathers. "Wake up. Something's wrong."

The creature's head shot upright. Nostrils flaring, he scented the air before building a visible shield around himself. *"They followed me,"* he said into my mind.

Fuck. *They* had to mean his erstwhile masters.

"Going to be a rough ride," Rhys cautioned seconds before the travel channel frittered to nothingness, leaving us in freefall.

I envied the griffon's gift of flight as I gathered air beneath me so I didn't smash every bone in my body. At first, I couldn't see shit beneath us, but then land came into view. Thank fucking god. We could have ended up over one of Earth's many oceans. The odds were not in our favor since they consisted of far more mass than the continents.

I ducked and twisted to avoid being knocked around by a thick canopy as we passed through trees before settling on the ground.

Rhys pushed upright. "Damn it. That could have gone better."

"Where are we?" Eh, never mind. I dragged out my phone. It was running on fumes, so I pushed a bit of magic into it encouraging the battery to do me one more favor.

One bar flickered to two then back to one. I clicked the map icon to switch over to satellites. In the flash of time between that and when my phone decided to die, I caught enough of a glimpse to say, "We're in northwest Utah."

"Too bad that gadget doesn't home in on time," Rhys muttered.

"Oh but it does." I resurrected what the home screen had

said. "2017. We're in 2017. Can't be winter. We'd be ass deep in snow."

The griffon plodded through thick foliage, wings folded tight against his lionesque rear end. "This is my fault. I'll find my own way to Sedona."

"No, you won't," I told him. "We're a team." My words surprised me as did the fact I'd actually meant them.

He opened and shut his beak. "Aye, I will."

"How do you know your masters can't get a bead on Alia even if you're not here?" Rhys asked him.

"They could. She should shield herself, but she is also more powerful than many of them. After her actions, they will proceed carefully, not so with me."

"What do they have in mind?" I asked.

"You are not cooperating, so they aim to destroy you. I have become extraneous, so I will suffer the same fate."

"Not on my watch." My voice rang with determination.

"Come on," Rhys urged as he built another spell, a far simpler one this time. "We're heading for Sedona."

"I thought the journey channels were damaged or perverted or something," I said.

"They might not be in this time frame. I'm hoping for the best since we're out of choices."

"No, we aren't. We can find a car and drive. It's not all that far."

"Oh really. How will you pay for it?"

I pulled a small wallet out of the same pocket where my phone had been. Opening it, I extracted a credit card before realization wrapped around me. I couldn't show anyone my ID since it held dates years in the future. Further, according to my driver's license, I wasn't yet quite old enough to drive, not in 2017.

"Driving is a decent idea," Rhys said. "I'll jump us to Logan, and we'll figure something out."

"I'll make my own way to Sedona," the griffon repeated. "Wait for you near the vortex we've been using." In a gush of feathers and magic, he was gone.

Rhys grabbed my hand. Moments later, we dropped into the center of Logan, a medium-sized city. People streamed this way and that. Why weren't they shrieking?

"Because we're invisible," Rhys informed me and guided us to a secluded spot where he released his enchantment.

"Maybe if we walk around a bit, we'll figure something out," I said.

"No maybe about it. We will."

Buoyed by his confidence, I strolled toward the center of town. We probably looked like one more scruffy, down-on-their-luck couple. The smells of food reminded me how long it had been since I'd eaten. A cursory search of my pockets turned up a twenty.

"The food is crappy, but cheap," I said and steered us into a fast food haven. There'd be time enough to map our next moves once our bellies were full.

CHAPTER TWENTY-TWO, RHYS

As ambivalent about me as she was about her magic, Alia was an enigma. Part waif, part sorceress; part innocent, part not, she was a study in contrasts. Despite our cursory attempts to clean up, the scent of lovemaking clung to us both. It tantalized and aroused me.

Had I not tried hard enough to ensure we weren't followed into the time channels? Or would no amount of effort on my part have defeated the Sumerians' link with the griffon. He must have a name. We'd have to ask when we caught up with him.

I sat across from Alia at a corner booth in a cheap drive-through that also offered limited inside seating. Stale grease permeated the air along with other chemical smells, a byproduct of overly processed foods.

She dabbed at juice dripping down her chin. "I know what's in these, but they still taste good."

"Welcome to the food industry working on killing us."

A laugh drifted across the table. "Not in their best interest. We need to stick around to buy more of their offerings."

"About done?" I wadded my napkin next to the paper wrappings that had held my meal.

"Yeah."

After standing, I extended a hand; we walked outside into what felt like late afternoon.

"Where to from here?" she asked.

"An ATM."

"Mmph. Do you have a card?"

I snorted softly. "No, but it shouldn't be an impediment." Halfway down the block, I spied a bank where I could test my theory.

"Should I get ready to run?"

I squeezed her fingers laced with mine. "No need. If this doesn't work, it shouldn't set off any alarms."

An ATM tucked behind a kiosk looked promising since it shielded me from view. Alia stood next to me while I punched keys, shaped power into an arc to trick the machine into believing I'd followed all the rules. Sure enough, $300 popped out, along with a receipt.

Alia waited until we were walking along the sidewalk to ask, "Whose money did we just take?"

"Mine."

"Huh? How'd you do that?"

"That's one of my banks. I know the account number, so I helped the machine recognize me and access my funds."

"Neat trick. You'll have to teach me."

"Happy to, but not right now. We have another

problem."

"Which is?" She arched a fair brow.

"My ID has the same glitch as yours. Can't rent a car without a driver's license. Mine expires in 2024 if I'm not mistaken."

"Aren't they good for ten years or something like that?"

I had one of those *duh* moments that comes from living through too many time periods. Stopping, I pulled a tattered leather bifold from an inner jacket pocket. All it held was ID. I've never been a big credit card user. Leaving the ATM card at the retreat center had been an oversight, but I'd been so focused on herding everyone into the bus, it was amazing I hadn't forgotten other things too.

Alia peered around me and pointed. "There. See? It has an expiration date and an issue date that actually works for 2017."

Bifold tucked safely away, I said, "Thanks for the reality check. Give me your phone so I can charge it."

"Can you really do that? If you can, it means I should be able to get more than a minute from it."

"Let's see." Holding the plastic-and-glass rectangle, I channeled a mixture of air and fire into it, watching as the battery bar edged to the right. Satisfied, I hunted for used car lots. The big boys like Hertz or Avis would require a credit card on file. Used car lots happily rented for cash.

To be on the safe side, I stopped at two more ATMs along the way. Despite not being "my" bank, they spit out funds just the same, but I did feed in data from different accounts I held.

An hour later, we were driving south in a past-its-prime

Ford pickup after arranging to drop it off at a sister lot on Sedona's outskirts.

"You've done this before," Alia observed.

"That obvious, eh?"

"Something like that." She laughed and consulted her phone. "It should take us about ten hours."

"Not a problem. We can trade drivers. You do drive, right?"

"I do." A sigh rustled from her.

"What is it?"

"All this." She extended an arm toward the passenger window. "Hard to believe it won't be here soon."

"I haven't given up on fixing this," I reminded her.

"We put it on hold," she agreed, "but I'm not hopeful. For one thing, I still don't get what's in it for them. No one could be sunk in a desire for revenge that lasts for thousands of years."

"They're immortal," I reminded her. "It puts a whole different slant on things."

After a pause, she asked, "Are you?"

"Long lived, but not forever." I waited, but she didn't pose the same question about herself. Made sense. Immortality is a huge burden, and I had no idea what her status might be. My fond hope was we could travel many centuries together, but I didn't voice it for fear of scaring her away.

The road stretched ahead splitting the darkness with occasional headlights. Even though it was a highway, we were one of very few cars. At some point, we'd need fuel, but not for a while. Neither of us had mentioned the previous night. Because I didn't want her to think I didn't value our time together, I said, "What happened in the cabin, well, it was special for me."

A glance revealed color creeping up her neck.

"Not wanting to make you uncomfortable." I reached toward her, hoping she'd take my hand. She did, but hesitantly.

"I don't have words," she mumbled.

"No need to respond. I just wanted you to know."

Her fingers had been tentative before. Now they gripped harder.

"I care about you, Alia. This isn't a passing fling."

"But we're so...unbalanced."

"What do you mean?"

She shrugged. "Big age difference. Big magic difference. Might be wise to take things slow."

Her words had a sobering effect. "We'll take them any way you want."

Because I was looking sidelong at her, I saw her wince. "Damn it. I'm sorry. Didn't mean to hurt your feelings. What we did together, it was perfect. I couldn't have designed a better introduction."

After a pause, she went on more slowly. "I want to leave the door open. You're not obligated—"

"I know that," I cut in, my tone sharper than I'd meant. "Sorry, but this is important to me. I wish we'd have met in better times. If Armageddon hadn't struck, you'd like as not have left Mexico, and we might not have seen one another again unless you wanted me to continue working with your power.

"Still events have a way of unfolding as they're supposed to."

"I don't want you to feel you're stuck with me." Her voice was low, sweet.

"Never."

A vista point was approaching. I turned into it, brought the Ford to a halt, and gathered her into my arms. She clung to me. We stayed like that as moments ticked past.

"Everything is so new," she murmured. "The extent of my power. Who I am. The end of the familiar." After a pause, she added, "Us. We're brand new. I have less than zero experience with men or relationships, or anything."

I kneaded tenseness out of her shoulder blades and felt her relax into my touch. "We're where we're supposed to be."

Tilting her head back, she met my gaze. "How can you know? The Sumerians seemed to view you as so much trash. Something they hadn't bargained for, something to get rid of."

"Their prophets aren't perfect. No one's are. If they'd wanted to hedge their bets, they'd have shown up in your life as soon as your power blossomed and made certain to shape it to their liking. Arrogant and single-minded, it never occurred to them you wouldn't be putty in their hands."

"I don't see why," she sputtered. "It's not as if you can swoop into someone's life, drop a totally unbelievable line of crap on their heads, and expect they'll trot off behind you like an obedient puppy."

I chuckled.

"What's so funny?" She swatted the side of my arm.

"A few hundred years ago, that's precisely what you'd have done. To be chosen by the gods is an honor, not something to be dismissed or taken lightly."

"Yeah, except they're not real."

I was still chuckling. "What part about *not real* would you assign to the ones we've run into so far?"

She extricated herself from my embrace. "Eh, you know what I mean."

I did. Dropping the transmission into drive, we rejoined the interstate. Alia snuggled next to me. Soon the rhythm of her breathing suggested she'd fallen asleep.

Good. I had no idea what waited for us at the vortex power point. The griffon would like as not be there, but his masters might be as well. They'd clearly come to some conclusion that boded ill for us. It was a familiar song dating from long before the time I was born. If acolytes didn't toe the line, they were dealt with summarily. Banished at best, executed otherwise.

That Innana wasn't more compassionate surprised me. She'd been stripped of everything, her station, her dignity, even her clothing when she requested audience with her sister, Ereshkigal, queen of the underworld.

Still, the times were very different. In Innana's, blood ties had trumped everything. Minor relatives were bound to deference. Hell, even significant ones were expected to obey, usually without question.

An hour clipped past, followed by a couple more. I pulled off the highway, intent on an open all-night truck stop.

"Sorry," Alia mumbled as the truck ground to a halt.

"Didn't mean to fall asleep. Want me to drive for a while?"

"Sure. Just going to fuel up."

"I'll hit the ladies' room. Want anything from inside?"

I considered it and handed her a couple of twenties. "Coffee and something to snack on."

She flashed me a smile and pushed tangled hair over her shoulders. "Sweet or more foodlike?"

"Surprise me."

I'd just hung the fuel hose back on the pump when she crossed a well-lit strip of asphalt toward me. Damn but she was gorgeous with her tousled mane and tall, athletic build. Coming around the truck, she handed me a steaming cup of coffee.

"Wasn't sure what you wanted in it, so you got one cream and one sugar."

I took an appreciative sip. Black would have been fine, but this was too. A plastic bag hanging from her arm crinkled. "What else do we have?"

"Tacos and ice cream bars."

"A veritable feast."

She gifted me with a smile that made my heart sing before trotting to the driver's door and handing me the bag. "My turn to drive. Remember?"

Coffee in one hand, bag in the other, I crossed in front of the pickup and got in on the passenger side. The seat was still warm from Alia's body, and I settled into it while she checked over the controls before slotting the transmission into gear and guiding us back onto the interstate.

Her coffee sat in a cup-holder. I placed mine in the other one.

"While I was inside, I checked Google maps," she said. "Maybe only another two-and-a-half hours until we hit the outskirts of Sedona." After a brief pause, she asked, "What happened to your phone? I saw it a time or two at the retreat center."

"I never warmed to them. Probably left it in the bus. Or maybe in my cabin. Didn't feel important." After stripping off a paper wrapper and winding it around the stick, I handed her an ice cream bar.

She snorted. "What? Life's short. Eat dessert first?"

"Something like that. More like, life's short and ice cream melts."

"My mother would be shaking a finger at you." Alia took a generous bite of ice cream.

Insight flared. Beyond the brotherhood at my guild house, I hadn't had anything even remotely close to family for longer than I could recall. "You miss them, don't you?"

Her knuckles whitened where she gripped the wheel with her left hand. "It's so much worse than that. Hell, I'll never see any of them ever again. And I never got to say goodbye." She sighed and took another bite. "It sounds whiny, but they took good care of me, and I loved them."

She'd kicked the door open, so I asked a logical question. "Did you consider a side trip to see them one last time?"

"You mean during this junket?"

"Yes." I handed her a napkin and took the wooden stick, dropping it back into the food sack.

She scrunched her face into a grimace. "You caught me dead to rights, but what would I say? I can't tell them about what's coming. All it would do is terrify them, particularly since there's no way out. Besides, we've had our hands full. No spare time for sentiment. Also, how would I explain not being fourteen anymore?"

It was the right answer. In a different world, she'd have been able to ease into adulthood. That world was no more. I felt bad for her, but she didn't need my pity. It would only muddy the waters.

Reaching into the sack, I fished out a taco and folded back the wrappings so she could eat.

"Just a second," she said and grabbed her drink. Once she'd put it back, she took the taco.

I unwrapped one for myself. Midway through munching it, I asked, "How are you doing?"

"Okay so long as I don't think too long or too deeply about any of this. It still feels as if I fell into a sick fairy tale. Part of me expects to go back to college." She crinkled the wrapper and handed it to me.

Over the next hour, we finished the tacos and made small talk. She didn't want to dissect our situation, and I supported this small break from our new normal. She'd placed her phone in a small bin in the center of the dashboard. I took it, intent on checking our location.

"My passcode is—" she began.

"Don't need it."

"Of course, you wouldn't. What was I thinking?" Sarcasm sharpened her words.

It took me a few taps before I located the mapping program. "We're really close," I informed her.

"I know. Been reading road signs."

I rattled off an address. "Let's drop the truck there."

"But it's early. Maybe no one will be there."

Her words alerted me to the fact dawn had broken perhaps a couple of hours before. I'd been lost in planning and hadn't been paying attention. "Doesn't matter. There will be a key drop."

"So much I don't know," she mumbled, followed by, "I need you to dial in the nav system for directions."

I could have guided us, but I found the program and added the address. We were five miles and change out.

Alia had been right about the lot being deserted. A sign on the door said they didn't open until ten thirty. I dumped our trash in a bin and stuffed the paperwork and keys into a slot in the door.

"I locked up," Alia told me when I returned to where she stood next to the pickup that had been our home for the last few hours.

"Walk with me." I extended a hand and led us in the general direction of the vortex until I found a secluded spot.

"What are we doing?"

I draped a sound shield around us in addition to a spell that rendered us invisible. "Mini jump spell to the power point. Be ready."

"For what?"

"Damn near anything. If there's trouble, we're not sticking around."

"But then how will we get back to the others and the caves?"

"One problem at a time," I cautioned and kindled my spell.

The city vanished, replaced by the now familiar steep

track leading to the power point. I'd brought us out here on purpose in case a greeting party had stationed themselves at the top.

So far, so good. I started up the track keeping Alia behind me.

A low moan stopped me dead in my tracks.

"Aw crap. It's the griffon." Alia sprinted around me right through the protective perimeter of my castings.

I raced after her, but she was quick. By the time I caught up, she knelt at the edge of the vortex, cradling as much of the griffon's body as she could in her arms.

Ragged breathing was reassuring. He was still alive.

Was whoever attacked him still there? Had they left his broken body as bait to lure us?

I threw my body over the two of them and wove power into a tight dome. None too soon. Darts, or perhaps arrows, pummeled my shelter. My power isn't bottomless. Sooner or later, something would penetrate.

Back to plan B.

Alia's focus was on the griffon. Magic shimmered as she struggled to heal his damaged places.

"Don't fight me. I'm moving us," I told her.

"All of us," she said without removing her gaze from her beast.

"Of course."

Maybe I'd learned something from my failed attempt to access time travel without using the vortex, but we didn't have a whole lot of options. The caves were a safe haven. Connor, Joss, and Nola needed us. For all I knew, Karen and Moriah had returned.

"Two steps." I spoke deep into Alia's mind. *"First the caves here. From there, we'll bump up half a dozen years and hopefully hit the time where we started."*

"Hurry. He needs food and water. And a safe place."

We all needed the latter. Along with a foolproof solution to keep the Sumerians on the run. Somehow, they had to believe they'd be worse off pursuing us than leaving us be.

I'd figure that out later.

Adding more fire to my spell than I'd done before, I was gratified when the grassy knoll shattered leaving us in darkness. I pushed it, shaped it, cajoled it to my bidding.

None of this was easy. Something fought my magic every step of the way.

"Why is it taking so long?" Alia skipped telepathy.

I didn't have the energy or concentration to reply. All at once, the barrier between me and my skill burst. The familiar entryway to the caves rose before me. A few words broke the enchantment guarding the place, and I ushered us inside taking care to seal the caverns against everyone except us.

Alia and the griffon were in the cave with the pool. She must have moved him with magic while I barricaded us inside, since carrying him was out of the question.

The griffon drank from Alia's cupped palms. She glanced at me, her brow creased with concern. "He's stronger than when I found him."

"Good. We shouldn't bide here long."

"Why? We need a break."

"We'll get a break once we're back to the others." I picked up a rock and drew an equation in the dirt.

Not pleased with the outcome, I tried again, and then a third time. By the time I looked up, the griffon sat on his haunches appearing much more alive than dead. Alia had an arm slung around him.

Their partnership had been cast in blood millennia ago. It was coming full circle.

"I believe I can move us up a few years. Figured out what went wrong last time."

"Mostly, we had unexpected company," Alia reminded me.

"Might have taken care of that too. Trust me enough to give this a whirl?"

"I do," the griffon squawked.

Vote of confidence from an unexpected quarter. "How about you?" I eyed Alia.

"Of course, I trust you." Leaving the griffon, she joined me.

"Can you walk?" I asked the beast.

In answer, he lumbered close.

"We're going to the oldest part of these caverns," I told them. "To leverage Earth's power more easily."

By the time Alia and the griffon caught up to me, my spell was ready. Glistening, it hung suspended from my hands.

"Is there a downside?" Alia asked.

"There's always a possibility. Avoid negativity. Rule one of magic is believing you can do something."

"Oh yeah. You've said that a time or two."

"Have I, now?" I chuckled and loosed my casting. It would either work very quickly—or not at all.

CHAPTER TWENTY-THREE, ALIA

My first clue the griffon was in trouble was low moaning. Not bothering to question why I was so all-fired certain it was him, I raced upward. When I spied him lying on his side, I was terrified he might be dead, but then I reminded myself he was still communicating.

Last I checked, the dead don't do that.

Heedless of my own safety—for all I knew his enemies had left him like this to set a snare—I drew power around both of us and reached within his body searching for damage. I was clumsy. No one had taught me healing magic, so all I had to draw on were simple things I'd done to fix my own wounds.

His anatomy was unusual, a mix of avian and feline. The configuration had probably saved his life, or maybe he was one of those magical creatures who couldn't die. Regardless,

I located broken blood vessels and gently knit them together again.

Could he have healed himself?

Impossible to say. Since I was here, I took over. After a time, I felt Rhys's power surround us. The griffon guided me to a broken wing bone I'd overlooked. Leaving me to my task, Rhys moved us to the caverns. I focused enchantment into a primitive bier and dragged the griffon close to the pool where I could cup water in my palms for him to drink.

As he gently pecked water from my hands, I marveled at the transition from wanting him to go away to protecting him with everything in me. How had it happened? The nanosecond I realized he was in trouble, I'd sprinted to the rescue. Were we truly bonded by some eldritch magic that ran both ways? The woman in the cavern—and Rhys—had intimated the griffon was supposed to protect me.

"What's your name?" I asked him.

"Cleyn."

Before I could question him further, he added, *"'Tis a clan name belonging to my pride. I may be the last one left."*

The protectiveness that had surged earlier burned brighter still. He'd been tasked with caring for me. That burden had separated him from hearth and kin.

"It's all right," he murmured between slurps.

I didn't reply, but it was not *all right* in any of my universes. He'd been stripped of free will and lost everything. Because of me.

Rhys was mumbling and scratching what looked like equations in the dirt with a rock. Finally, he beckoned for us to follow him after explaining we were heading for the most ancient part of the cave system to better access Earth's power. It made me wonder if Earth was his strong suit much as fire has always been mine.

He asked if I trusted him, which seemed like an odd question. If I didn't, I'd never have shared my body. Had our lovemaking meant less to him than to me? Not the time to bring it up, particularly not with his exhortations to remain positive, so his spell had the best possible chance of working.

He'd also asked earlier if I'd considered a side trip to visit my family. I'd soft-pedaled my answer, so he wouldn't know the depth of my internal struggle not to do just that. Once we returned to our own time, my family would be dead. I'd tried to soothe myself with reassurances I could time travel on my own to see them, but I knew in my heart I'd never have that kind of latitude or time.

Not with us fighting for our existence nearly every waking moment. Plus, I had yet to solve the age problem. I'd have to hit damned close to the summer I'd gone to the retreat...

Rhys ducked through a slit of a doorway into a smallish cavern with a low ceiling. The same glowing lichen provided muted light. A crumbling altar streaked with what might have been blood—or charcoal—took up most of the middle of the place. Enchantment thrummed, beating against my eardrums. Rhys hadn't been kidding about guiding us to a power spot.

He stood next to me. Cleyn squatted on my other side. He seemed to have made a full recovery.

"If this works," Rhys was saying, "it will be over quickly."

"And if it doesn't?" I scrunched my face into a grimace. "Sorry. I'll radiate positivity from here on in."

"It's a reasonable question," Rhys said. "Worst thing should be we end up where we started, which is right here." He eyed the griffon. "Do you sense anyone who shouldn't be here?"

The creature shook his head from side to side. "I've been looking ever since Watchers jumped me."

Surprise scuttled down my spine. While I was healing him, I hadn't bothered culling through his memories for who'd attacked him. "But they're ghosts," I protested.

"It's a common error," Cleyn corrected me. "They only appear to be spirits. They're capable of, well, of what happened to me. One inconvenient aspect is since they're long dead, killing them isn't possible."

Good to know.

"Back to the problem at hand." Rhys's tone was firm. "I'm ready to do this. Come closer."

I flanked him on one side, Cleyn shuffled to the other. The familiar touch of Rhys's power formed around us, tucking us into his spell. If I squinted through my third eye, bands of power circled the walls before wrapping around the three of us.

Breathe, I instructed. *Breathe and believe.* We'd had such rotten luck, surely it was time for something to go off without a hitch. Never mind returning to the spot we'd left held its own set of problems. At least, we'd be there for Connor, Joss, and Nola. For all I knew, the wolf-shifter sisters had had enough of freedom and returned.

What I didn't let myself think about was we'd done all

this essentially for nothing. No victory dance. Not this time. Just three weary pilgrims slogging home against steep odds.

"Do not let your guard down," Rhys cautioned.

Fuck. He was in my head again. He'd told me to get used to it, but I hadn't taken him literally.

"I will protect her." Cleyn's tone was solemn.

The cavern took on a glittery aspect before ceding to darkness. Should I be looking for nodes? Or was this the iteration where there wouldn't be any. I bit down on my lower lip to stem a tide of questions.

I could ask later—if I remembered.

Rhys took up a chant in a guttural language peppered with consonants. His spell pressed against me, gentle at first and then so firmly I stifled a whimper. A low growl from Cleyn suggested he was none-too-comfortable, either.

Words tore from Rhys, louder and louder. The second he loosed them, they turned into sparkling runes that circled us. Fascinated, I reached for one.

"*Nooooo!*" thundered through my head.

Relegated to a child whose hand had been slapped, I swallowed a heated reply. Rhys was doing the best he could, shaping unfamiliar power. He deserved better than being bombarded with my hurt feelings.

"Soon," he mumbled between spewing runes.

Beautiful in an arcane sort of way, they lit our travel channel like a clumsy lightshow.

The transition was abrupt. One moment, we were swathed in runes and his spell. The next, breath swooshed from me. If I'd been punched in the guts, it would have had a similar effect.

The same tiny cavern we'd left shaped up around us complete with the crumbling altar. Had it been used for sacrifices? Or was my imagination running overtime?

What did it even matter? The important part was if we'd hit the right time frame. Out of so many possibilities, had Rhys pulled off a miracle?

He'd shifted his power to jets of seeking magic as he sought to determine what lay in the tunnel. The griffon fanned his wings and swished his tail. I threaded my skill in with Rhys's and found an empty corridor.

"So far, so good," he said softly and started toward what passed for a doorway.

I fell in behind him, nostrils twitching as I sought our companions.

Cleyn was so close to me I felt his breath on my back.

We rounded a significant bend I didn't exactly remember from the 2017 version of this cave system, but then I hadn't been paying close attention.

In the distance, shouts, screams, and thuds sounded.

Crap. Were we too late? Were these even our companions?

Rhys accelerated with a magical assist. I bumbled a bit before doing the same. We flashed past the big cave with the pool. A quick peek suggested Rhys had hit the proper time since our dishes and bowls littered the back counter. Or maybe they were someone else's. We were far from the first group to shelter here.

As we grew closer, the noise of a battle in progress twisted my stomach into a ball of hot acid. Bile splashed the back of my throat. I swallowed once and then again.

The griffon slithered around me. I gathered power into a defensive arc and held it at the ready.

One more bend in the tunnel, and all would be revealed. I sucked air and fed fire into my casting. Rather than stopping there, it formed a shield around me burning brightly.

Rhys bellowed; the griffon roared.

I skidded around the final corner. In another world, another time, the one so recently lost to me, I'd have turned tail and run for shelter. The new me could puke later.

At least six werewolves and three vampires had drilled through the barrier keeping the cave system safe. How in the hell had they managed it? In hawk form, Connor dripped blood from one wing. Joss had walled himself behind a blend of earth and air, but two werewolves were taking big paw swipes out of his protection. Nola was nowhere to be found.

Had a vamp already turned her?

No time to think. Only to act. What I'd done before had worked handily. I summoned silver. The first batch of stakes melted in the heat from my fire. I dialed it back and tried again. Just like last time, no rhyme nor reason to what showed up.

With silver-bladed knives in both hands, I addressed myself to the nearest vamp. He must have been expecting my frontal attack. Maybe what I'd done to the others had become an urban legend. Regardless, he didn't make it easy. He kicked me so hard I flew through the air, narrowly missing impaling myself with the blades meant for him.

The snick of metal on rock suggested Rhys had a blade of his own, but I couldn't look. Straying attention would be the true kiss of death, even before the vamp got his fangs into me.

Cleyn barreled into the vampire from behind, pushing him into the dirt. A sideways leap landed me on his back. I didn't hesitate before driving a blade between his ribs and hoping to hell I got the angle right to hit his heart. My answer was immediate when he crumpled into a pile of bones.

No chance to savor victory. Two of the fuckers piled on top of me. The griffon pecked and slashed with beak and claws. Noxious black blood burbled. It burned where it touched me. Gasping with effort, I yanked the blade from between rib bones that no longer had space between them.

Facedown, I was at a distinct disadvantage. Hot breath seared my neck followed by the brush of fangs. Christ. The vampire was toying with me. Or maybe this was a she.

An outraged shriek suggested I'd been right the second time. The weight on top of me shifted enough for me to jackknife myself around and bury a blade through a breast and on through. At first, the tip caught on a rib but I jockeyed it until it slid home.

Breath burned my throat. There wasn't enough air in the universe to feed my racing heart. Two down. How many had there been? A furious howl suggested Rhys had dispatched a werewolf. Good. More of them than vamps, but they weren't as deadly.

Or maybe they were.

My head felt fuzzy.

"Twist away," Cleyn shrieked. The shadow of his huge wings hovered over me.

I jerked first left and then right, shocked to feel something withdraw from the junction of my neck and shoulder. Running on fury and adrenaline, I got my feet under me and launched myself at another vampire. I nailed that one with both blades, stopping only after it morphed from dead flesh to rotting bones.

Rhys spun in a circle. Power flowed from his hands as he dispatched werewolves. The last two took off at a run, preferring freedom to annihilation.

"Her neck," Cleyn shrilled.

Jumping over a fallen werewolf, Rhys was by my side. Curses in yet one more unknown language fell from his mouth. He slapped a hand on the side of my neck. Power augured into me, burning like liquid fire. The sounds—howls, shrieks—coming from me were so alien I didn't recognize them.

I wanted to see to Joss and Connor, but it was all I could do to stay on my feet. Had a vampire nailed me? I didn't see how. I hadn't felt anything—except for something needlelike withdrawing from my flesh. The heat factor escalated until I didn't understand why I hadn't turned into a pillar of flames.

Things grew hazy, merged together. After a very long time, my mind grew a wee bit clearer. And then clearer still. I didn't realize Rhys still had his hand on my neck until he withdrew it. His palm was dotted with putrid black bits.

"Think I got it all." Breath rushed from him.

"Another minute, and you wouldn't have," Cleyn growled.

I still didn't quite understand, but I shook them off.

Connor had shifted. He crouched working on healing a gash in his upper arm. Joss was helping.

"Sorry I wasn't more assistance," Nola began, followed by, "Aw shit, you came back."

We'd never been the huggy type, but she threw her arms around me. "Where were you?" I asked and hugged her back.

She jerked a thumb toward the courtyard. "Trying to help Karen and Moriah."

"They changed their minds?"

She let go of me and shook her head. "Not of their own free will. The local werewolf pack captured them and tortured them until they revealed how to breach the barrier."

So that was how the bad guys had gotten into the caverns.

"Goddammit," Rhys growled. "Are they still alive?"

"Moriah, barely," Nola told him.

He raced outside.

"Guess it didn't work," Nola mumbled.

It took me a moment to latch onto her meaning, which highlighted our failed reconnaissance. "Not this trip it didn't, no, but we'll try again."

The day's light was fading, but there was enough for me to see Nola's usually pale face turn even whiter. "If you do, we need better shelter."

I didn't answer. It was a topic for a different day. Besides, nowhere was safe. Not anymore.

Rhys ran past with Moriah in his arms.

"There," Joss said. "About done. How do you feel?"

"Tolerable." Connor's voice was gravelly.

"Help me," I told Nola.

"What are we doing?"

"Moving these remains outside. And then we're going to resurrect the barrier but with a different spell."

No one had left me in charge, but I picked up the banner anyway. A couple of Watchers materialized. They did what I told them, a fact I filed away since they'd assaulted Cleyn. Half an hour later, we all trooped along the tunnel.

Rhys had propped Moriah near the pool. She was sitting up and crying, probably mourning Karen.

"I'm sorry," Rhys said. "She was already dead."

"You just left her body out there," she shrilled.

I came close and knelt in front of her. "This is hard. When we were moving vampire remains out of the cave, I found Karen. She'd shifted. She looked peaceful."

"You can't leave her out there," Moriah insisted.

Rhys stood and strode from the cavern. Joss and Connor had begun to work on food preparation. Good. Running through power drains me. Since I had nothing else to do, I followed Rhys's route. Cleyn started after me, but I waved him back into the main cave. He'd had a rough go, and I didn't require a bodyguard.

Rhys had unraveled the spell I set to keep the caverns safe. Sheesh. If he could do it this fast, others could as well. I needed to up my game.

Karen lay in front of him, and he probed the inert wolf with visible rays of power. Stepping to his side, I followed the beams and did them one better auguring deep within her.

The wolf growled. Ears twitched. I fell back a step and

tossed a protective barrier around Rhys and me. Had the shifter been absorbed, turned to evil by one of the weres?

Moriah must have heard the growl. Half shifted, she barreled into the rounded entryway.

"Stop!" Rhys followed the word with shielding.

Fully shifted, Moriah attacked the barrier with fangs and talons. It bent but snapped back.

Karen's wolf whined, ears pinned against its skull as Rhys dug deeper than I'd gone. Something must have satisfied him because he cut the flow of his magic on all fronts.

Moriah bounded to Karen's side whimpering and whining. The two wolves licked muzzles.

I addressed myself to adding several layers to what I'd hoped was an impenetrable barrier protecting the cave system,

"It's good enough." Rhys closed a hand around my forearm and almost dragged me toward the corridor.

"Shift and come eat with us," Rhys told the sisters before we trotted along the passageway.

"What were you so worried about?" I asked.

"Had to make certain there was no werewolf taint. Could have happened while they were being tortured."

"Did you check Moriah?"

He nodded and ducked into a smallish cave off to our right, presumably to finish our conversation.

"I was certain Karen was dead," I mumbled. "Checked thoroughly."

"Which was why I had to make damned good and sure

she hadn't been subsumed by something we did not want in our midst."

I slumped against a wall. "This won't ever end, will it?"

Not sure what I'd hoped for, soothing words maybe. Stupid of me. What I got was vintage Rhys: straight from the hip, absent sugarcoating.

"If by *this* you mean one enemy right on top of another one, no, it won't end. Not for a long while."

"Someday?"

"I don't know." Stepping close, he drew me against him and stroked my hair back from my face. It fell in greasy tangles, reminding me how filthy I was. Old world problems. After a time, we rejoined the group.

Karen and Moriah were there. They'd dressed and wiped some of the grit off their faces. Everyone was gathered close intent on hearing what happened. I caught the tail end of Karen saying, "...not sure how, but once I shifted I was certain death wasn't far off. My wolf howled the song of her people, the special one reserved for fallen comrades."

"And?" Connor prodded.

She shrugged. "I woke up. Rhys and Alia were jabbing me with the most unpleasant magic, but I didn't care because it meant I was alive."

"Your wolf took care of you," Connor said flatly.

"What do you mean?" Karen arched dark brows.

"The animal side of our bond can push us into a type of stasis. Not forever, but sometimes it's long enough for danger to pass. Did your mentors not teach you that?"

Karen and Moriah shook their heads. Color stained

Moriah's cheeks. "We, erm, didn't have mentors. All we've ever had is each other."

Mmph. It explained a lot, both about their bond and their primitive grasp of the power available to them.

Weariness washed through me in waves. To keep me on my feet for a little longer, I plodded to the pool, cupped water, and rinsed vampire blood off my face and hands.

"But that's our drinking water," Nola protested.

"The cave's power will purify it," Rhys assured her.

After a time, Joss placed a cracked bowl next to me. Picking it up, I ate mindlessly. Things might not look any better tomorrow, but at least my power would have had a chance to regenerate.

It's the small things.

Yeah, because that's all that's left a caustic inner voice snarked.

No one had much to say during our meal. Being reunited was enough for now.

CHAPTER TWENTY-FOUR, RHYS

Two days passed. None of us left the caverns. Eventually, we'd have to, but if the werewolves and vampires had been on the prowl before, now they'd be out for blood in more ways than one.

Watchers oozed in and out, traveling byways only they knew. Alia had been stern with them, and there'd been no further unprovoked confrontations.

I'd half expected the Sumerians to approach her again, but it didn't happen. Maybe they viewed her as trapped and were taking their sweet time.

Though the group talked of many things, we scrupulously avoided bringing up the future. They all looked to me for guidance, but I had scant wisdom to impart. On the good news front, my power was robust, as was Alia's.

We grabbed the odd moment together, but stopped shy of actual lovemaking. It didn't feel right in such close quarters. Plus, magic is vulnerable then, and I wasn't willing to let down my guard. So far, no one had tried to break inside, but they had all the time in the world.

We were who'd have to scuttle out in search of provisions.

Alia found me standing—or actually sitting—watch near the entry point. I'd set up rotating guard duty that included us all.

"What a lovely surprise." I got to my feet.

"Sit." She waved a hand at the ground and squatted next to where I'd been leaning against a wall.

I did. "What's up?" I asked.

"We need to kick around what happens next. Do we stick together? Do we send out a team to see how Sedona's shaping up? Cleyn is restless. He says we need to make a move before someone forces our hand."

"The griffon?" At Alia's nod, I went on. "Figured he had a name. How long have you known?"

"Does it matter? He said it was some kind of clan name, and he was probably the last of his kinsmen."

The information about the griffon was intriguing, but I refocused. "The way I see it, we have a few options. We can stay here. We can use jump spells to check out nearby locations. We can time travel either forward or back."

She frowned, creating a crease between her fair brows. "If we went back, everyone would return to their lives. The ones we had before the...the incident."

I held up a hand. "Nope. If we voted on that choice it would be with the understanding we'd stick together and work as a team to bend the future in a different direction."

An audible sigh rattled from Alia. "Yeah. We'd all agree until we actually got there, and then I bet everyone would scatter. The temptation would be irresistible."

"Then that's off the table."

"Is it?" Her hazel gaze augured into me.

"Yes."

"Why? What do you know?"

"Not much, but Micah seemed to view me as a harbinger of the end of the world, so if my guild has access to prophecies sketching out Earth's non-future, other mages will as well."

"Why haven't they prepared better?"

I squelched a smile. The question was vintage Alia, ever practical. "Seers sift through many possible futures. They tend to pick the ones they prefer, not necessarily the ones that will come to pass."

Straightening from where she'd been leaning into me, she snapped her fingers. "That's it. We go back, not very far, only a few years, but we make good use of the time by tapping as many brotherhoods and sisterhoods of mages as we can. Surely, if we all work together, we can forge a different outcome."

I doubted it, but one look at her expression, so earnest and determined, stayed my tongue. Instead, I murmured, "Can't hurt; might help."

"Thanks for the vote of confidence." She made a face and stuck out her tongue.

"Knock, knock," Connor said before he joined us. His arm had made a solid recovery, an ugly red scar the only remnant of his wound.

"Join us." I patted the ground.

He arranged his lanky limbs in a cross-legged sit. "The others and I were talking. The griffon too. He's amazingly chatty. Reminds me of a shifter even though he's not." Connor paused for a moment. "We liked your idea about returning to the past to try to change all this." He spread his arms for emphasis.

"It is one option." I spoke slowly. "Others are remaining here, aiming for the future, or sticking in this time frame but moving away from these caves."

"We covered that ground," Connor said. "We think the past is our best bet."

I snared him in a truth spell. He flinched but didn't complain. "The temptation to return to your lives will be huge, potentially overwhelming."

"We know."

His words pinged cleanly off my casting.

"Did you discuss ways to counteract the desire to be normal again?"

"Sort of. Not in so many words." He switched to telepathy. *"I suspect Karen, Moriah, and Nola will hunker down and wait this out hoping against hope the rest of us pull off a miracle."*

As he spoke, my mind traveled divergent tracks. Returning to the retreat center was inviting. Since I had a specific time and date for the apocalypse, we'd plan better, stock in supplies with the thought of holing up in the Sierra Madre mountains. No more precipitous bus ride down the mountainside. Also, I'd pick and choose my participants with an eye to what loomed over us.

A sharp prick suggested for once Alia had invaded my thoughts.

"That's counterproductive," she said. "You're assuming we're powerless and are simply planning better for the inevitable."

Busted.

"Huh?" Connor's brows shot up. "What'd I miss?"

I stood. "Let's rejoin the others. This conversation requires us all."

An hour later, consensus eluded us. Everyone voted for the past, but that was where agreement crashed and burned.

"Magic can't be forced," Cleyn squawked. It was the first thing he'd said, and he was abundantly correct.

I made my way to the pool, cupped my hands, and took a long drink.

"Since we can't decide," I said, "this is what we're going to do. I will move everyone a couple of years into the past. That's two years before the retreat. You will return to your lives—if you choose. Pushing you to remain in this group would be a mistake. Your ambivalence will impact anything I try to do magically to alter the..." I almost said inevitable but stopped in time.

"How will we find you?" Nola asked.

"The only sure way is to stick with me," I replied in as even a tone as I could muster. Crap. She couldn't have it both ways. Either she lived out additional time in whatever way pleased her, or she bent her magic—limited though it was—to the cause.

"You'll be able to find us," Alia said, "because Rhys and I will spend at least some time at the retreat center. If we're not there when you show up, you can leave us a note."

"I'll be with you two," Connor said.

"Me as well," Joss chimed in.

The griffon clacked his beak, but I hadn't had the slightest doubt about his allegiance. Alia's words soothed a nagging fear she'd trot back to her college campus.

"Can we tell anyone?" Moriah asked.

"Depends," I replied.

"On what? Come on, Rhys. Don't toy with me."

"If you tell anyone without magic, they'll chalk you up as having lost your mind."

The wolf-shifter's mouth crumpled into a frown. "Oh yeah. There is that. But we could rally other shifters."

"That's my plan," Connor informed her.

"Our only hope is a critical mass of magic," I clarified. "If we gather enough mages, we may have sufficient magic to take on the Sumerians."

"Don't count on it," the griffon hooted.

He may have been right, but his attitude grated. "How about if we rustled up a Celtic god or goddess?" I pressed.

The beast spread his wings and flew to the other side of the room.

"Is that even possible?" Karen asked. She'd been quiet since her near brush with death.

"I have no idea," I said. "Hundreds of years ago, they were not exactly available, but they'd occasionally rally support if the need was great."

"Maybe we're missing the boat," Alia said. "What if we aimed for, say, the 1500s."

Cleyn swooped back to our side of the cavern. "Even if my masters agreed on the surface, it leaves a lot of time for them to revert back to their original plan. Humans didn't get serious about trashing Earth until the latter part of the 1800s."

There was that. All bets would be off when faced with polluted oceans and climate chaos.

"Enough discussion," I cut in. "We're leaving for the near past." I focused on Alia. "If you join your ability with mine, we should be able to transport everyone."

"I'll take care of myself," Cleyn chirped.

No reason to tarry. Plenty of food, shelter, and water where we were headed. "Follow me," I instructed, left the cavern, and turned hard left. My aim was the small cavern in the very back of this cave system. Its magical linkage with Earth would provide a powerful assist.

"Why here?" Moriah asked as she joined us.

My temper has never been my best friend. "Either you trust me by now, or you don't," I snapped.

"Touchy, touchy," she mumbled plenty loud enough for me to hear.

I turned to face the group absent Cleyn, who'd presumably already left. "I will test each of you. If you carry the slightest taint of negativity, I will leave you here. Is that understood? This will be difficult enough without adding doubts to the mix."

No one argued. The bit about leaving them must have been a strong bargaining chip. I beckoned Alia to come close. Her troubled expression suggested I'd been a tad on the heavy-handed side, but where I hail from, the weak don't question master mages.

Showing rather than telling, I led her through her part in our joint spell. She asked a couple of questions that pointed out holes in my plan.

Half an hour later, we were as ready as we were likely to be.

The group had been silent. No coughing, no rustling, no shifting from foot to foot. I motioned them near and draped the edges of the time travel spell around them.

"No matter what you see or feel or hear," I cautioned, "maintain a neutral mindset."

A series of *got its* echoed through the small cave. Before I launched the spell, I did one last check for Watchers, but didn't find any. They could have stashed themselves in shadows waiting to report to their masters. Or not.

Can't control every variable.

I extended a hand. Alia clasped it. The cave vanished, replaced by darkness. This shouldn't take long. Longer than when it was just Alia and me and the griffon, but not by a whole bunch.

A faint grinding noise gradually grew louder. Alia's grip tightened. I'd forbidden questions. No one asked any.

Fire flickered on Alia's end. Her power element. Meant she was feeding more magic into the mix. Concerned the casting would lack balance, I did the same but with Earth.

Minutes ticked past. Too many for my liking. Time to pull the plug. We'd take wherever we ended up.

"*Calling it,*" I told Alia.

"But we're not done."

"How can you know?"

"I don't." Even her mind voice was tense.

No nodes to check the passage of time periods. It wouldn't have been as convenient since we'd have had to leave the caves, but perhaps I should have used the vortex.

Too late now.

I counted off five more minutes. *"We have to end this,"* I told Alia and spoke words to curtail our spell.

At least that part worked. The dark channel we'd been suspended in burst outward, leaving us tumbling downward. It had been daytime when we left. Now it was night, which didn't bode well.

I trusted everyone had sufficient self-preservation instincts to buffer their fall.

It took a while to round everyone up. The distant howling of wolves and coyotes made me cautious. I didn't want to levy power to hold packs of predators at bay.

Alia reached into a pocket and dragged out her phone, a bellwether of how well we'd done. I edged next to her and peered over a shoulder. The spot in the upper right remained stubbornly blank. No carrier logo.

Annoyed by even modest reliance on modern anything, I dug deep, accessing my innate knowledge of time and location. The answer that popped up was inconceivable, so I checked again. And then a third time.

"Well?" Joss asked. "Where are we?"

No one likes to admit failure, but I had no choice. "About a week before we left."

Groans rose. "How?" Nola demanded. "Time travel worked for you before."

"Yeah, why not now?" Moriah chimed in.

Coyote yips drew closer.

"Quiet," Alia cautioned and tossed a *don't look here* spell around us. It wouldn't deter a determined coyote, but it might slow them down.

APPARENTLY, something major had changed. My next task was to determine exactly what it was. Or maybe there'd simply been too many of us. That's the thing about magic. It's far from an exact undertaking.

A second check of our surroundings convinced me we were closer to Flagstaff than Sedona. Why our longitude and latitude had changed absent instructions from me was baffling.

Our immediate need was a sheltered spot to sit out the night.

"We need to move," I told everyone.

"Where are we going?" Joss asked.

"Shelter for whatever remains of the night. Then we'll regroup."

"Can't we do a jump spell back to the caves?" Connor asked.

We could, but given my colossal failure with time travel, I wasn't about to take anything else on until I'd had time to dissect what went wrong. A man has pride— misplaced though it might be—so I didn't spell out my concerns.

"Maybe there's a deserted house that hasn't totally collapsed," Alia suggested.

Rather than guess, I sent rays of power spinning in a full circle. The ones to the southwest suggested a structure, so I set a course for it. Shortly, a commercial hanger came into view. After breaking the padlock, I shooed everyone inside and kindled a mage light.

Bales of hay lined the walls. A couple of tractors sat off to one side. I resealed the door. It would be good enough for now. "Get comfortable, everyone," I said and went to work clipping wire to free hay for bedding.

Everyone settled in. "I'll take the first watch," I told them. "Two hours, and then we'll switch."

Back against a bale, I spread power in an arc and set about monitoring it.

Alia joined me. "Feel like some company?" Her voice was soft.

"If it's you, always."

"*What happened?*"

"*No idea.*"

"*I think we were too many.*"

I draped an arm around her shoulders. "*It's a better explanation than someone didn't want us leaving. Any idea where Cleyn is?*"

"*No, but he'll find me. What happens in the morning?*"

"*We go somewhere without spies.*"

"*The Watchers?*"

I nodded. "*It's one explanation for our spell being subverted. Get some rest. I'll wake you when it's your turn to keep an eye on things.*"

She snuggled next to me, head on my shoulder. *"It's a deal."*

Alia by my side, I kept watch. I've been in worse spots. Much worse. Tomorrow, we'd move on. Staying in one spot had been a mistake, one I wouldn't make again. I'd been looking forward to returning Nola and the shifter sisters to a simpler time. For now, Fate had other plans for us. Prophecy has never been one of my talents, but the next pool we found, I'd do my damnedest to scry a primitive future.

Ultimately, we needed to move far enough into the past to rally other mages to the cause, but it was a problem for another day. Left to my own devices, I'd have let Alia sleep, but she must have set an internal alarm.

"My turn," she said sleepily.

"You can rest longer." I cupped the side of her face in one hand.

"I could, but you need to replenish your power too. If I run into problems, you'll be the first to know."

I could have argued, but I was tired. After settling a protective barrier around us both, I scratched hay into a pile and lay on my back. The last thing I saw before my eyes closed was Alia's striking profile. With bone structure like the goddesses she was formed from, she cut a formidable figure. Beauty holding darkness at bay.

"That's lovely, but you should sleep," she murmured.

No one had ever taken care of me. To my surprise, I rather liked it.

You've reached the end of *Conjuring Fate*, book one of

Sanctuary. It's tough to know where to break these long tales, but this is as good a spot as any. The story continues in *Conjuring Chaos*, book two of the series. I hope you enjoyed the tale so far. Please take a moment and leave a review. They mean so much to authors, and are a way of sharing what you loved about this book.
Read on for the first chapter of *Conjuring Chaos*.

CONJURING CHAOS, BOOK DESCRIPTION:

If this were a normal nightmare, I'd wake up, dust myself off, and forge a path. Nightmare, yes. Normal, not so much. After the world imploded, none of the usual rules applied.

They say finding your roots is freeing. In my case it was like nailing a coffin shut. Everyone has a few rotten relatives. Mine created me to serve their purposes millennia ago. Except nobody bothered to tell me, not until my world shattered. When I rebelled, they labeled me extraneous, so now I'm on the lookout for them along with every other evil thing that's risen to populate Earth.

All the mortals are dead. In theory, those like me, mages, survived, but outside our small group, we haven't stumbled on any of them beyond a lone skinwalker. Rhys is a bright spot. Who'd have thought I'd find love amongst the ashes of civilization. Sometimes, I want to cling to him and run away, but Earth needs us.

And there it is. Along with love, I'm coming into the full extent of my power. The more I push it, the brighter it burns.

We tried once to alter the cataclysm that ended everything. It didn't work, but we haven't given up. Between Rhys and an eldritch griffon tasked with protecting me long before my birth, we'll tackle my masters. They're behind the disastrous event that blew up the world.

If we could figure out why, we might turn the tides in our favor.

CONJURING CHAOS, CHAPTER ONE, ALIA

I checked the gas gauge once more. We weren't quite running on fumes, but almost. Ever since we abandoned the cave system outside Sedona, we've been on the move. Seven isn't all that many people, but we split up a couple of weeks ago. The shifter sisters, Karen and Moriah, wanted to take to their wolf forms and hunt. Nola, a weak-as-dishwater witch, is holed up in a farmhouse in southwestern Nevada where the previous owners laid in enough food to sit out eternity.

Their cellar reminded me of advertisements for the Doomsday crew. Who would have guessed Armageddon would play out in our lifetimes? Some days, I'm used to the status quo. Others, not so much.

Mostly, we've been in survival mode. We have yet to meet a mortal who escaped destruction. All their abandoned cars and trucks have come in handy, though, since the highway system is mostly intact. Enormous cracks and potholes have blocked roads in some spots, but nothing a determined four-wheel drive can't manage.

The engine sputtered. I'd hoped for five more miles, but it wasn't going to happen.

From long habit, I pulled to the side of the road while the wheels were still turning. It scarcely mattered since no one else was likely to come along. Chanting from the backseat suggested Rhys was conducting one more interminable magic lesson. I swear, that man has the patience of a saint, but we are improving.

Not that I need more magic. I don't. My problem is a surfeit that's mostly out of control. Too much when I don't need it; too little when I do.

"What's up?" Connor called. He's a dark-haired hawk shifter with blue eyes and pretty levelheaded.

"Out of fuel."

Rhys cut the flow of his lesson. "Odd. I was certain we'd have enough to hit the next town."

I grabbed the paper map sharing the front seat with me and stared at it. After the wolf shifters defected, group consensus had been to head north. We weren't breaking any speed records as we meandered up a north-south highway spanning the eastern escarpment of the Sierra Nevada mountains.

Towns were few and far between. That would change once we crossed into Nevada, for a while anyway, but it hadn't happened yet.

I flipped the ignition to off and pushed the driver door open. Rhys, Connor, and Joss, a druid, piled out of the back of the white Toyota 4-Runner. It was the middle of the afternoon, and a chill wind battered me. Shading my eyes with a hand, I scanned the skies for my gold-and-brown griffon sidekick but didn't see him.

Bound to me by eldritch Sumerian enchantment, he chose to use his wings to travel. Being confined in vehicles made him uncomfortable. The era that spawned him had used oxen, horses, and carts to get around.

I wrapped my arms around myself. We needed to find a clothing shop and stock up on warmer garments.

"Grab whatever you don't want to leave," Rhys instructed. "I'll move us away from here."

The only possession not on my back was the map. I reached into the cab and retrieved it. Nearly every gas station had them, but who knew when we'd find another. My useless cell phone was a weight in my jacket pocket, but I couldn't bring myself to throw it away.

Stupid, huh?

Above us, the clouds turned gray and menacing. Rain spit in violent bursts pushed by escalating wind. I zipped my faded green jacket to the chin and wished for a hood.

An eerie howl was followed by several more. Great. Was a wolf pack bearing down on us? Not that I couldn't immobilize them, but I hated to. Unless they were werewolves, but we hadn't seen any of them since leaving Sedona.

No vampires, either.

Surprisingly, we hadn't run into any trouble. It was one reason Karen, Moriah, and Nola had cited for jumping ship. They'd downplayed the danger we faced to convince themselves it would be okay to pretend things weren't as bad as we feared. So what else was new? They'd been reluctant recruits from the moment our world imploded.

I jammed my hands into my pockets before my fingers froze.

"Alia." Rhys's tone was tense.

"Yeah?" I scuttled to his side.

"Try a jump spell."

I angled a sidelong glance his way. "Uh, why? What happened to yours?"

"For god's sake, woman, for once do what I ask without questioning it."

Oops.

Whatever was going on wasn't good. Not that Rhys couldn't be temperamental, but his comment was unsarcastically strained. With thick ice-blond hair and blue eyes, he was tall, well-muscled, and lean. He was also my partner and lover, although we'd had precious few moments to ourselves.

I still harbored reservations—big ones—about the lover part. We're so different, and he's like a bazillion years older than me. Although, apparently, I'm far older than I'd thought since the Sumerians kept me in some sort of unnatural stasis until they tucked my essence into a human woman so she could birth me. I'm still unsure what all that means. It's kind of like the "next life rebirth" gig but on steroids.

I cleared my head and focused power into a simple jump spell, one designed to move us a few miles north. Not so far we needed the usual journey channels, which had been perverted by evil, but away from here and nearer the next town.

The men pressed close. I goosed my casting fully expecting it to take off.

We didn't move. What in the hell? After forcing vision through my third eye, I tried again.

And ended up with the same results. An old saying about doing the same thing and expecting a different outcome swatted me broadside.

"Not good," Rhys muttered. "Same thing that happened to me."

"Then why'd you set me up?" My tone was testy, but worry gnawed a hole in my guts.

The look he skewered me with made me feel about an inch tall. "Don't be so edgy. This wasn't a set up. Christ, Alia. I wouldn't do that to you, but I was hoping a different style of magic might turn the tide."

"So the bottom line is we're stuck walking?" Joss asked. He tossed flame-red hair over slender shoulders. "If so, we'd best get to it. Nightfall isn't far off."

The pain in my midsection intensified. Night brought vampires and werewolves and god knew what else. We needed shelter. Even the car was better than nothing. Maybe we should stay put.

"I'll fly reconnaissance," Connor offered and started to strip off his clothes.

"Good idea." Rhys gathered the discarded garments and slung them over an arm.

Eh, guess we weren't remaining here.

Connor's hawk spread shapely brown wings and took to the skies. We plodded north. I spread magic all around hoping it would provide some level of warning since we were terribly exposed. The only living things around.

"Where's Cleyn?" Rhys asked, referring to the griffon.

I shrugged. "Not here, but it's not unusual."

"Don't you have some kind of link with him?" Joss asked.

I did, but it wasn't as if we were connected at the hip. "Doesn't mean I know where he is," I replied. The rain had settled into a steady drizzle. Cold leached every scrap of warmth from my body. My feet were turning into chunks of ice. I started to shiver. Worse, weariness dragged at me, made it hard to think. Despite walking, I was having a tough time not falling asleep.

What the hell? I'd slept decently the night before cradled in Rhys's arms. Because my eyes were at half-mast, I stumbled and would have fallen if he hadn't grabbed my upper arm.

"Are you all right?"

Trying to form words was a struggle. By the time I managed, "Not even close," Rhys had spun me to face him. He placed a hand on both sides of my face. The familiar touch of his power flooded me. It was a wakeup call, but after an initial jolt, I slithered back into the pit.

"What's wrong with her?" Joss's voice came from a long way away, which was odd since he stood next to me.

The shrouding I'd erected to check for bad shit folded around me effectively rendering me blind and deaf. Rhys and Joss were there, but I could no longer sense them.

I should have been terrified, but all I wanted was to lie down and shut my eyes. Peace would reign. All would be well. No more running with an eye over one shoulder. No more struggling.

A vision of an oblong ball of light filled my visual field. It was crystalline with pale pink and lavender highlights. I knew that sphere. Realization punched me in the guts; I twisted from side to side. The light coffin was where the Sumerians had dumped me—or my essence. I'd lived out millennia within its clutches. Guttural moans ripped from me. Wrenching my head out of Rhys's grip, I vomited onto the asphalt.

Someone was shaking me. A short, wicked blade materialized in my hand. I still couldn't see through my earth eyes, but my third eye was functional. Somehow, I ended up in a crouch, head whipping from side to side and knife at the ready. The reek of puke was strong in my nostrils.

Rhys glowed where he'd surrounded himself with something. Joss did too. Why were they protecting themselves, but not me? And then it dawned they'd erected a barrier I couldn't penetrate.

Were they abandoning me to my fate?

Did they know about the crystal that had held me prisoner between my making and when the Sumerians decided my time to serve had arrived? I made a grab for anger, but it eluded me. The same thick, sticky mud I'd been drowning in returned with a vengeance.

My stomach burned, throat too. Dry heaves subsumed me, but my stomach was empty. Despite how cold I was, foul-smelling sweat beaded on my body and trickled down my sides.

Ghouls circled me, staring with empty eyes. I recognized

them. Watchers. Servants of the Sumerian gods. Was that what this was about? Were they sick of my insurrection and calling me home?

I had to fight this, but when I hunted for motivation, it eluded me. Simpler to sink into the crystal and let it take care of me as it had for many a long year. No more hunger. No more thirst. No more cold…

"Alia." The voice in my head was hypnotic, mesmerizing. *"We'll take over now."*

"Leave this place. Immediately," Rhys thundered in one of his many languages, except I sort of understood this one. No wonder. On closer examination, it was Sumerian.

Something must have swatted him since he flew through the air. The next glimpse I caught of him, he ran toward me, fists swinging. I did my damnedest to marshal words to tell him there was no hope, not for me, but he could save himself if he left now. Joss too. At least Connor was safely away, flying somewhere above this mess.

I tried, but nothing beyond a squeak emerged from my throat.

The shining crystal edged nearer. I wanted its gentle confines, its nurturing. My longing horrified me. I shuffled away, fighting its pull. A goddess-like figure formed behind my third eye. She might have been the same woman I'd seen deep underground. She carried a lantern. Her silvery eyes were warm, inviting as she herded me toward the crystal.

If it reached me, I'd never escape.

Fight this, a faint inner voice cried. *You cannot give in. You know what awaits if you do.*

Of course, I knew. Why didn't I care more?

Had I been drugged? I didn't see how. Our last meal had been canned peaches and tinned bread scrounged from the remains of a small market in Independence, a tiny town squatting in the shadow of enormous mountains.

Thinking about the food inserted a ray of objectivity. It wasn't the food. How could it have been. No. This was about running out of gas. Someone had finessed it, and they'd done it in a specific place. This area must house a gateway or a power point amenable to their control. It also explained the griffon's absence. Either he couldn't break through, or they were holding him prisoner.

The latter explanation broke my heart. Cleyn has lost everything on account of me. I'd be damned if he'd add suffering to the mix.

The crystal coffin wasn't more than a foot away. How had it come so close? Breath burned my abraded throat. I finally understood what I had to do to break free. Could I manage it?

"Distance," I panted, but the word emerged so garbled it was unrecognizable. No wonder our jump spells hadn't worked. They'd been tainted right along with the Toyota.

"Got to get away from here." I reverted to mind speech.

"I'm trying," Rhys gritted.

Somehow, I was still on my feet but disoriented. How broad a net had the Sumerians cast? No one's magic is limitless. I couldn't go back toward the Toyota. Pushing ahead on the road didn't feel right, either. Running on instinct, I forced myself into a shambling run at right angles to the highway into sand and sagebrush.

At first, it was impossibly difficult. The lantern goddess

blocked me, except I stepped through her. Whoa. Hadn't expected that. Ghouls brushed against me. I ignored them and kept moving. They'd attacked Cleyn, but so far they'd left me be. If I were right, the horridly debilitating exhaustion would lessen as I inserted space between me and the highway.

If I was wrong, at least I'd go down swinging. I did not want to drag Rhys and Joss into the muck with me. Wings swooshed past just before talons closed around my shoulder. Their sharp points made me yelp, but they also pushed the fog around my brain back a little.

"Nothing is out there," Connor squawked. "Keep moving, Alia."

I'd suspected as much. We'd been waylaid and done the expected: walked in the same direction as we'd been driving. Shit. How had we been so stupid?

Not stupid, complacent. My inner wise woman was back, and she was right. We'd let our guard down in the absence of werewolves and vampires as if they were the only bad things in the world.

Awk. Bad things. Where was the coffin?

Staring through my third eye, I still saw it, but it was maybe twenty feet away. I felt like crowing. It wasn't about to snatch me into another dimension.

"Damn straight," I muttered and plodded on.

Manzanita branches tore at my pants. I was soaked to the skin and had passed beyond the point of cold, but I was moving more easily. Relief sluiced through me. I'd guessed right. Emphasis on *guess*.

This could have so easily gone another way.

Another 500 paces and I felt more like myself. The crystal orb and the amorphous goddess had vanished. Connor still rode on my shoulder offering moral support.

"Thanks," I murmured. "I'm good."

Rhys and Joss caught up. Connor fluttered to the ground and shifted grumbling about how wet his clothing was as he dressed.

"Bet your jump spell would work now," I told Rhys. "But I'm worried about Cleyn."

"You can help him from anywhere," Rhys pointed out. "We need shelter. I figure maybe only half an hour before nightfall."

I glanced skyward. Crap. He was right. How had I burned through a couple of hours trekking due east? Because I'd been moving with all the speed of a land tortoise until about half an hour back.

Power surged, illuminating the droplets around Rhys. "I need to hear everything," he said, "but not just now."

His words were so typical I smiled. He was far better at triage than me. Aiming at the problem burning brightest.

"Liked it better as a hawk," Connor mumbled as he wrung water out of his pant legs.

"Do n't take us too far," I urged. "Bishop is the next town on the map. We were only about five miles away when the Toyota broke down."

As he worked on his casting, I shielded my eyes with a hand and stared at the skies. Where was the griffon? Since Plan A hadn't worked, were our erstwhile masters holding him hostage and planning to use our link force my cooperation?

More importantly, would they ever leave me alone?

When the answer, a resounding *no*, came, my spirits drooped. I'd considered separating myself from Rhys and the others more than once. Trouble dogged me; no reason to drag the others into my personal hell.

"No fucking way," blasted through my mind.

I snorted. Ever the consummate mage, Rhys could craft a spell and track my thoughts without breaking a sweat. Before I dredged up a snappy reply, the sagebrush shimmered and vanished. Moments later, we stood on the outskirts of one more trashed town. Rows and cars and trucks were promising as was a mostly intact Quonset hut that had once housed a tire business.

Too burned out for subtle, I focused a blast a power at the hut to ascertain if anything living bided within.

"Well?" Connor arched a dark brow.

"We're good," I said and led the way toward a side door hanging open on bent hinges. If we got lucky, there might be a can or two of food. Anything fresh would have long since rotted.

After a bit of hunting, I located a small kitchen off a work area. The others pushed in after me. It was a tight fit for four of us. Joss, our *de facto* cook, rustled through cupboards.

Rhys turned me to face him. "Strong work."

My damp face warmed. "Thanks, but more like a strong guess."

He shook his head. "Nope. You followed your intuition."

"Score!" Joss cried and held up a box of Triscuits and a round of some kind of hard cheese. Bits of mold grew along the edges, but those could be cut off.

My more-than-empty stomach growled. I'd eat, and then address myself to the missing griffon. Rhys wouldn't want me outside at night, but leaving the beast to whatever fate awaited didn't sit well. He'd have come after me if he could. I'd be damned if I abandoned him.

Rhys took a cracker with cheese layered on top and handed it to me. "If Cleyn isn't back soon, I'll help you find him through your link."

The day had been rougher than I expected; my eyes filled with tears. I brushed them aside hoping no one noticed. Sorrow was an old-world luxury; my tears wouldn't help Cleyn—or anyone else.

Connor had been rifling through cabinets. He set a can of tuna on the counter, followed by a jar of what looked like home-canned pears. At least our bellies would be full.

Faint scratching drew me to my feet, head cocked to one side as I pinpointed the noise.

"I heard that." Connor shot upright, nose twitching much as his hawk's might have.

"Not magical," Rhys said as he, too, stared at a spot on the far side of the kitchen and added a drawing spell to the mix.

Because the creature couldn't help itself, a smallish gray rat scuttled forward, whiskers twitching.

"How'd it survive?" I blurted as it edged toward a pile of moldy cheese Joss had left next to the sink. Rodents are smart. Somehow, it knew not to dive into the round we'd fed from. At least, not while we were here.

"Good question," Rhys muttered. Power surged as he

tested our temporary home, searching for whatever it is mages hunt for.

Yeah. I'm still new and green. Nowhere near dry, I prepared to trade our shelter for somewhere safer. Joss wrapped the cheese in a chunk of butcher paper. Connor returned to the cupboards to see if he'd missed anything. Our invited guest hunched over the cheese scraps eating methodically.

Colors swirled around Rhys, blues and violets, before he reeled in his spell. "We're good," he announced.

"Good how?" Connor stopped searching long enough to eye Rhys.

"Energy fields coalesce around this area," he explained. "It's what saved the rat, and probably a bunch of his relatives."

"Could it have spared any people?" I asked.

"Good question," Rhys said. "Let's look, shall we?"

"Maybe we shouldn't be eating their food." Joss put the cheese back.

"Premature." Rhys flapped a hand his way and started out of the kitchen.

If we did anything, we should be hunting Cleyn, but I didn't call him back. Instead, I activated my link with the griffon and held it wide open.

Please let him be there. Please.

It was selfish, but I'd lost so much, even one more defeat was unacceptable.

ABOUT THE AUTHOR

Ann Gimpel is a USA Today bestselling author. A lifelong aficionado of the unusual, she began writing speculative fiction a few years ago. Since then her short fiction has appeared in many webzines and anthologies. Her longer books run the gamut from urban fantasy to paranormal romance. Once upon a time, she nurtured clients. Now she nurtures dark, gritty fantasy stories that push hard against reality. When she's not writing, she's in the backcountry getting down and dirty with her camera. She's published over 100 books to date, with several more planned for 2024 and beyond. A husband, grown children, grandchildren, and wolf hybrids round out her family.

Keep up with her at www.anngimpel.com or www.anngimpelbooks.com

If you enjoyed what you read, get in line for special offers and pre-release special reads. Newsletter Signup!

Broken Line

Circle of Assassins

Shira

Quinn

Rhiana

Kylian

Grigori

Coven Enforcers

Blood and Magic

Blood and Sorcery

Blood and Illusion

Demon Assassins

Witch's Bounty

Witch's Bane

Witches Rule

Dragon Heir

Dragon's Call

Dragon's Blood

Dragon's Heir

Dragon Lore

Highland Secrets

To Love a Highland Dragon

Dragon Maid

Dragon's Dare

Dragon Fury

Earth Reclaimed

Earth's Requiem

Earth's Blood

Earth's Hope

Elemental Witch

Timespell

Time's Curse

Time's Hostage

Gatekeeper

Shadow Reaper

Rebel Reaper

Untamed Reaper

GenTech Rebellion

Winning Glory

Honor Bound

Claiming Charity

Loving Hope

Keeping Faith

Ice Dragon

Feral Ice

Cursed Ice

Primal Ice

Magick and Misfits (Fall and Winter 2020)

Court of Rogues

Midnight Court

Court of the Fallen

Court of Destiny

Rubicon International

Garen

Lars

Sanctuary

Conjuring Fate

Conjuring Chaos

Conjuring Promises

Soul Dance

Tarnished Beginnings

Tarnished Legacy

Tarnished Prophecy

Tarnished Journey

Soul Storm

Dark Prophecy

Dark Pursuit

Dark Promise

Underground Heat

Roman's Gold

Wolf Born

Blood Bond

Wayward Mage

Hands of Fate

Jinxed

Hunted

Salvaged

Tiana

Wolf Clan Shifters

Alice's Alphas

Megan's Mates

Sophie's Shifters

Wylde Magick

Gemstone

Lion's Lair

Unbalanced

STANDALONE BOOKS

Branded, That Old Black Magic Romance (paranormal romance)

Edge of Night (short story collection, paranormal and horror)

Grit is a 4-Letter Word (nonfiction)

Heart's Flame (post-apocalyptic romance)

Icy Passage (science fiction romance)

Marked by Fortune (post-apocalyptic coming of age story)

Melis's Gambit (historical paranormal romance)

Midnight Magic (paranormal romance)

Red Dawn (post-apocalyptic paranormal romance)

Shadow Play (historical paranormal romance)

Shadows in Time (Highland time travel romance)

Since We Fell (contemporary romance)

Warin's War (paranormal romance)